Broad Street Goddesses

DeAnna Carol Williams

Broad Street Goddesses

Copyright © 2013 DeAnna Carol Williams

All rights reserved by the author. No part of this publication may be reproduced, distributed, or transmitted in any form or by any means, including photocopying, recording, or other electronic or mechanical methods, without the prior written permission of the publisher, except in the case of brief quotations embodied in critical reviews and certain other noncommercial uses permitted by copyright law. For permission requests, write to the Author, addressed "Attention: Permissions Coordinator," at the address below.

Deanna-williams@comcast.net

ISBN-13: 978-1481960892

This book is dedicated to the women in my life who have shaped and inspired me... questioning my sanity, but *never* my integrity.

Mom, Mamo, Gimmy, Nainy, Auntie Nancy,

Launa, Brenda, Jeani, Lisa, Gloria

and my beautiful daughters,

Megan and Emily

You will find yourselves sprinkled through these pages and rooted firmly in my heart

~ Always~

Acknowledgements

This novel would not have been written without the endless patience extended to me by my husband, Billy, who shoved sandwiches and chocolate under the office door and fiercely protected my work space.

Jeani Ambrose, you are an incredible sage and an irreplaceable voice of reason. Thank you for your editing of content and attitude.

Lisa Huntzinger, you inspired me to the finish line.
Thank you for the final edits.

Charlene, I appreciate your support more than words can ever say.

CHAPTER 1

Paige stumbled and fell into the comfort of an overstuffed chair and reached for a cocktail glass in the dark. She slopped the remains of the cheap fruit flavored vodka over the rim and cringed with the burn in the back of her throat. She intended to drown out the gnawing clench of failure or at the very least kill the brain cells that cared about it. A seductive ache lured her with the bliss of going to sleep and never waking up. In the depth of her downward thoughts, she wished for her final breath, which in her opinion couldn't come soon enough.

She spied a bright orange carton cutter teetering on the last box she'd packed. Grabbing the unlikely weapon, she sized up the razor's edge in the light of the moon shining through her bare window. She placed the blade to her wrist and pushed till it hurt. The harsh reality of how she'd be found flashed in her mind like a crime scene photo. Paige sucked in a sharp breath. Her lungs burned as she hung onto betrayal and heartbreak until it came gushing out of her in a howl that should have been heard on the moon. She flung the blade across the room to bury it deep into the lath and plaster wall with a dull thunk.

The truth was she couldn't bear the thought of bleeding out on her travertine floor tiles. She hadn't sealed them in over eighteen months, six months past their due date. Being a naturally porous stone, travertine required the care she hadn't supplied. Her tragedy would not leave the stains of desperation on her greatest creation. That was one exit strategy she simply could not die with.

~

"Truck's ready to go," a man's voiced boomed into the emptiness. There was no response. He lumbered past her delicately carved Victorian screen door searching for its occupant. The ominous sensation of gloom crept into his lungs and stopped him cold. Waiting, his ears perked for any sound of her. He braced himself and tentatively stepped into the light filled cottage.

He called into the vacant spaces of the house, "Paige." Holding his breath, he searched the room looking for a sign that she was still there. The rhythmic thumping of his own heart pounded in his head as he took a few more steps and called out in a panic, "PAIGE!" Soft rustling sounds off in the distance and moving closer created a flutter in his chest, thank God.

Sam had been dodging the pangs of guilt for weeks. Avoiding Paige, his old friend, his first love, felt like self preservation. The anticipation of seeing her before she left town had kept him up most of the night. She sauntered into the foyer carefully examining the empty rooms through her dark glasses. Seeing Sam, she slid the glasses up into a pile of curly auburn hair on top of her head and squinted toward his face. He couldn't help but notice the deep worry around her beautiful green eyes. In her face he recognized dread, fear and the threat of tears. Desperately trying to avoid the latter, he disregarded his official capacity, "What's in Nevada City?"

Paige threw her shoulders back, meeting his compassionate eyes, "Distance, Sammy."

Masking the gut kick to his ego, he forced a smile and nodded. Feisty, she'd always been feisty. Even if she didn't recognize the power of her own resilience at that moment, Sammy did and he knew she'd be alright.

"Just need a signature here." Sammy held out paperwork for her to sign.

"And that's it?" she breathed out numbly.

He nodded, "Any questions can be directed to Carl."

Her mouth pinched a firm line, nostrils flaring to hide the ache of hearing his name. He reached out to retrieve his pen, impulsively grasping her hand. Warmly, she squeezed back. Sam swallowed years of missed opportunities to tell her how he felt about her. He looked at her signature and then back to her face feeling his last chance was right in front of him. The sweetness of her smile and the wild tendrils of auburn hair that had been the star of all his dreams were right in front of him with undivided attention. He'd rehearsed all night what he'd say in these final moments. He sucked up a huge breath of courage and felt a twinge of panic in his heart that stopped him cold. His brain took over, "You sure that truck's had a safety check?"

She laughed nervously, "I'll be fine, Sam," and pulled her hand back quickly brushing away the hair that had fallen into her eye.

"Be safe, Paige." He let himself out, disappointed in his habitual lack of courage where his feelings for Paige were concerned. He whispered quietly to any omnipotent force that may be listening, "Be happy, Paige." Sam's prayer silently wafted inside and circled around her. She looked out the door as Sam turned the corner and smiled after him. He'd been a good friend.

Fanning herself with the roadmap she looked around her sweet cottage. It appeared so much bigger without her belongings. Not a box, bag or dust bunny left anywhere. Her pride didn't allow her the satisfaction of leaving anything stripped of its value or untidy in any way. Every corner had been cleaned and polished while she'd been intoxicated the night before; Quite an act of futility knowing that her cottage would be demolished in less than a week. It was a pride thing.

A tangle of sadness lingered thick in her throat as she stood in the middle of her emptiness. Every color, fixture and fancy thing was her vision. From the neighborhood eyesore with boarded up windows, she'd gutted disgusting bathrooms, pulled off splintering siding and bled for days after wrestling blackberry bushes to get to the bones of the house. Completed now for years, she'd lovingly selected stained glass dormers and marigold carnival glass light fixtures. Paige was solely responsible for every amazing detail. It stood as a testament of her dedication to the intrinsic value of the past and of course an epic stubborn streak.

She eyed the map in her hand and wondered what kind of crazy person buys an old house, sight unseen from the internet in a town over six hundred miles away. Against the advice of her friends and family Paige was moving to Nevada City, California with no plans to return. Ever. Paige was convinced the life she'd been trying desperately to create was gathering for her over six hundred miles away. She could see it unfolding in her dreams at night as she walked through the mansion she'd only seen through internet photos. In her desperate attempt to outrun bad decisions Paige was convinced the move was exactly what she needed. No old flames around every corner, only hard work to restore a great old house. One more failure was not an option. Her new adventure may kill her but she would not allow it to be a mistake.

Slapping the map against her leg, "It's off to Nevada City," she stated loudly and listened to the echo of her voice bounce around the empty room. Maybe it was her imagination, but Paige felt lighter for the first time in months.

Wally protested from the cat carrier with an angry MEOWWW prompting Paige to speak, "I know you think this is cat abuse." Picking up her long haired black and white roommate she headed for the door. The tick tock of her heels resonated from the floor as she made her way through the foyer. Without the self indulgence of a look over her shoulder into her heart's work, Paige allowed the bright red wooden screen door to slap shut. She was too pissed off to cry about it.

With Wally loaded in the passenger seat, she hefted herself up into the driver seat of the humongous moving van. Adjusting the rearview mirror and the stereo, she lowered her sunglasses over aching eyes. Annie Lennox sang, "No more I love you's". Paige cranked the volume and raised her voice to match Annie in melody as Wally wailed out a helpless cry from his cage.

Perfect.
She grinded the truck into 1st gear rolling away from her failed life.

After nine hours on the road, Paige wiggled uneasily in her seat. She'd stretched her legs at three gas stations along the way, but with a foggy hangover head and her tingling butt waking up from the last leg of the journey, Paige wanted to be there already. She peeked in to see Wally lying sprawled out to allow maximum air coverage on his body. "Soon, Sass-Master, we'll be there."

~

Turning into the foothills of California, the landscape transformed from crowded and dirty to the eerily familiar sight of a forested winding road. She cracked the windows to breathe it in. Her stomach lurched with the uncertainty of what lay down the road. Impatient to blow her anxiety away, Paige rescued her unruly auburn hair into a clip on top of her head and rolled both windows completely down. The scent of pine and blooming dogwood landed on her tongue with the sweetness of Christmas and cotton candy. The flavors poured into her like an elixir soothing the sting of her disillusioned life.

Once in Nevada City, Broad Street was steep and led straight up through the middle of town. Long standing buildings with hand painted signs and bay windows displaying, candies, bakery goods, books and clothing lined both sides of the street. Paige could feel every building bursting with a story untold from over a hundred and sixty years of time in the same spot. Nevada City was in integral part of the California gold rush. Images of miners and madams swirled though her head as she looked in her rearview mirror at the perfectly preserved historic city bustling with modern day people. Squinting to read her map, she rolled along looking for the turn toward her destiny on the impossibly cramped street. One tight three point turn and a block up the road, she cautiously maneuvered the moving truck along streets originally created for a horse and buggy. The truck moaned to a lumbering stop as she examined the address on a mail box. Paige held her breath until she realized it matched what she held in her hands.

Dumbfounded, she looked up to the top of the four story turret all the way down to the wraparound porch with its carved trims. She was humbled by the magnitude of the house. It wasn't a house, it was a mansion. *Her mansion...* something she'd never imagined as part of her vocabulary, not even in her wild imagination.

She scanned the painfully impossible ribbon of a driveway to find a place to park the moving truck. Paige tried to back down the drive to get the truck out of the street. Several attempts with jerky stops and starts produced the heart stopping cringe of metal on metal. Dollar signs flashed in her head as she recalled refusing the additional insurance from the truck rental place. She shook off a niggle of dread and focused on seeing her future for the first time. Slowly she rolled down the drive, resolutely checking the side mirrors. Finally she set the brake, grabbed Wally and hopped down out of the cab.

From the cool shade of the back of her mansion, imperfections were quickly apparent. Big cracks in the concrete stairs had settled into deep crevasses. Tired shutters hung askew. Grey lap board siding clung to shards of peeling white paint that was quickly flaking into drifts along the foundation. Walking all the way around to the front of her mansion, things only got worse. Stopping at the base of the eight foot wide stairway leading to the expansive front porch she looked up to the highest peak of the roof and back down to the crumbling walkway under her feet. Paige was instantly in love.

And that was always the problem... Paige fell in love.

CHAPTER 2

Hidden beneath the overgrowth of snarled climbing roses and craggy wisteria, one porch post teetered, barely attached and several ballasts were missing. Paige precariously climbed up the creaking stairs and made it to the door without falling through the rickety boards. The rusty mail slot promptly fell off in her hand as soon as it was touched. The hidden key bounced on the porch teetering between two boards, balanced, but poised to fall clean through. Instantly, Paige imagined what was under the porch; spiders, dust, dead things and overgrown brambles. She cringed at the thought of crawling through it to retrieve her only key.

"This is why I didn't tell anyone..." Paige flopped down onto the top step. Wally groomed himself, unconcerned. "Typical, you let me worry about everything." She reached to feel the comfort of his fur under her hand, while she eyed the key perched on the edge of falling into a nasty abyss.

"I don't recommend it as a pastime." A deep friendly voice startled her.

"Excuse me?" She looked up to see him sitting on a bicycle.

"I mean worry, I don't recommend it. Something I can do to help?" Very blue, earnest eyes and dark blond hair curling around the edges made her heart ache. His muscular legs looked like biking was his mode of transportation and the sight of him made her decision to give up men suddenly the most foolish notion of her life. The last thing she needed now was a gorgeous man. Stop it, Paige, her head screamed to her heart. Dimples, he had dimples.

Paige blinked from his tanned muscular legs back to his face. "I'm new." Her mind moved slowly, "I…I…I'm Paige." She stuttered. Standing up to clear her head, "And this is Wally." Introducing the cat with a wave of her hand she felt ridiculous but kept her head high in spite of her failing composure.

He was off the bike and halfway up the stairs extending his hand, "Jake Jenkins. Welcome to Nevada City. It'll be nice… someone living here." Genuine kindness could be felt in the warmth of his firm hand. Humor, sunshine and time showed in the crinkles turned up on the outside edges of his eyes. He was possibly the sexiest man she'd ever met in person.

"I broke it before I even got inside." She held up the rusty mail slot with her free hand, gently retrieving her other hand from his friendly hold.

"Ah, the ole' key behind the mail slot trick…" He bent down and picked up the key, handing it to her with none of the drama she'd conjured up.

She stared at the key in her hand, "Thanks, I think I'm overwhelmed. Things will look better in the morning." She looked at the old wooden screen door drooping from a broken hinge, "Maybe," she forced a smile and blew at the wild tangle of hair hanging over one eye.

"Well Paige, we're a friendly bunch here; A little odd, but always helpful. The old dudes are crusty at first, but they always warm up to a pretty face. Wally fits right in." His smile slipped into a lopsided grin as he watched the cat stalk a blue belly lizard.

"Thanks for the welcome, Jake." She was breathing easier.

"Do you need anything? It'll be dark in a few hours. Power turned on?"

"Oh." She grimaced, looking at the key in her hand, kicking herself for not thinking ahead. Electricity wasn't at the top of her list. She'd had a lot on her mind.

"I'll give you the number for the power company. My best girl, Betty should be able to fix you up today." He wrote a number on the back of his business card, handing it to her.

He had a girl. Paige felt a confusing mixture of relief and disappointment as Jake continued, "Be sure to tell her you're a friend of mine. Hey look, Wally's got dinner covered." He called over his shoulder referring to the dead lizard on the stoop. Paige watched as his manly strut moved his fabulously firm behind away from her. She was mesmerized by his easy nature and incredible good looks. Before Paige realized she'd been standing there brainlessly soaking up his essence he was on his bike and gone. With a disgusted sigh, she tried to shake off the feeling of fascination he'd sparked in her. She clenched the key tightly in her hand and looked at the leaded glass door. "Well Wally, here we go..." Paige pulled the screen door from its resting place and the scream of deteriorating metal hinges shot painfully through her aching head.

The key slipped solidly into the lock, it was the door that wobbled and then stuck tight. She shoved her hip into the ancient slab of a door which released, flinging her into a whiff of musty dust swirling into her sinuses. Pursing her lips and wrinkling her nose she mentally prepared for what she was about to find. With eyes adjusting in the darkness, she slowly moved into the foyer. The banister and stairs looked intact and passed the wiggle test. Pale ghosts where pictures once hung lined the walls. The allure of the parlor's rounded turret of float glass windows pulled her closer to examine the rare find. Through tiny bubbles and water-like waves in the glass Paige looked out onto the front of yard. A blur of pale blue slipped into and then out of her peripheral vision. When she turned to look there was only Wally blinking lazily at her. Tingles of cool air covered her neck. Rubbing her arms against the unsettling sensation, Paige cursed her hangover.

Eight foot tall glass pocket doors led into the library with dark wood floor to ceiling shelves complete with a rolling ladder. Nothing but dust and some very impressive spider webs on the shelves. Paige closed her eyes imagining the room brimming with books and art. The adjacent dining room was an enormous space with floors reaching far enough for at least eighty people to dance. As her eyes adjusted, the deep carved crown moldings around the ceiling gleamed, gold even through the years of grime.

Examining the kitchen, Paige stared out over the sprawling black and white tile floors and countertops. Pale pink enameled cabinets with black porcelain knobs barely clung to the walls. Over the farm sink a huge filthy window framed by raggedy café curtains looked out over the back yard. Appliances, rounded and chromed, a fabulous look in 1925, looked so decrepit she'd be afraid to turn them on. Turn anything on? Paige scrambled for her phone and made the call to Jakes girl, Betty. Mentioning Jake was magic. Until that point in the conversation nothing was going to happen until

Monday. The sound of Betty's angelic voice had Paige conjuring images of a petite beauty queen with a sugary nature. Paige instantly despised her. Betty assured her the power would be on before the close of business that day. Mystified, Paige shook her head in disbelief and smiled into the phone, matching the honey tone coming from the other end and thanked Betty. Imagining Jake was shallow enough to couple up with someone perfect and plastic like Betty made her feel better. Reminding herself once again that her "no men" policy was a solid choice for her peace of mind. Paige recognized the essence of smugness when she caught her own reflection in the dirty window.

"Most unbecoming for a beautiful face." A woman's voice circled her head creating a buzz in her ears and shiver down her back. Paige looked around to see where the woman's voice came from. Stillness hung thick in the air making it hard to breathe. She grabbed for the wall to steady herself and her eyes darted into every corner. She was alone in the mansion and she had a powerful hangover. Paige threw her shoulders back and looked up the stairs to the top.

Powder fine dust caked onto her hand as she stepped up the grand sweep of stairs. Paige recoiled, listening to the moan of protesting stairs all the way to the mezzanine, a majestic area with at least a dozen doors that led into hallways on either side. The first bedroom was small in size and a ghastly gold color that once might have been cheerful yellow. Pulling back the tattered sheers on the window she watched the bustle on Broad Street wondering how long it would be until she fit into such a small world. She'd never really fit in anywhere, but the draw to belong in Nevada City had become a nagging issue she could not explain.

The second bedroom overlooked the back yard and was larger than the first. With its faded bird house wallpaper the room felt tired and sad. Practically no light came in through the closed window shade. A quick tug to the wooden handle of the shade and the brittle fabric crackled and spun shards of crunchy linen above Paige's head, which sounded like peals of laughter. From the window of the "blue room" she looked out onto the lawn and spotted an arbor or gazebo, it was hard to tell what lurked under the overgrowth of blackberry bushes. The feeling of someone standing behind her crept over her shoulders and she pulled herself away from the window.

Abandoning the upstairs exploration, Paige's descent down the stairs stopped short when she heard a faint voice. Standing very still she listened closely but heard nothing more. A quick chill of nerves prickled her skin. Paige dismissed the feeling and justified the voice as neighbors chatting in the yard. She laughed at herself. Her house in Oregon had been so quiet, she'd have to get used to having people closer to her now. She decided in that moment that she would not allow the noises and creaking of the massive old mansion to put her on edge.

Following the rear staircase back down to the main floor behind the kitchen, Paige found a rather large bedroom and bathroom where mermaids flaunted silver and gold tails amongst the turquoise sea weed printed on pale mauve walls. Beautiful in its day, she wondered if there was a way to salvage it. A large claw footed tub just like in the internet photos was a pleasing find, followed by a gasp of horror at the rings and rings of filth inside of it.

She closely examined the aged tub. The scent of lavender and pine filled the air, as Paige strained to hear something so slight it was almost undetectable, but it sounded like water running and singing. The imaginings of a desperately tired and hung-over woman were running amuck! It was in that moment that hunger pains and a headache hit her hard.

No food at hand, Paige set out to explore her new city. Beyond the expansive sloping lawn, the sidewalk in front of her mansion was raised nearly three feet from the road with an aged metal guard rail, something she'd never seen. There were long-standing cement stairs with metal railings going down to the street level at the corners. She walked a block and then turned onto Broad Street. There spread out before her was a whole new world. The street itself was a vertical slope down through town and out the other side into a heavily treed are. From where she stood at the top of the hill people moved in rhythmic colorful patterns on both sides of the street. Cars crept slowly looking for a prized parking space. Each shop had its own design and retained the integrity of its history, with awnings, hand painted windows and colorful trims. When she considered it all together she was reminded of a Norman Rockwell scene. This is what she chose and this is where she would make a new beginning.

Just as she thought of pinching herself, a man came up fast behind her playing a guitar and singing. With hair in dreads and clothes woven from knobby hemp, he nodded as he passed her on the street continuing to sing. Down past a sidewalk Café, the aroma of marijuana wafted through the air. Well, not quite a Norman Rockwell moment, but definitely interesting. Paige smiled out loud.

CHAPTER 3

There was knocking in her head. So strong, she thought it must be the results of a resilient two day hangover. Quickly, she stretched to get her Barings. More knocking, damn knocking, it was coming from the kitchen door. Pain radiated through her hips as she wiggled out of the sleeping bag on the hardwood floor, stood up, took two steps and realized that her legs were asleep. Squinting her eyes for clarity she waddled to keep her legs steady and made it to the kitchen door, grasping the glass knob for balance. She looked sideways against the bright light of morning to see the silhouette of a woman through the shabby curtains. Practically incoherent, Paige cracked the door, peeked through the slit against the brutal light. On her back porch was someone clearly not of this world. The woman wore a loose patchwork tunic over jeans. With a scarf in her hair, sandals on her feet and no makeup, a cake in one hand and a French press pot of coffee in the other. She was quick to smile and Paige had never seen anything more beautiful.

"Are you an angel?" Paige croaked. Tasting the garlic from her pizza last night, she tried not to breathe on the poor unsuspecting bearer of salvation.

"I'm Etta Jenkins, from next door. Welcome to our little corner." Her smile seemed familiar.

"Come in." Paige stood aside, "What time is it?" She searched the room for a clock that wasn't there.

"Nine-thirty or so. I thought you'd be awake."

"Yeah, me too", Paige looked back to Etta's face... Jenkins... slowly her mind came to life and she was able to connect Jake's smile to this woman. "You must be a relative of Jake Jenkins. I see the resemblance."

"Jake's my brother," Etta placed the yummy looking cake on the countertop and poured Paige a cup, "Cream or sugar?"

"Just cream. Jake stopped by yesterday and gave me a hand."

"He is a handy one... that Jake." Etta studied Paige's eyes with a drilling intensity.

Wally slinked into the kitchen to pounce on imaginary prey and then began to eyeball the coffee cake. He looked away when he was caught. What a little sneak Paige thought shooting him a cautionary glare.

Etta laughed, "Just like a kitty. Does he eat sweets?"

"Like a fiend, especially ice cream." Paige watched Wally edge closer to the plate of cake. "Would you be offended if I gave him a little piece?"

"I was going to do it, if you didn't." Etta shoved the cake plate toward Paige.

Taking a pinch for Wally and a pinch for herself, "I'm not really into delayed gratification myself."

"Amen sister!" Etta looked around for a fork and then used her fingers to dig in and leaned easily on the edge of the counter.

"Oh my God, this is so good." Paige sighed trying not to let anything fall from her mouth as her eyes rolled in exaggerated joy.

Her shoulders relaxed and she entered into an easy chat with Etta standing over the kitchen counter eating cake with their fingers and drinking tepid, strong coffee. Paige examined her closely, with her long blond hair and crystal necklace, Etta was an odd creature, a genuine hippy-chick.

"Your truck!" Etta's eyes were huge as she bolted out the kitchen door, down the stairs and ran for the slowly creaking, rolling moving truck.

"SHIT!" Paige yelled as the truck moved in triple slow motion towards the overgrown gazebo. She flew down the back stairs right behind Etta, who heroically climbed up onto the slow moving truck, threw open the door, hopped in and set the emergency brake a few seconds after the sound of splintering wood echoed through the back yard. In the bright light of morning wearing only her red rocker t-shirt and hot pink panties Paige stood breathlessly cursing the stickers in her feet as Etta jumped down dusting her hands onto her jeans.

The newly acquainted women stared at each other breathing heavily and began to laugh hysterically. "Oh My God! Thank you!" Paige yelled out of breath.

"Your pergola is a gonner." Etta pursed her lips at the creaking structure.

Paige glanced quickly over the mound of lumber and bushes intertwined, "well it saved me from having to tear it down."

Etta eyed her new friend, scantily clad and shooed her back to the house, "Don't you start a scandal on your first day...you've got plenty of time for that!"

"What just happened?" Paige asked.

"Tommyknockers!" Etta said with a conspiratorial wink.

Even with the help of four hired hands, Paige made dozens of trips up and down the stairs. Her muscles ached with the torture of being out of shape. Her bed was made with crisp linens, washed before she packed them up. She scrubbed the muck out of the tub which took opening the window, wearing rubber gloves and a can of scouring powder. It was definitely going to be refinished. Towels and all the necessities were stocked in the bathroom. With the last project of her day completed, the needs of her stomach pulled her to the kitchen. The only thing she'd eaten all day was cake, coffee and tap water that tasted like iron. Rubbing her aching muscles, Paige rummaged for something, anything to eat.

Out the kitchen window she detected movement. Etta was setting candles on her patio table, arranged the chairs and fussed like she was about to have a garden party. With daylight fading into the glow of candles, she created an ethereal scene. Etta even had a bouquet of daisies on the table. A hippy Martha Stewart! Wally was napping on a cushioned patio chair, no doubt resting up for the gala.

From the back porch Paige shouted down, "When does the party start?"

"I've got wine, BBQ'd salmon and salad from my garden. Come on down when you're ready. I thought you'd be starving."

Paige contemplated changing out of the jeans she'd been wearing for the last two days, but the thought of another move without food drew her straight down the stairs and to the beautifully set dinner table.

"You're a picture down here in the candle light, Etta... a

garden Goddess." Paige looked around. Her overgrown gangly yard was suddenly enchanting. With brambles and wild roses illuminated by the warmth of flickering glow, deep purple clematis vines intertwined with honeysuckle, ivy and sweet peas climbing over every bush and tree trunk. What had appeared by the light of day as a wreck had been transformed by Etta's beautiful table setting, candles and loving touch, "When do the fairies show up?"

"You mean you can't see them?" Etta winked slyly.

Filling two glasses with wine, Etta handed one to Paige, raising her glass, "To new beginnings…" they toasted.

"How appropriate," Paige leveled a look across the table into Etta's eyes that glistened in the candle glow. An intimate connection crept between them; an unfamiliar feeling to Paige, who had never been close to other women. Not even her mother.

The first glass went down easy and cool, the second settled on her like a silky blanket, muffling the tension in her body. "This is amazing wine!"

"Our local Winery, I thought it would be a good welcome." Etta smiled.

"Well, of course you have a winery here." Paige laughed, "Is there a chocolate factory? How about Christmas tree and flower farms?"

Etta beamed proudly, "I'd be happy to show you all of that once you're settled."

"Seriously, you have a chocolate factory and a Christmas tree farm here?"

"Yep, we grow a lot more than Christmas trees around here" Etta said as a matter of fact as she loaded the salmon onto a plate for

Paige and one small piece for Wally, who had a place setting at the table! Paige looked straight at Etta who took the cat's place setting in stride.

"Unbelievable!" Paige grinned. She'd landed in an unusual place.

Etta served them the most incredible salmon she'd ever eaten. With a hint of BBQ smoke and garden herbs, it was heavenly. Halfway through the meal Paige smiled at Etta who was watching her eat.

"This is so good! Sorry, I'm eating like a trucker." She looked at Etta who was smug with satisfaction in the flickering light. Wally had inhaled his salmon and was licking his empty plate and paws, occasionally giving Etta the misted over gaze reserved only for a cat messiah.

"I love to cook." Etta picked a piece of salmon off her plate and put it in front of Wally who had exhibited excellent table manners for the hooligan Paige knew him to be. "Truth be told, I usually eat something cold right over the sink if I'm not fixing food for someone else... this is nice."

"No someone special in your life?" Paige asked.

"You mean a significant other?" Etta looked off in the distance, hesitating. Paige was immediately concerned that Etta might be interested in more than just a friendship. Was she a lesbian? Where in the world had that come from? Why should she care about the sexual orientation of a woman who'd just fixed an amazing candle light dinner for her and was now plying her with wine and conversation? Strange territory indeed.

Etta looked Paige in the eye with a half smile, "There hasn't been anyone… well… in a while, and to answer your inquiring mind, I'm not gay. I've considered it, and while I'm quite fond of the female form, having sex with a woman isn't something that appeals to me."

"Oh, lord, I didn't think you were coming on to me. I just…" Paige paused taking a drink of her wine, "wanted to get to know you. Sorry."

"Nothing to be sorry about Paige, I spend most of my time with my clients or in my garden. I have a gallery on Broad Street which doubles as my office. I love to cook, garden and tend to the little things that make life more enjoyable. I'm very intuitive; I hope that doesn't put you off."

"Having my needs anticipated before I know I have them is huge! I just don't know how I'll repay you for all your kindness." Paige settled back into her chair enjoying the contentment of a full belly and the buzz of wine.

"I liked you the moment you pulled into the driveway with Wally." She slipped her furry devotee another nibble of salmon, and cast an intense look at Paige, "Now how about you? Significant other? What's your profession? Do you have children?" Etta placed her chin into her open hand, dramatically batting her wide grey eyes waiting for Paige's response.

Paige weighed how much she wanted to share with Etta during a contemplative breath, "Well, there is no significant other. I'm 39 with a bullet. I could write a book about my bad choices where men are concerned. I come from a small town in Oregon called Sisters." Paige hesitated to continue, but something in Etta's easy air urged her on, "After 20 years of dating, everyone at the store or the bank was related to someone I had been intimate with. My last bad decision, who I found out after our last date was married, got freaked out that I might rat him out to his family and well...long story short, he condemned my sweet historic cottage via eminent domain so his clients could build a shopping mall."

"Ouch!" Etta looked as though she could feel Paige's emotions.

"I didn't have any fight left in me after that. I just wanted to get as far away from that pain as I could. I bought this old mansion on an internet auction site. It was the weirdest thing; I became absolutely possessed by it. I looked at thousands of houses but kept coming back to this one. The morning after I dreamed of walking through the halls of this mansion, I sat down at my computer and clicked the mouse until I owned it. Now I don't care if it was a smart investment or not, I feel like I've been waiting to get here my whole life. It's a bizarre sensation of..." Paige hesitated to find the right word.

"Belonging," whispered Etta.

"Yes, belonging." She examined Etta's face for an indication of how much farther to go.

"It's going to make an amazing bed and breakfast." Paige sat back in her chair rubbing her arms against the chill in the air, "How's that? Oh and I don't have children, although I think some of them grow up to be wonderful people, as a whole, I find them demanding, loud and sticky. I don't think Wally's fond of them either."

"I love children." Etta looked wishful, "I was hoping to have a family by now. There aren't a lot of choices in our City, and the one chance I had at love disappeared... literally."

Paige exclaimed, "I must sound horrible! Here you want

kids and I tell you I don't like them!"

"Nope, not horrible at all, you're an honest woman with a past... I find that absolutely delicious! I can't wait to hear the stories!"

~

Paige looked into the claw footed tub and admired her handiwork. The slick clean insides were going to feel amazing once she slipped into liquid hot yummy-ness. A wave of deJaVue pulsed through her like the flicker of a candle. Placing her fingers under the stream of water, she waited for the hot. Kicking off her jeans and pulling the shirt over her head she tested the water again. She pulled her hair up into a clip and waited, bare butt against the cold edge of porcelain with a finger under the spigot. Eerily familiar feelings gnawed the edges of her awareness while Wally perched himself on the edge of the tub watching her every move. When the hot water finally showed up Paige slipped in, a few degrees above comfortable, just the way she liked it. Every muscle in her body was melting like hot wax. She closed her eyes and let her body float. Three days of fatigue, one extreme hangover and at least a year of anxiety radiated out of her into the water. The feeling was divine.

As she watched the red and orange swirls a screen unfolded behind her closed eyes. She began to feel the sensation of pulling a bath tub out the side door of the mansion into the secluded garden into a group of men who'd gathered. She talked sweetly to the men as water was brought out in buckets and quietly poured over the white rolled enameled lip. The men came forward boldly tossing gold nuggets into the tub until it gleamed in the sun and the entire bottom was covered with glittering gleaming gold. The men easily parted with their weekly wages for just a glimpse of what had proven to be a very valuable commodity... her smooth, firm body. With her robe loosely tied, she stood before appreciative eyes filled with desire. The sense of power filled her with a wicked thrill. Slowly, she gathered her waist long red hair unto a bundle and pinned it up. Allowing the neck of her robe to slip off of one shoulder and baring the top of one bosom, she grabbed for the silk, giggled and checked the appreciation level among the crowd of at least three dozen. She felt her smile become wide and sweet concealing her calculating eyes that danced from face to face looking for the one who had the most to offer. There was a certain gleam in a man's eye when he's got a larger than usual pocket full of gold. She recognized it instantly. Against the groans of highly aroused men, she smiled brightly at one freshly scrubbed man with his hat in his hands. He stepped forward and gently handed her a walnut sized gold nugget bowing as if she were the queen of England. She smiled appreciatively and handed him a long handled bath brush. Turning her back to the crowd of men, she allowed her robe to slowly slip into a brilliant blue silk puddle on the bare ground. The feeling of a breeze hardened her nipples. She turned toward them and heard the appreciative moans, pointed her pretty foot toward the tub and slipped into the water.

  Stabs of chilly water woke her up. She was disoriented and cold to the bone. As if she'd done it a hundred times before, she flipped the drain with one foot and used the other to turn on the hot water, never opening her eyes. Warmth crept back into the tub. She was back in the naughty dream of bathing before miners for gold. The bump against her leg brought a lazy grimace. Must be Wally batting at soap bubbles… another bump against her side, weird. She opened her eyes to shoo the cat but he wasn't there. Paige stared into the water at some kind of black and brown goop swirling up through the drain. She flailed out of the tub, squealing and slipping to the floor on the wet tiles. Her bare skin felt like squid sliming over the cold marble floor.

"Holy Hell! What *is* that?" she checked to see if anything had stuck to her legs. Clinging to a towel she crawled back to the tub and looked inside. Her nose crinkled up. She was unscathed. Whatever it was could be classified as foul and obviously what she scrubbed out of the tub earlier in the day. Wally appeared, leaned down to the water taking a sniff and sneezed, his nose twitched in disgust. From Paige's vantage point on the tile floor she noticed rollers tucked beneath the claw feet on the bottom of the tub. It became almost impossible to shake the chill of curiosity after that.

CHAPTER 4

"A barn dance?" Paige laughed. She was still shocked by her picturesque little town.

"Sure, we do it every year at the old fire station; it's a fundraiser for the cowbells." Etta said rifling through Paige's closet.

"And the proper attire for this affair would be?" Paige raised an eyebrow.

"Don't you have a square dancing dress?" Etta jabbed, flipping from one garment to the next in Paige's closet.

"Hell no I don't have one. What color is *your* square dancing dress?" Paige was trying to picture Etta in crinoline skirts and pigtails.

"Well your Donna Karan will be totally unappreciated by the crowd." Etta pulled out the little black dress, "Great lines though." Shoving it back into the closet she pulled out a denim jacket and a pair of jeans. "You have any boots?"

"Pointy little cowboy boots?" Paige blinked her eyes and then squinted at Etta daring her to confirm.

"Whatever you have will work. I'll be back in an hour. Will you be ready?"

"Yeah I just have to saddle up the donkey, then I'm good to go."

Etta smirked and patted Paige's hand, "It's your debut!

Everyone's heard about you, now they're dying to meet you. It's been two whole weeks since you rode into town. Best you show them who you are before they make up stories. Besides there are eligible men, and they know how to dance."

"I'm not dancing. I not dating and I'm not sure it's a good idea to go at all."

"You can't be a remodeling hermit forever Paige. Just don't dance with Ernie from the hardware store, he's got roaming hands… well unless you're into short balding men in overalls."

"I do have a thing for overalls… bought two pairs just last week!" Paige watched Etta move toward the stairs.

"See you in an hour."

Etta returned an hour later in a pretty peasant skirt and an off the shoulder top, hair pulled up with some configuration of scarf woven through and casually falling to her shoulders. Paige didn't know how she managed to embody the image of a free spirited Goddess every damned day. It was mystical and part of what she had come to love about Etta.

"Denim and diamonds…nice choice," Etta said as she examined Paige carefully, "Beautiful actually. Can I reconsider the non-lesbian clause in our friendship?"

"Sure! If I can borrow that top next time."

True to prediction, there were hay bales to sit on, a country swing band playing on a makeshift stage and decorations made of red and yellow crepe paper, so authentically sweet it made her smile. Women in jeans with fringed shirts wore cowgirl hats complete with glitter and spangles. Ornate dresses with full skirts and pointy little cowboy boots were everywhere. Men duded out in their finest cowboy shirts and boots and hung out around the beer keg at the wine barrel bar as women set up the dessert table.

"Etta, this is unbelievable!" Paige said in awe.

"Told ya'. Come on let's get a beer."

Paige was definitely the center of attention as they walked through the party. She didn't feel critiqued really, it was more curiosity. The smiles she received felt sincere. She had a flashback of the adoration she felt in her bathing dream and blushed at the memory.

"Can I offer you a beer young lady," the timid voice of Ernie spoke behind her.

"Thanks Ernie, I'd love a beer." Etta grabbed the long amber neck and raised an eyebrow to Paige, jerking her head toward Jake, who was leaning on the bar lazily drinking a beer and smiled right at her. She looked around and sure enough, he was smiling at her, so she smiled back, with a slight wave. Jake grabbed a crutch and came hobbling over to her.

"I'm afraid I'm a lousy dance partner tonight, but I'd love to buy you a beer," Shoving the brim of his hat up with the tip of his bottle, his infectious wide smile flirted with her.

"This is all just too much. You guys are out of some kind of novel... I've never been part of anything like this." She accepted a beer.

"That looks painful!" Paige looked at the crutches in his hand.

"Basketball... It's a long story."

"Where is Betty?" Paige asked, "I want to thank her for

helping me out. She saved me the other night."

"Yeah, she's a sweetheart. I saw her a few minutes ago... I think she's in the kitchen. Her fried chicken's so good it'll break your mouth." Jake looked around the room with a goofy grin, "She was the prettiest girl in the place until you walked in." His comment lurched in her gut.

Paige glared back at him, "I'll talk to you later, Jake." She had no tolerance for an outrageous flirt who had a girlfriend in the next room! There would not be a repeat performance of her relationship drama here in her new city. Common sense told her to start walking home, which she did, but Etta grabbed her arm and steered her back into the party.

Paige politely met dozens of folks and tried to remember their names. Ernie, true to prediction, asked her to dance. He was at least two inches shorter than Paige. His thin grey hair had been slicked to one side and he was wearing Brute aftershave. Pearl buttons strained on his shirt that was just a size too small. Paige was flattered that he looked so proud to be dancing with her. Even though he glanced into her cleavage a few times, his hands never roamed. Ernie was actually a very good dancer. Paige shot Etta a sly look from the dance floor as Ernie spun her around. Etta laughed so hard Paige thought beer was going to come out her nose. Paige rolled her eyes at Etta over the top of Ernie's head, and then thanked him for the dance with a little curtsy and tilt of her head.

"You made that look effortless and sweet." Etta said handing Paige another beer.

"Ernie was almost chivalrous," Paige raised one eyebrow, "Almost."

"I don't know why you chose to dance with Ernie when you clearly had Jake's full attention. He'll be off those crutches in a day or two."

"He's not my type." Paige said shortly.

"All the women here adore him. He's very likeable." Etta quipped.

"Apparently..." Paige felt pissy and ready to leave. She took a swig of beer and looked away from Etta and straight into the eyes of a woman approaching from the kitchen.

The woman walked directly up to her, extending a delicate hand, "Hello Paige, I'm Mim." There was a slight hint of southern drawl in her voice that was petal soft. She was about sixty years old. Her hair had gone completely white-silver and was cut into a bob, no bangs, one side tucked neatly behind her ear. Barely over five feet tall, she was elegant and eclectic.

"Pleasure to meet you, Mim," Paige hesitated hoping she'd pronounced her name correctly.

"The pleasure is all mine," Mim cooed back. The darkness of her eyes shined like she knew the secret to everything. In a sea of red plastic cups and crate paper decorations, Mim stood in a long russet velvet duster fringed at the wrists and hemline with aurora borealis beads dangling and catching the light as she moved with a crystal glass full of deep red wine. she was clearly the queen of the dance. Her jewelry was unique, gold, amethyst and carnelian bent into flowing and circular shapes.

Etta turned toward Mim and kissed her on the cheek, "Paige you'll just love Mim's art! She's got several pieces in my gallery and her jewelry is simply the best!"

"Is this one of your pieces?" Paige reached out to touch the medallion hanging from the long chain.

"Yes, I call it 'the mother'. I'd never sell this piece, you see I was inspired by the harvest rituals of the Celtic culture while I toured Europe a few years back." Mim waved her wine glass into the air as if the memory of the ritual unfolded before her. Paige was mystified as Mim started to tell the story.

Etta, not wanting to get drug deep into the conversation interjected, "Paige has taken on quite a project, Mim, she's bought the old girl uptown. Going to turn her into a Bed and Breakfast," Etta said raising an excited eyebrow.

"Fabulous!" Mim opened her arms widely, slipping carelessly from her story to making eye contact with Paige, "You look perfect for the job! I bet you'll bring that old girl a shiny new face and a whole new life." Mim winked in slow motion, and then pulled Paige into an unexpected hug. Paige felt as if she'd been blessed by the Holy Mother herself.

CHAPTER 5

Tearing off the damaged and splitting pickets and posts of her front porch, the boards radiated heat in the afternoon sun through her thin canvas tennis shoes into her feet. She was infuriated by her constant preoccupation with Jake. Paige pulled a ballast from the railing and threw it into the dumpster off the side of the porch with gusto. How in the world could he have come onto her at the dance? She ripped off another piece of shoddy wood and tossed it. She'd been furious about it for days. Wondering why she didn't see Jake and Betty together, she came to a romantic conclusion; they were so comfortable they didn't require constant contact. A little streak of jealousy ran through her. Of course her attraction to him was bothersome. She damn sure wasn't going to get into an emotional gut bucket with an attached man again! She assessed her work and flipped on the Shop-Vac to clean up her mess before she began priming the wood of the new ballasts leaning against the mansion.

In the high pitched whirring of the vacuum cleaner she heard a clear and unmistakably female voice, "You're still a fool..."

She jerked her head around and the only other life form on the porch was Wally. In the six years they had been roomies, he had never talked. Walking down the front steps she scanned the yard, no one there.

"Hello?" Paige looked down the side of the house. Invisible fingers touched her hand, sending chills up her arm and across her shoulders. She shook off the uncomfortable sensation and laughed, returning to the task at hand.

Mastering the art of the saws-all, the drill and the pneumatic nail gun was a piece of cake compared to the stubborn can of primer that refused to be opened. She'd used a screwdriver, a hammer, and now she looked at the tortured rim chewed all to hell realizing it had gotten the best of her. Wally looked at the can, fell on his side and started batting at it.

"Nice try," Paige eyed the cat.

"Always have the right tool for the job." He was in her yard again! "Try this." Jake tossed up a funky looking tool on his keychain and it worked like a cinch as she popped open the can.

Her shoulders fell and she looked at him standing at the base of her stairs, leaning heavily on the rail. His crutches were gone, but she could tell his foot was still giving him grief. Paige looked him square in the face, "What is it about you? Do you have some deep seeded hero envy? I really am able to do this on my own."

"I know you are. I just had the right tool," he looked satisfied.

"Why is it on your keychain?" She called down the stairs at him.

"Well it's called a church key and it's been on my key ring since I was in high school. A guy's gotta' have a way to get into his root beer quickly. At least that's what I used to tell Auntie Mim." He winked at her.

"Ah yes, Mim..." she said on a breath. Jake climbed the stairs with a wince here and there until he was at the top and eye level to Paige.

"Well my Aunt by proxy. She went to high school with my mom and they'd been great friends. She raised us after our parents and grandparents died." He looked out over the yard quickly and cleared his throat, "Anything else I can do? Any jelly jars you're having trouble with?" His crooked smile was intentionally charming and flirtatious, Paige was sure of it. She narrowed her eyes at him but thought immediately about a stuck door in the upstairs hall.

"Actually, I can't seem to get..." she stopped short the instant she began to talk and looked at his foot, cursing herself for finding him easy to talk to.

"What is it?" he saw her gaze was on his foot, "Come on, I've been advised that moderate exercise is what I need at this point."

"Well, there is a door stuck in the hallway upstairs. What kind of tool do you recommend for that job? Or do you have something on your keychain?" She smiled raising one eyebrow, crossing her arms. Flirting, she was flirting with him and she couldn't stop!

"Sounds like its either wood swelled up or paint sealing around the edges. Do you have a utility knife?"

"The curiosity is killing me." she said, "I'll grab it in the kitchen."

"I'm free for the rest of the day... closed the office early," holding the door, he limped in behind her,

"It's the only stuck door upstairs, I'll get the knife."

The door was standing open by the time Paige got up the stair. Jake was nowhere to be seen. She looked past the opened door up a flight of stairs. Naturally, there was an attic. Every house she'd ever known had a crawl space to the attic. She grabbed onto the railing and went right up.

"It's pretty cool up here!" Jake yelled when he heard the squeak of her steps coming up.

The stairs were walled in on both sides until she ascended into an open space filled with dingy light. Benches and shelves were in one corner flanked by windows. One of several doors on the other side was open and she assumed that's where Jake could be found. Walking though the doorway, trying to soak it all in, she looked for Jake.

"Wow," was all Paige could say. She leaned in through the open door and looked inside to see trunks and boxes stacked high through the room. She didn't see him, so she yelled out. With a sharp whomp, everything went sideways. The next thing Paige knew he was hovering over her prone body, surrounded by the smell of him, spicy and warm. They were arguing in her dream. Her heart hurt, the love she had for him was all consuming. He was telling her something that hurt her, he wouldn't look into her eyes. She wished him closer. She could never get close enough. His voice cut right through the dream she was in.

"PAIGE!" Her eyes fluttered. He was just inches from of her face, "There you are." He looked horrified.

"What happened?" She blinked against the light in the room.

"You called out and when I jumped up I slammed that door right into your head. You went down like rock, scared the hell out of me!" Relief spread over his face.

"Let me see the damage." Gently he brushed the bangs away from her forehead, "Oh not that bad. You were only out for a second or two."

The heat of his touch crept into her skin, reminding her how cold she felt, even though the attic had been hot when she walked into it. The dream she had still lingered in her heart and it ached. Confused, she blinked hard trying to focus. The scent of him surrounded her until she realized how close he was. Her eyes were wide and panic hit her hard as she crab walked backwards right out of his arms scuffling to stand on her own, which ended badly as her legs buckled. He wrapped his steady arms around her. Despite her protest, he helped her back to a bench.

"That's it, I'm calling it a day for you." He got puffed up and manly.

"Who do you think you are, anyway?" Thinking he looked ridiculous, she stood up too quickly and flopped right back down.

"I'm taking you down stairs. Have you eaten anything today?" He asked.

"Yes, I had a banana and a box of juice earlier."

"Well you're running on empty, its four thirty." He was helping her stand and get to the stairs.

"I'll make a sandwich or something..." She certainly didn't need anyone to take care of her.

"Nope, no PB&J, not on my watch," He squeezed her arm as she tried to wriggle past him, "tonight you'll have filet mignon, baked potato and salad."

"Jake, there is no way... besides I'm watching my carbs." She said feeling the steel cold warning in her gut.

"Ok, I get the potato and you eat half of mine. I know how it works..." he smiled.

"What about Betty, don't you have plans with her tonight?" She asked pointedly and started down the stairs.

Jake followed right behind her, "Let me see, well its Wednesday, so yes I do, we play pinochle on Wednesdays. I'll call her and cancel... no big deal."

"You will not!" She stopped halfway down the stairs and turned quickly, which planted her face right into his chest. He stopped short and grabbed her arms to stop another tumble.

"Jake there's something you have to take seriously about me..." She stopped talking and looked up into his face. He lowered with a wince to the step she was on which brought them much too close; she could see the silver flecks in his eyes even in the dark, tight stairwell. Her nose almost touching his chin, electricity built as their breath merged, he lowered his face to her.

"Get out!" She gasped.

"What?" he wrinkled up his face, pulling away from her, but he didn't let go of her arms.

"You heard me, Jake, just go." Paige pointed her finger at the door and stood aside, shrugging his hands off of her arms. Jake limped down the stairs and out of her sight.

She immediately called Etta, "Hey, I need a girl night. You in?"

"Oh that sounds great, but you'll have to come to the girls. It's mahjong night at Auntie Mim's!"

"Is there some kind of city ordinance that says Wednesday night is game night?" She felt tired and ill tempered, "I mean, what should I bring?" Paige laughed out loud at the absurdity of a town wide ordinance for game night.

"You bring yourself, but you have to dress appropriately, Mim's rules. I'll bring you something. Red or gold?"

"Gold." Paige said without deliberation even though she had no idea what she'd ordered.

"I'll be here to get you at six. You're driving, I'm drinking..."

"After the day I've had that's probably a wise decision."

CHAPTER 6

All the way down the winding roads Paige weighed in her mind how she could possible start a conversation about her strange dreams and her uncanny connection to the mansion. She couldn't come up with one. She didn't want to be branded the crazy new woman in town.

"Oh, turn in here." Etta said after they had traveled quite a while on a narrow windy road.

"You have got to be kidding me! Wow," Was all Paige could say.

Between two stone pillars, ornate wrought iron gates stood open to a long driveway lined with crepe myrtle trees. The house, completely made of stone, stood as a testament to all good fairy tales, with its tall chimney and long sweeping 'A' framed porch. They pulled into the circular drive and walked up the cobblestone trail to the front door, which was made of heavy wood with big black iron hardware. Etta grabbed the handle and went right in. Sitar music filled the house. Her mouth watered as the delicious aroma of oriental spices welcomed her. Mim appeared wearing pale blue silk pajamas with huge sleeves almost trailing the floor.

"Paige, Darlin' welcome to Mahjong night," She opened her

arms and met her with a kiss on the cheek; "You come on in and meet the girls."

Mim slipped her arm through Paige's and led her through the foyer that opened up into a large room lit entirely by candles. Mim had not picked a style and stuck to it in her decorating. She was a collector of interesting things. An antique, eight foot tall carved statue of the Goddess Durga presided over the room. A chaise lounge covered in deep beautiful blue brocade stretched across one corner, anchored by antique green slag glass lamps and pewter candle sticks with well used candles alight and dripping.

The art was fascinating to Paige and she stopped in front of a huge canvas to examine the details. "Mim, is this one of your paintings? I don't see your signature." Paige asked.

"Why, yes, I call it 'intermission'." Mim commented, stopping to check Paige's reaction to her work.

"It's so unique." Paige stated looking at it from a different angle.

"It's from the nekkid years." Mim said softly.

Paige turned to her hostess and waited for an explanation, "Well, during menopause, I would wake up in the middle of the night and lay in bed furious that I couldn't sleep. After a few months of that nonsense, I decided to get up and do something instead of lay there getting madder by the minute. So, I started painting in the middle of the night. While painting this one, I got started getting hot flashes so I stripped my clothes off and painted naked. No one was awake, the whole world was quiet and eventually I moved my easels outside onto the patio." Mim glanced up into Etta's face, "Only once did I get found out by my boys. But that taught them to stay in bed if they didn't want to catch me nekkid in the moonlight, nipples to the breeze." Mim patted Paige's hand before turning toward the group. Paige blushed at the knowledge of that feeling.

"Look here, chickens, our own Paige is joining us!" Mim took her arm and walked her outside onto the magical lanai like a proud mother.

Paige recognized the group from the barn dance and was charmed at the sight.

"Paige, this is Addy, She has the little bakery at the top of the hill, not far from your house." Addy rose from her pillow on the ground, she was tall and lean with long dark curly hair. She was in her late fifties, wearing a red Japanese style jacket with black slacks and no shoes. Abby extended a hand over the table to Paige.

"This is Della, she owns the dinner theater." Della was barely five feet tall, rounded in all the right areas and soft spoken. Also in her late fifties and wearing a cherry blossom print robe tied in the front. Her shoulder length big hair had so many colors of blond, auburn and brown it was hard to tell what was original. Della took short quick steps around the table to give Paige a warm hug, waving her tiny bejeweled hand toward the only male at the table, "This is Patrick, we call him Patti, and he's in charge of tourism in Nevada County." Patti wore a spring green kimono and had a silk tie around his head with a Japanese character on it. She instinctively smiled when she looked into his beautiful green eyes that had been lined with black. His glossy pink lips pouted as he batted his eyes and extended an animated hand to her. She didn't know if she should shake it or kiss it. She clasped his hand in both of hers thinking it was the safest reflex. He beamed at her, "Oh Honey, you're all that and a sip of sake!" The women laughed in unison, easily. Paige felt welcome as if she'd always been part of the intimate little group.

Over dinner Paige listened more than talked to the chatter of women who had known and obviously loved each other forever. They spoke their own language, a kind of verbal shorthand that she was slowly picking up on. Patti's blond hair framed his face like a sun sticking out on all directions. His eyes flashed mischief as he grabbed the second bottle of Sake with a flourish and said, "Paige, you've been so quiet. You look like a woman with a story to me." He popped the cork on the bottle, "Spill it, Sister, we're all listening."

Paige looked around the room which had taken on a fuzzy glow, "I have friends. But it never felt like this to me."

"You mean our grand costuming?" Della asked reaching into her pocket and pulling out a jeweled cigarette case and lit up like a glamorous movie star. Mim rolled her eyes and Patti reached over, snatching the cigarette and sneaking a puff before he handed it back to her with a bat of his eye, lifting his chin to dramatically exhale the smoke.

"What I mean is I can sit here with you and feel so at ease. I've just met most of you."

"I bet there's a story about a man..." Addy said, brushing her wild curls away from her eyes.

Paige snorted, covering her nose with her fingers, "I'm not sure you're ready for my man stories." She blinked apologetically over her hand feeling the effects of the sake.

"We've all got 'em. We all know 'em. Your secrets are safe with us." Della said softly, edging Paige to tell the story they all wanted to hear.

Paige looked around at the faces surrounding her, glowing in the flickering light of paper lanterns, "My last romance ended badly..." Paige tried to hold back a grin as the women leaned in closer, "I had just broken up with Josh who was seventeen years younger than me." Nodding heads were all around her and Addy passed the sake bottle again. "The day he showed up on a skateboard instead of his truck the age difference hit me hard. He was getting serious and very comfortable. Coming into my house opening my fridge, you know, expecting me to be an extension of his mother. He mentioned babies and that he wanted a whole house full. I don't even like children! I am almost forty years old and there is no way I want to have kids now. So, I broke up with him." Paige said, "I met Carl the next week when my car wouldn't start at the movie theater. After he jumped the car, he asked me if I wanted to get some coffee. We talked about so many things and the conversation just flowed... no uncomfortable silences. He sent me flowers the next day, Daffodils, dozens of Daffodils. I swear to you I thought I would melt every time that man came around. He had smooth good looks, an investment broker, always in an impeccable suit. He spent money on me, which was nice after Josh. I almost always paid."

"Men in suits...how delicious, you don't find many around here..." Patti placing his chin in his open palm listening for more with a dreamy sigh...

"So he jumped your car and then he jumped you!" Addy laughed.

"I did make him wait for about three dates." Paige said sheepishly.

"At our age honey if you wait for the third date..." Patti

started...

Mim hushed him. "Stop it Patti, She gonna' think we are just a bunch of common alley cats here..."

Paige laughed but continued her story, "So we dated but never in our town. We always went for long weekends, or dinner at my house. I was never invited to his home. He told me I was too pretty to keep home. Then on my birthday, he called forty five minutes before we were going on a weekend trip and canceled. The next week he called and wanted to take me out and make it up to me. He was the king of 'make it up to you baby'. He wanted to go to the next town over but I made reservations at my favorite Italian restaurant and although he agreed I could tell he wasn't happy. Anyway, I wanted more of him. I wanted it so bad it became a pain in my chest that never left me. We'd been seeing each other for a little over nine months. I figured it was time to, you know, move forward, or get out!"

Heads nodded all around the table and Patti sat back in firm agreement folding his arms across his chest.

"So I bought this incredible dress with peek-a-boo cleavage, four inch red high heels with little straps at the ankles and I dotted on the perfume that drove him wild. When I got there, he was leaning against his black Lexus SUV." Paige closed her eyes, shaking off the memory, because she couldn't believe he still affected her. "Can you call a man beautiful?" Paige looked around and they were all nodding with wide eyes in agreement.

Patti rolled his eyes, held his hands up, "HELLO!"

"He was dark and dangerous, the most sensuous man I've ever known. I knew by the look on his face he was drinking in every detail, gazing over the strappy shoes, the way the silky material flowed over me. I felt, sexy and invincible! His hands reached out, but it was his lips I felt first, he whispered against my cheek, 'my God you look good enough to eat.' The feeling of his breath against my skin started the buzz, you know, deep in your belly. I was so dizzy next to him I had a hard time walking in those shoes.

We sat there in a quiet corner on the patio, in the sunset, the kind that turns from orange to purple... and the candle light, it was one of the most romantic nights of my life. He kept looking around like he was robbing a bank or something, but he ordered wine in perfect Italian," Paige rolled her eyes at the memory, "Then he looked right at me and said, 'you look a thousand miles away precious.' I asked him if he knew how long we'd been seeing each other and I could see a panicked look roll over his face. Then he kissed my hand and told me, 'I could know you a hundred years and never tire of loving you.'" she shook her head, "So I was looking out at the sunset trying not to tear up at the thought of him always with me" Every eye was fixated on Paige and waiting for the finish to her story.

"Then he got this look on his face, like, he knew what I wanted and he was going to give it to me. He slid a jewelry box across the table and sat there looking at me. I picked it up and held it to my chest, because I just knew it was the ring I had been waiting for. I said a little prayer and opened the box. It was a necklace... beautiful, diamonds, huge emerald in the middle of an extravagant Victorian design. All I could see was a noose, no promise. So I stared at that damned open box until tears fell on my arms. I closed the box, put it into my purse and walked away. I felt guilty about keeping the necklace. I was almost ready to give it back when I found out he was married and had three kids."

The women were silent, caught in the web of Paige's story.

"When I threatened to 'out him' to his wife and the community of which he was the cornerstone, he threatened me with imminent domain for my sweet little house. The city had been begging me to sell it to them for years, but I refused. Less than thirty six hours after I demanded him to come clean, I got the notice of imminent domain. I fought it but each time I appeared before a judge, who was also his brother, I lost my appeal. It broke my heart." Paige sat quietly. Reliving the hurt pulled her down. She wiped away an unexpected tear.

Finally, Mim raised her Sake glass and toasted, "Here's to Carl, smokin' a turd in hell for what he did to you, Honey."

Every glass was raised, "To Carl, smokin' turds in hell" they said in unison.

Paige began laughing hysterically, "How did that just make everything ok?"

"It's our witchy way Paige, you'll get used to it." Etta cooed.

"What is it that brought you to Nevada City, Honey?" Patti asked.

"Well, my mother told me I was born here. I was curious so I did a little research. I found a picture of the mansion online and I fell in love. Well, I don't think I fell in love until I got here, but I was obsessed with that house. I looked at it every day for a week. Once I got the notice of imminent domain, I started to think seriously about buying it. Before I really knew what I was doing I owned it! I don't remember living here; I think we left when I was two."

"Of course you remember it, Darlin', you're a child of red dirt. You belong here... don't you feel it? What is your mother's name?"

"Maggie Hamilton. She never told me much about this place. We moved to Oregon to be closer to my father's family when I was two."

"What's her maiden name dear?" Della asked.

"Oh, sorry, it's Matheson." Every eye perked and curious smiles widened across the table.

"Of course it is," exclaimed Mim, leveling off a knowing look at Paige," You're the great great grand daughter of Hal and Gigi Matheson. There is a strong family resemblance. Your great granddaddy's picture is hangin' in the courthouse today. He was one tough judge here. He brought justice back to the town when it had gone crazy, at least that's how the story goes. He's a legend around here."

"I felt so peaceful when I arrived, like I'd been waiting to get here my whole life." Paige said quietly.

Mim reached behind her, plunging her hand into the flower bed and grabbed a handful of earth, holding it out to Paige, "It's a cellular response to red dirt. Once it's in you, you long for it always. Your family tree is so deeply rooted here, Paige, it goes back to the gold rush! I moved from here once," Mim's eyes dimmed a little, "we all have at one time or another. I thought I'd lose my mind. Tragedy brought me back and I never wanted to leave again." Mim reached for Etta's hand on the table. "We're all waiting for some of our kids to come back. You know they leave for college and get out there in the world that's all nasty and crowded. They come back eventually...

most of the time." Mim looked away from Paige and gave Etta a quick smile.

"We can hope..." said Etta.

Examining the dirt in her hand Paige felt her smile reach deep into her gut, "So you're telling me that I've been drawn back here by the longing to be living on red dirt?"

"That's exactly right." Addy said everyone nodding in unison.

"So how's that explained?" Paige asked

Mim narrowed her eyes as she said, "Well, scientists will tell ya' that it's just a higher concentration of iron in the dirt. But I'm telling you if you're born here you'll always have the need to smell it, hold it, and build upon it."

"Interesting, my mother never mentioned this to me." She said quietly.

"That's because your Mamma wasn't born here. If I remember the story right, your grandmother married a man who moved her to San Francisco. So your Mamma was not born here."

Glasses were raised and a toast, "Welcome home, Paige."

~

"You were awfully quiet tonight Miss Etta." Paige said on the drive home.

Etta smiled and gave Paige a shy look, "Reflective I guess. What did you think of our gathering? Aren't they just the best?"

"There is something engaging about each one, but when you put them all in one room, well it's mind blowing. I feel that I've just crawled out of the rabbit hole in Wonderland. They're fabulous...and Mim, painting naked in the moonlight" Paige shook her head, imagining what that would feel like to be naked under the stars.

"The boys only walked out there one time, but you know, I used to sneak out and watch her paint all the time. To this day was the most magical thing I've ever seen."

"How many paintings came from the 'nekkid years'?"

"Only a handful, but she won't sell them, she says they feel too personal."

"You're all Goddesses."

"Now you're one of us, Paige. You can never go back." Etta Laughed.

~

Seven O'clock that evening, Jake walked through his kitchen ignoring the bag of groceries on the counter that needed to be put away. Grabbing another beer, he turned at the creaking of his back door and saw Will come in, who was still wearing his basketball shorts and jersey.

"Hey what's in the bag?" Will didn't wait for an answer, but rifled through it like he lived there, which he did not, he was just "staying" for an undetermined amount of time.

Will and Jake had been great friends their whole lives, raised like brothers. William was Mim's son, one year younger than Jake. Opposite to Jake's light complexion, Will had dark Mediterranean features, a chiseled strong face giving him an intensity that cracks wide open when his smile releases dimples and a mischievous nature. Jake knew there was the spirit of a Newfoundland puppy inside Will's picture perfect body that women drooled over. It was hard to take him seriously. Half the time he was a goof ball. But there was never a doubt in Jakes mind that Will had his back. His year long absence hadn't affected their friendship, if anything it made Jake appreciate Will even more.

"Hey, you fixin' me dinner? Steak and salad, wow and baked potato with all the guts... Dude, there's only one, but I'll share." He started to unwrap the stakes.

"Have you no pride?" Jake asked flopping down onto a kitchen chair against the wall.

"Nope, none."

Jake held up his beer, "This is my dinner."

"NO, no, stop, you're hurting my ears, look at this food! I'll even start the Webber. This is date night food, how'd I score..." Will slowly sat the steak down and looked closely at Jake, "Oooooh, bad night?"

"Misunderstanding, that's all." Jake raised an eyebrow cautioning his friend he wasn't talking about it.

"Gotcha, I'll start the fire and let's get this party rollin'." Will grabbed a beer and headed for the patio. Jake knew Will wouldn't let the situation rest, so he followed him outside.

"Is this about that woman from the barn dance that has you brooding? Did she stand you up?" Will had only been back for a day and already he had his finger on the pulse of all things Nevada City.

"It's a long story and Betty's probably mad because I cancelled our Pinochle night." Jake stared at the decking under his feet.

"Betty was in bed thirty minutes after you called her. She'll get over it. I'll bet she gets up in the morning and bakes you cookies."

Jake smiled. She probably would and that made him feel like an even bigger heal.

"How long are you going to lurk in the shadows before you let your mom know your back?" Jake asked, deflecting the conversation, and then took a long chug of his beer.

"I figure I'll give her a call and invite her to dinner. When the scolding stops, she'll be glad to see me."

"You're going to take her out instead of holding out for one of her exotic meals? Men die for less you know."

"Ah, but you underestimate me Sir, I'm going to woo her into forgiveness for the way I left, then she'll have a huge gathering out there and we'll all profit from my good fortune." Will nodded, holding up his bottle.

"Your right, Auntie Mim can't hold a grudge, not against you, the prodigal son."

"I've got a lot of groveling to do."

CHAPTER 7

Paige took the long way to town, past Etta's house. The quickest route, which she had always taken in the other direction, had shielded the vision of Etta's cottage that stood before her. The body of Etta's house was cornflower blue and the shutters were yellow with raspberry trim. The gingerbread on the eve of the house was painted tangerine and the little details sprinkled here and there were a mixture of bright and brilliant colors. Etta's house was alive! It had character and a voice on their street that said, 'I'm bold, loud and beautiful! I don't care what you think.' How in the world had Etta captured her own personality in the painting of her house?

"The style is called Painted Lady." Etta yelled from her garden on the side of her house, reading the look on Paige's face.

"Amazing... Did you do this all by yourself?"

Etta rose up from her weeding and walked toward her gate to meet Paige, "I did the painting. I had the help of an artist when I chose the colors. He is actually quite famous now; he's planned the color pallets of the truly beautiful houses in Nevada City and Grass Valley."

"I'd like to hire him," Paige's eyes brightened, "This is amazing."

"He's pretty hard to track down. I don't think anyone's seen him in almost a year." Etta's eyes darted back to the eves of her house, "I'm sure Ernie can help you chose a good color pallet." Etta's voice broke softly, "I have a lot to do before it gets too hot out here… have fun in town, Paige." She turned and walked away leaving Paige gawking at Etta's home which exploded in colors.

Etta's house inspired her to get cracking on the colors of her Bed and Breakfast mansion. Painting was one thing she could plan herself. Walking a few blocks out of her way she enjoyed every step savoring the details of each Painted Lady she walked past. They stood out like pretty party dresses among wall flowers of simple white or yellow. Some had only variations of one color, but after careful consideration you could see the tiny details that had been tended to. All of the houses had their own personalities. If she stood still each house had a private story. Her house was among the very few that had fallen into ill repair. She now felt it was her duty to bring her old girl back to life and let her have another hundred years of glory in the historic city.

Once on Broad Street, she found the hardware store. She pushed at the heavy brilliant blue door. The brass bell hanging from twine rang to announce her presence.

"Paige, what can I do ya for?" Ernie asked with a toothy grin.

He made her smile, "Paint. Do you have a wheel or paint chips or something I can choose from?"

"Sure enough…" he walked her to a wall of paint, "Interior or exterior?"

"Exterior," She said looking daunted, "Wow there's a lot to choose from."

"Yep, I've got the best selection in Nevada County! And I'm an expert color mixer." Ernie walked back to the register to help a man who didn't look familiar to her.

She scanned over the colors, trying to imagine what each one would look like. A couple of years of art classes lodged in the back of her mind only confused what she was looking at. In her hand she had chosen a grey base and blue accents. But she wasn't happy about it.

"May I?" The man at the counter had wondered over to her.

Paige snapped out of her color trance and looked at a man who was examining her choices, "What?"

"I just think your making a mistake with these colors." He said with an air of confidence.

"Really?" Paige gave him a sharp warning look and stood back crossing her arms.

"Yes," he recognized a woman who didn't want to be messed with but preceded with tenacity that Paige found just a little irritating.

"These colors are depressing. If I were to choose a pallet for you I would choose rich muted colors, something deep and soft. Here, how about this..." She watched him select one and hold it up, deliberate and then handed her "Garden Spot" his head tilted sideways and then he pulled out "Wood Violet" and "Enchant". That's a good start, but don't use white, go with something warm and creamy."

"Thank you." She said looking at a color pallet that made her smile. All of her favorite colors in the perfect shades to complement each other. "How'd you do that?"

"It's a trade secret. But I can tell by watching you that you don't show yourself easily. Your deep and thoughtful... takes a while to get to know you." He handed her another chip, "For little details."

She looked at the chip which read, 'Ember glow,' "Nice." She said smiling at the encounter.

"You must be Paige." He extended a hand, "I'm Will."

"Will, I'm so sorry I don't remember meeting you."

"Will you walk with me? I'll buy you an ice cream." He offered.

"Bribery." she glanced sideways at him and thought for a moment. Who was this mysterious paint magician? He was drop dead gorgeous and goofy all at the same time. An air of confidence vibrated from him but his kid-sized smile told her he wasn't too full of himself. Paige was curious, "Sure, I'll go for ice cream." Besides, she thought it would give her something to think about besides Jake, the cheater and the bizarre dreams of the gold rush days.

With ice cream in hand they stopped in the park to sit on a cement bench.

"I just rolled back into town yesterday. My buddy told me all about you though... you're making him sweat it out! I can see why he's so upset." He leaned back on the cement bench and nodded, eyes flirtatiously searching her face.

"Who would your buddy be?" Paige had no idea what he was talking about.

"Jake Jenkins. He's at work right now wondering what he did wrong. He's been trying to get your attention for weeks and apparently you're not biting."

"Biting?" She was so confused! Why did everything in this town have to come back to Jake Jenkins, it was infuriating!

"So you see Paige, my friend Jake is a fisherman, he's not a hunter."

Her shoulders fell and she looked him straight in the eye, "I am having a hard time following you."

Will's flirty look faded quickly, "Jake doesn't hunt, Paige. A fisherman puts himself out there and figures if the woman doesn't bite, he'll change lures and keep trying until she's interested. Most of us knuckle draggers hunt down and club what we want and drag it back to the cave. With Jake, he's got to know you're interested. So, why aren't you interested?"

"I don't hang out with men who have other interests." She took a bite out of her ice cream cone, "What about Betty?" She said around the ice cream in her mouth.

Will burst out laughing, "He's loved betty since he was 5 years old!"

"So it's more than just high school sweethearts..." Paige felt confused and deflated.

"Oh yeah, it's much more than that." Will licked his ice cream, contemplatively, "do me a favor and get to know him. He's one of the good guys, Paige."

"Are you visiting or do you live here?" Paige asked him trying to change the subject.

"It's the call of red dirt... I couldn't stay away any longer. Have reason to put my roots back into it and let them spread out."

"I recently had a friend tell me about red dirt and the draw to those born here." Warmed by the memory, she looked back to Will.

"My Mother has the same theory. She'll be happy to see me again."

Paige leaned back to get a good look at him, "So you were born here, grew up here... that's how you know Jake?" He nodded.

She burst out, "So you know Etta!" Will's head fell back and a lazy smile spread across his face and up to the sky, "Yes, Etta." He looked lost in the statement. Then it all started to make sense.

~

With morning coffee in hand, Paige contemplated the color chips plastered to her refrigerator door. There was no way to improve on them, they were perfect. Warm, rich and muted, all the colors that felt safe and happy to her. "Thank you." Paige heard a woman say. She jumped almost spilling her coffee. Wally was unaffected by the other voice in the room.

"Hello?"

"Thank you for tending my house." The voice was soft and small.

"Where are you?" Paige look around, "What are you doing in my house."

"It's my house, dear." The voice answered, but there was no one there.

"Who are you?" Goose bumps rose all over her body.

"I'm Georgia." The small voice tinkled like a bell in her head.

Paige looked again to Wally who was paying no attention to the voice crisis.

"What are you doing in my house?" Paige asked again.

"It's always been my house dear; my Grandmother had it built for me."

"So, you're a.... a ghost?" the coffee in her cup began to tremble.

"I don't know... I've always been here. It's where I belong."

Paige thought fast. She wasn't above sharing her house with the ghost of the woman who owned it previously. A conversation with a ghost! What was next, a gypsy telling fortunes in the parlor? Paige reached for the phone and dialed Etta immediately.

"Etta, can you come over, I've got a situation here..."

Paige was afraid to say anything out loud that would prompt the suddenly gregarious Georgia. She poured a cup of coffee just as Etta was walking through the door, "Here..." Paige thrust the cup at her friend.

"Thanks, there's a coffee crisis?" Etta looked wide eyed at Paige and ruffled Wally's fur.

"Don't think I'm crazy but I'm hearing the voice of a woman who's not here. She says her name is Georgia." Paige braced herself for Etta's response.

"Oh you met! I've seen her wandering for years. I wasn't sure of her name. She obviously likes you or she'd have run you out like the previous owners." She frowned into her cup. "They weren't very nice people."

"What are you saying?" Paige clung to her coffee cup like a lifeline. "I'm not following..."

"When this house went through probate, which took decades, some shirt tail member of the family sold it. By that time this place was a wreck! The new owners weren't happy here. I think your ghost helped run them out of Nevada City, if the truth be told." Etta looked out the window thoughtfully.

"You're asking me to believe in ghosts?"

"Well, you're telling me you're talking to Georgia and I'm telling you she died decades ago. I think you already believe. Now what does she want? That's the question!"

"She wants to thank me for tending her house." Paige said softly, "So, I'm sharing my house with a ghost?"

"Spirits on this plane usually have something left unfinished. She'll probably go quietly once she sees the house restored. Until then talk to her like she's your friend."

"She'll *probably* go?" Paige's eyes widened.

"I'm fairly well versed in the area; I'll read up on it some more and when the time is right, we'll help Georgia on to the other side." Etta rambled until her gaze landed on the paint chips on the fridge, "Nice choices Paige. This is a beautiful combination."

The thought of telling Etta about her meeting with Will brought an immediate grin, "Oh I yeah, I met someone yesterday…"

"Paige!" Etta stopped mid stride and looked up to the ceiling at nothing, "I think there is more than one spirit here. Georgia has ties to you!"

CHAPTER 8

The sign hanging over the door of Jake's cabinet shop read, "Jenkins Fine Cabinetry." It had been hand painted beautifully in gold show card paint by his Auntie Mim as a gift the day he re-opened the doors without his granddad. The building and its contents had been willed to him five years previously when his teacher and mentor passed away. He loved being in the shop. It brought him closer to his granddad and the impact he'd had in his life. Mim also painted the sign that hung in front of his law office with the same gold paint.

"I'm not kidding, Jake, she thinks you and Betty are an item, that's why she's giving you the cold shoulder." Will was playing with a wood file, tapping out a beat on the edge of Jakes workbench.

"Seriously man, she's not interested in me." Jake was measuring for a miter cut.

"Don't count her out. I think she's perfect for you. She's a thinker; a nice surprise waiting inside that up-tight package."

"Have you offered to help her with that house?"

"Every chance I get." Jake was getting annoyed.

"Have you tried pulling the unbelievable romantic thing yet?" Will wasn't giving up easily.

"Dinner in the bag..." Jake paused, made quick eye contact

and creased his forehead at Will.

"Right, well it wasn't a lost cause," Will patted his stomach.

"Go over there tonight. I'll go with you. Come up with some reason and we'll tag team it... then I'll slip over and see Etta."

"Yeah, then there is Etta, you piece of work, she only cried for months after you left with no warning Bro... she'll be thrilled to see you." Jake picked up an axe and made psycho noises with it.

"So, I've got some ass kissing to do... I'm ready," Will gave him a boyish grin.

"I don't think ass kissing is going to cover it." Jake laid the axe down, looked at his friend dead in the eye, "Don't hurt her again, Will, she's too good for that shit." Jake walked out the back screen and let it slam, ending the conversation.

Paige was tangled up in the rose bush with flakes of white paint flying everywhere as she passed the flat silver scrapper over the peeling and aged paint of her house "This is a lot harder than it looks," She brushed flakes from her safety goggles. Wally found it fascinating and rolled in the piles of what Paige could only imagine was lead based paint, "Oh, Wally, NO!" With the leg of her overalls hopelessly hung on the thorns she tried to scoop up her kitty and get him in the house away from the paint, but he was cagey when he didn't want to be caught. He ducked out of the shrubbery and ran across the lawn. "Fine, but stay away from my paint!"

"I'm calling Jake, he's got a pressure washer." Etta yelled from across the short fence separating their yards.

"Don't you dare! This is like a meditation for me." Paige realized she was ass deep in a rosebush, wrestling a cat covered in toxic paint chips. The safety goggles were so dusty she could hardly see Etta across the yard. Ripping her leg loose from the thorns, she tripped out of the flower bed and stood on her freshly mown lawn, slipped off the goggles and shook like a dog. The rain of tiny particles catching color through the air fluttered to settle around her feet. Then she blew a short breath up into her bangs for the final dusting and coated her lips even further.

"I hope your hair doesn't start glowing in the dark! Paige that's not healthy. At least wet it down so you won't breathe it."

Feeling ridiculous, "I'll call him. I've got to catch my cat, he's covered in this!"

Etta chuckled, "What's your plan tonight? I was thinking south of the border...Carne Asada Tacos?" Etta snapped her finger close to her head.

Wally's movement caught the corner of Paige's peripheral vision. She followed him around the back side of the house and placed a piece of tuna on the bottom step to tempt him close enough for her to catch. Once he was in a tuna coma eating his treat she nabbed him and ran a damp towel over his fur to remove any paint chips that he'd come into contact with. As long as the tuna kept coming Wally allowed the indignity of a public bathing. When Paige released him from her grasp, he meandered away stopping short of the corner to shoot Paige an accusatory glare. It was a clear message; Wally had given his mother the equivalent of the cat finger.

Once she called Jake, things happened quickly. He offered to bring the pressure washer by the house that evening. No flirting, no date invitations, he was all business. She was relieved as she stepped into the steaming shower to wash the work of the day away. Being with Etta came so easily, it was like they had always been friends, sisters separated at birth and reunited again. Paige searched her past for anyone who had touched her life like Etta had. She had her high school girl friends, but after they married and had kids things we never the same again.

"Bound by red dirt," Georgia said.

"It's starting to make sense to me." Paige whispered, "Well, not really... but I'm trying not to think too much."

"Good girl," Georgia cooed, "now open your heart."

"What are you talking about? You don't know anything about my heart." Paige argued as she toweled off her hair.

"Open your heart, Paige," the air around her head became lighter and she knew Georgia was gone.

Her recently acquired status as medium was still unnerving when she thought about it. She'd be walking through the mansion and suddenly see things as they had been in the 1800's. When Paige didn't think about it, talking to a dead woman who used to own her house was part of an ordinary day. The peculiarities of eclectic Nevada City crept into her life, welcoming like a quilt waiting by the fire on a cold night. But it was still damned weird.

Wally sat on the pile of clothes suspiciously watching Paige go through her closet like a tornado. She didn't want to look like she dressed for him. She didn't want to look sloppy either. Jeans, she decided, and a pale blue tank top that showed just a little cleavage. She slipped into the jeans and reached for the tank. Having her arms bare felt too sexy so she pulled a denim shirt over the tank, nodding in approval. Her hair was wrecked, half dried and all curly, so she put it up in a clip. It was a casual, 'oh, didn't know you were dropping by' look she was going for. Paige shook off the feeling she was getting ready for a date.

It was getting harder to deny her attraction to Jake; he'd become a constant visitor in her dreams. He didn't always appear as the Jake she knew. It was his pale blue silvery eyes shining out of a stranger's face. It was startling. When her mind wandered she could conjure up his smell surrounding her, the way his embrace drew her into him, how his face so close to hers felt when she looked into his eyes and relaxed for the kiss... she'd woke up wanting him more than once. Being burned by a taken man wasn't going to happen to her again. She may not have been able to control her dreams, but she was going to take charge of the situation and nip it in the bud. She heard a truck pull into her drive. Damn, why did he have to be so punctual? She slipped into her flip flops and ran out to meet him.

Bonnie Raitt was singing "Are you ready for a thing called love," when she walked out the kitchen door to meet him out back. He was casually leaning on the side of his truck, music lulling, smiling like a cartoon cat. He too, looked showered clean and charming, "*I ain't no icon carved outta soap, sent here to clean up your reputation...*"

"I just love Bonnie," Jake said over the music.

Her smile was immediate, "Me too."

"Wow... that smile! I don't think I've seen that from you before, well, not aimed at me."

"Thanks for coming over on short notice." She tried to wiggle away from the compliment.

"It's just a machine, sitting all alone in the back of my shop. It'll do ole Freddy good to be useful."

"You named your pressure washer?"

"All of my tools have names." He realized quickly what he'd said and looked away to hide his blush, "You know Paige, I think we may have gotten off to a rough start." His eyes were the most perfect shade of steel cool blue. She swallowed hard as he continued, "I would like to be your friend, if that's ok."

Bonnie was singing "Nick of time" behind him; *"When did the choices get so hard? With so much more at stake, life gets mighty precious when there's less of it to waste..."*

"I've learned that you can never have too many friends." She softened cursing herself for the weakness. She planned on blaming Bonnie.

"Hey Jake!" Etta was coming across the yard wearing her BBQ apron.

"Hey beautiful..." He reached out to kiss his sister's cheek.

"Stay for dinner, I've got enough for an army." She said without hesitation.

"Is that what I smell?" His nose was in the air, eyes closed, smile widening.

"Yep, you go get some Corona's and we'll eat in about an hour. Carne Asada!"

"You've got enough for an army you say... ok to bring someone?"

"Plenty..." Etta waved him off to get the beer. Bonnie was singing "have a heart" when he pulled out of the drive.

"How does that just happen? One minute we're scraping paint and the next we're having a Mexican dinner party?"

"I woke up with a hankering for Mexican food this morning, and while I was at the store

I had the urge to buy much more than we needed... I try to not question my intuition when it's working." Etta shrugged and pursed her lips, "It's a gift."

They were walking towards Etta's back yard when Paige said, "So, you just follow what your gut tells you?"

"I try." Etta opened the gate and held it for Paige.

Etta's back yard had all the colors of a carnival carefully organized to create the peace of a sanctuary. Huge oaks shaded overhead and bushes had been carefully selected to soften the edges. Flowers exploded from old wine barrel planters, ground cover cushioned the steps and Spanish moss grew obediently between the stones on her walkways. Tiny lights sparkled in the bushes surrounding the patio; four grottos located inside the entertaining area illuminated statues of women. It was evident that every blade and petal had been tended tenderly by Etta's extraordinary hand.

Paige's eyes couldn't get enough. Blooms and blossoms everywhere! The water fountain looked as though it had been there for hundreds of years, covered in moss, flowing quietly in the corner. It was alive with a magical earthiness known only to flower fairies and water babies. How had she known Etta for weeks and not experienced this backyard wonderland? She'd been too wound up in her own projects to see what was right next door. The table was set with brightly colored linens and plates.

Etta said, "I better grab two more."

Paige sat down on a cushioned wicker chair taking in the beauty of her surroundings. How had she survived her whole life without this particular feeling? She reached down to touch a striking pink azalea blossom and then went straight for the dirt. Placing her hand on the lumpy soil she tried to feel it, tried to draw from it the answers to her endless questions.

"You ok, Paige?" She looked up and Jake had entered the patio with a twelve pack of Coronas under his arm. He also had a pink box which she could only imagine held dessert. She drew her hand away from the dirt and patted it off against her jeans.

"Just taking it all in," she said honestly. "Didn't you say you were bringing someone to dinner?"

"Wanted to shower first, but he's not one to pass up a great meal." Jake headed toward the kitchen door and handed Etta the pink box. Paige had to smile. He'd definitely been raised right.

"Adult beverages" Jake came to the patio with a bucket full of ice and Corona's.

"My Hero!" Etta grabbed one before the bucket hit the table and plopped her bottom into a turquoise metal chair between her two guests.

Jake opened a beer, handing it to Paige, "Senorita," His masterful grip instantly created sweat on the bottle. Paige blushed with a flush of naughty thoughts.

"So, tell me Jake, what purpose does a power washer serve a cabinet maker?" Paige decided to take the conversation into safe waters.

"It belonged to my Granddad. The whole cabinet business does actually, well did, until he died a few years ago. Ole Freddie hasn't been run in a long time so I thought I'd come by in the morning and fire him up, show you how it all works."

"Tomorrow is Saturday. I don't want you to spend your day off working at my house."

"The truth is, I want to spend some time with you." He was being straight to the point.

Paige's hackles twitched and a surge of anticipation covered her immediately, "Listen Jake..."

"Wait just a minute Paige," he said softly, holding up his hands, "I think we have a misunderstanding..."

Etta took in a sharp breath, "Jesus," she gasped. They both looked at her to see tears welling in her eyes. They followed her line of sight to Will who was coming up the walk with a dozen pink roses. "That wasn't fair, Jake..." she ran straight toward the door shaking her head and ducking inside.

"Buddy!" Will called out to Jake, "Ah, fair Paige." He reached over to take her hand, grazing a kiss across her fingers. "Was that Etta making a quick getaway?"

"Don't, Will... this was obviously not a good idea."

"I'll talk to her... I got it." Will went through the kitchen door like he'd done it a thousand times... maybe he had, Paige thought. She certainly didn't know any details of his connection with Etta. He had never been mentioned, not by name anyway.

"I'm assuming there's a story?" Paige said quietly, shifting uncomfortably in her chair.

Jake met her eyes with a sorrowful look, "Yeah, there's history. If he comes back out with all his limbs, my guess is she'll forgive him. If not... start looking for a shovel." He took a long drink from his beer.

"A shovel?" Paige didn't quite follow.

"I love Etta enough to bury my best friends' body." His tone was somber.

"Sounds messy, not like Etta at all..." Paige said softly looking at the kitchen door for the answer.

They finished their beers and waited, voices could be heard from inside. There was no yelling. When the door opened, Will left with the roses in hand, saying nothing to either of them.

Etta came out moments later, her eyes freshly wiped and carrying trays of food, "I simply do not want to talk about it. Not with you," she looked at Jake, setting the trays down, "and I'll tell you about it later..." She looked to Paige. There was no argument. "So, tonight we drink." She raised her beer and they joined her in a toast to "To crimes of passion."

CHAPTER 9

"No, no... I think that should be just a smidge higher. Yes right there. Hang that sucker!" Mim waved her petite hand and Jake hammered in the last picture fastener of the morning. His head felt a little thick and pounding from the beers at Ettas the night before. Jake made a promise to Auntie Mim and there he was at 7am helping her add new art to Etta's gallery. Perched on a ladder he turned to get her final approval before he got down. Mim's gaze was fixated and tearful staring at the door, hands over her heart, "William!"

"Hi Mom," Will ran to pick up his mother, swinging her around in his arms.

"You wretch!" she smacked him with her balled up fist, "You are not the son I raised! You put me down this instant, I can't believe you just waltz in here, thinking I'm gonna' make all over you." Mim's eyes were blazing fire lasers. Will carefully put her tiny kicking feet back on the stone floor. "The fruit of my own womb...I can't even look at you!" Mim slammed her heals with purpose on the stone floor and disappeared into Etta's office and blasted the door shut.

"Way with the women, Bro..." Jake shook his head.

"Hey, your girl seems to like me ok." Will shot back squinting his eyes.

"First of all, she's not my girl, and you need to mend some fences quick my friend or I sense your life-force running low."

"I'm workin' on it."

"Flowers ain't gonna' fix this one, man."

Will was already knocking lightly on the closed door of Etta's office, "Come on Mom…"

Paige was humming in her kitchen. Raisin bran and yogurt in her bowl, coffee in her cup, she was ready to start the day. She sat down and tried talking to Wally who had assumed his position in the sunny window and was incommuni-cat-o.

"That's why I never had a cat." Georgia said.

"Good morning, Georgia."

"I always had dogs. They are happy to see you and forgive you anything."

"Forgiveness," Paige whispered under her breath, "great."

"It's the path to a peaceful heart."

"Was that little piece of advice for Etta?"

"Whoever needs it…So simple, really…Simple as pie!"

Georgia left the scent of berries in the air as she dissipated.

Jake's truck was slow down the drive, no music. He parked behind her little car and walked right to the power washer.

"Down in a minute," Paige yelled out the door.

"Bring an extension cord." He yelled back.

Paige bounced down the stairs wearing old athletic grey sweats, hair in a pony, no makeup, dragging fifty feet of orange cord from the kitchen. She wasn't going to fix herself up when she knew Jake was around sending the wrong message.

"Perfect!" Jake had the hose hooked up and they were dragging the machine over to the side of the house where Paige had been scraping the day before. "Okay, Freddy, make me proud..." Jake turned it on and a blast of water came out strong enough to strip the paint off the house in one pass.

"I'm impressed!" Paige reached for the handle.

"I don't mind helping." He passed the washer over three more boards exposing grey naked wood underneath. "I was hoping you would do something for me while I get this side of the house done..." Jake looked deep into her face for some empathy and turned off the washer.

"What is it?"

"Etta. I'm worried. Will you check on her this morning? I was an ass to invite Will last night. I don't think she really wants to talk to me about it. Maybe you can check in with her."

"Yeah, sure," She immediately turned and walked toward the gate connecting their back yards.

"Paige..." Jake called out, "Thanks,.."

Humble Jake, that was new.

The side door to the kitchen was open so she knocked on the screen and called into the house, "Good morning". There was no answer.

Paige peeked in through the screen. Dishes from last night's party were stacked high in the sink. She could hear water running and assumed that Etta was taking a shower. Cleaning up gave her something to do while she waited.

By the time Etta shuffled out in her robe, Paige had most of the dishes done and put away. "Now who's the angel?" Etta said softly running fingers through her wet hair.

"We should have done this last night." Paige turned to see her friend's puffy eyes and blotchy face. Her heart ached as Etta's shoved her shaking hands into robe pockets and slumped in a kitchen chair.

"Oh Dear," Paige said going straight to her side, "What can I do?" Placing her hand on Etta's shoulder she closed her eyes and remembered what Georgia said.

"Georgia wanted me to tell you something."

"Oh yeah, a direct quote from the other side?" Etta smiled weakly.

"Forgiveness is the path to a peaceful heart."

"Oh Paige, he's so easy to forgive. He's like a great big slobbery dog that you love and can't quite train. Forgiveness isn't the issue... I have to forget that he left me less than 8 hours after he said he loved me for the first time. I never got a letter or a call from him in all this time. He just went away." Silent tears were running down her face.

"Did you ask him why?"

"No, I just asked him to leave last night. He said he needed to talk to me and I was just struck stupid... I wasn't ready to hear anything he had to say to me."

"If it helps, he looked pretty defeated when he walked out of here last night."

"It doesn't help to know I've hurt someone I love. I just couldn't talk to him. But I will, and he'll explain, and I'll forgive and we'll move forward... it's just so hard to forget. I don't think I'll ever forget." Paige listened to every word but couldn't think of one thing to say about the situation.

"Jake's at my house blasting all that old paint away. It's amazing how fast that thing works!" Paige tried to lighten the conversation.

"He's a good guy Paige. He really is... why don't you get over there and tell him I'm okay. Thanks for doing the dishes." Paige was satisfied that Etta looked lighter.

Half of the south side of her house was exposed raw by the time she got back into her own yard. Jake was blasting away until she tapped his shoulder, "She's ok."

He turned Ole Freddy off and wiped the back of his hand across his forehead, "That's good. What's for lunch?" His boyish smile was intentionally trying to charm her.

"Good question." Paige mentally scanned her pantry, "How about Pizza?"

" I have strict rules about what I'll eat on a pizza."

"Really?" Paige put a hand on her hip waiting for his terrorist demands.

"Yeah, no fish, no fruit, it's a simple rule that many have a hard time with."

"No fish, no fruit, got it." She headed for the phone.

By the time Louis pulled into the drive with lunch Jake had finished the south side of the house and was relocating to the back. "Hey Lou, Glad to see you buddy, we're starving!" Jake pulled out his money and paid for the pizza before Paige had a chance to grab her wallet.

"Place is looking great" Louis said smiling widely at Jake.

"She's comin' right along." Jake said proudly.

"Miss Paige, glad to see you looking well," Louis said as he passed her getting back to his truck.

"You too Louis..." Jake was trying to sneak a piece before he got to the table.

"I was going to buy lunch... it's the least I could do after all of this."

"Eat up champ, the back end is calling your name." He said around the slice going into his mouth, ignoring her comment.

Paige looked at the backside of the house and thought, what a labor of love it was going to be.

Jake pulled his cell phone out of his pants and made a call, "Yeah, I need a favor, Bro. Scaffolding, I need the frame works on the back side of the shop and the old planks inside of it. Can you get Woody to help you and come on over to Paige's? Paige has... I think so... but if I were you, I'd lay low for a while. You get things smoothed out with your mom? Man you're a piece of work."

He looked at Paige, "Will and Woody are going to bring over scaffolding. There is no way to get to the top without it... Woody's like a spider monkey, he can crawl up to anything. I'll bribe him with pizza to hit the high spots."

Paige sat there chewing her pizza and listened to Jake take charge, which she hadn't yet resisted. She tried to wrap her head around three men in her yard, one monkey-like crawling over the high spots while the heartbreak kid and Jake watched on.

"When does it end Jake?"

"When I've helped you put the old girl back together or you kick me out for making a pass at you."

"I'm not dating you. Believe me, I'm saving you a world of trouble. I thought we were friends. Didn't we have that conversation just yesterday?"

"Yep."

"I thought I was clear."

"Crystal clear. But, once I know you better, it won't be enough, Paige."

"Have you forgotten about Betty?"

"Nope. Betty will always be my best girl." He said with a cocky grin.

"You're infuriating! If you think I'm going to..." The compressor that was powering the washer kicked on with a loud and clanging whir as Jake said, "We're not..." The hose blew spewing water wildly circling through the air.

"Save the pizza Paige, I'll get the hose." Jake yelled. "Damn it." He turned everything off and looked at Paige who resembled a pissed off wet cat holding a pizza box. "You sure look cute with your hair all curling up." Jake was standing in a puddle, handle in hand, water running over his head and dripping off of his nose.

Paige couldn't help it; she busted out laughing, "What in the world just happened?"

"My fault, I should have checked the hoses, they haven't been used in so long they got brittle."

Pulling up the bottom of his t-shirt and wiping his face, Jake exposed his toned and tan abdomen which Paige had to blink twice against before she quickly turned away and found a dry spot on the steps to set the pizza.

"I'll grab a towel." Paige said as she flew into the kitchen and caught herself, stopping with both hands on the table, "Don't do this, Paige!" she whispered. She couldn't afford another mistake, not in her new town with a fresh start.

"Pie?" Georgia said with humor.

"Go away!" Paige called into the empty room.

After changing into dry clothes Paige felt helpless as she watched the scaffolding erected against the side of the house. Jake replaced the hose and immediately, Will and Woody got to the job at hand. Woody was a goofy guy with a tall wiry build. He didn't say much, but nodded a lot and was so nimble on the scaffolding Paige thought he could climb the house without it. Will worked deftly and quiet like a man with a lot on his mind. She decided to provide a thank you to them and headed to the market to buy beer and some chips and salsa.

By the time she returned from the store, Will was smiling and joking with Woody and Jake. Paige brought the bags straight to the patio table and called a break. Handing out beers into eager hands she said, "Thank you all for your help!"

"All the thanks necessary," Will held up his bottle.

"Yeah" Woody nodded and chugged his beer half gone.

"We'll be done here in no time." Jake announced shoving onto the bench next to Paige. His leg was intentionally resting up against hers creating heat.

She wiggled away, "So, Woody, have you known these guys for long?"

"Yeah, Yeah," Woody nodded, taking out a cigarette and lighting up.

"You know what sucked about growing up in a small town?"

Will asked.

"Having everyone know who you are? Not being able to get away with anything?" Paige volunteered.

"Exactly!" Jake interjected, "Will and I tried so hard to be bad. We tried smoking out behind my granddad's cabinet shop after school one day. Will took the smokes from his mom and we stood out there behind all that machinery and huddled down, swearing to God, no one knew we were back there. We coughed and choked and smoked a whole cigarette between the two of us. We were walking tall, swaggering and bragging about what we did. By the time we got to the house, Auntie Mim told us she knew where we'd been and what we'd done and slapped a pack of cigarettes down the table and told us to have a smoke. We shook our heads no but she insisted we smoke until we were sick. You know what?"

"What..." Paige said trying to stop herself from laughing out loud.

"We never smoked again. Not once since that day has smoking sounded like a good idea."

Woody looked at the smoke between his fingers and shrugged, taking a deep satisfying drag.

"Any idea who ratted you out?"

"Oh it could have been one of a dozen people. I'll never know. It might have even been my Granddad; he always had a knowing eye on us."

"A whole town of people who cared about you must have been infuriating as teenagers!" Paige felt herself relax and she popped open a beer.

"Well, let's wrap this up..." Will sat his empty bottle down and headed toward the scaffolding. Woody jumped up and followed closely.

"You be around for a while?" Jake asked her.

"I live here. What're you asking?"

"If I can talk to you before I go?"

"I... Jake," she stumbled, "Of course." infuriated that she was incapable of saying no. How could she after he'd helped her all day, endured the humiliation of being drenched by his own machinery and abused his friendships to finish the stripping project? "I'll be in the kitchen. Wally needs his dinner." Paige made a hasty getaway.

It was definitely a raspberry pie cooling in the window. It smelled incredible. Wally was nowhere to be seen and Georgia lurked in the kitchen with a smugness that infuriated Paige. Now what? She'd have to offer the pie to Jake as a thank you and he'd want to have a piece right there and it would almost be dark. Jake would lure her into a conversation, which was becoming much easier than she wanted it to be with him. She *wanted* to watch Jake's face as he told her a story and to get a little too close to him and feel her skin tingle in anticipation to be touched. The possibility of finding herself in exactly the same position she was in back in Oregon was the only thing that kept her from throwing herself onto him just to feel the heat they could radiate. How was she going to avoid this? And now a Raspberry pie, great.

"You made pie!" his eyes danced as he put his face close enough to breath in the sweetness of the pie.

"Why don't you take it home with you? You can share with the boys."

"I'm not sharing this with those wolves! I'm going to eat it right here..." he pulled out a chair from the table and sat down expectantly.

Right, thought Paige, if she had indeed made him a pie, which she had not, wouldn't she be anxious for him to have a piece? Her lips pursed up as she turned to get a plate from the cupboard, "Georgia, quit meddling." She muttered.

"Excuse me?" Jake said.

"Nothing!" she gasped, "Whipped cream?" she asked sweetly.

"Smells delicious! Did you have trouble finding Raspberries? Whipped cream, yes."

"No trouble at all," Paige answered truthfully.

The pie cut solid, showing no signs of its transcendental origin. She held her breath as she inspected the filling and placed it onto a plate with a squirt of whipped cream on top. Jake took an eager bite and released a moan bordering on obscene. He reached for the whipped cream can and liberally covered the rest of the piece with a white mound of creamy sweetness.

"It's ok?" Paige had been holding her breath.

"God yes, I haven't had pie this good since before Auntie Mim gave up carbs in the 90's. We all suffered when she stopped baking the good stuff. Have you ever had a sugarless cookie?"

"Actually, I don't recommend it." She agreed.

Fascination washed over Paige as she watched him eat. An artful tongue darted at the tiniest wayward crumb. He ate with his whole body savoring every drop. Paige looked forward to watching him lick the plate with guilty anticipation, but he stopped short after licking his spoon. Apparently, Georgia was a great baker.

"You have to serve this at the Bed and Breakfast. What else do you bake?" Jake's question seemed to be self-serving.

"I haven't decided. I've got a few more months before I have to put energy into a menu."

"Well, not trying to boss you, but the menu is pretty important. Why not leave the dirty work to those with proper tools and focus on the details that are going to make your place shine, like menus and marketing."

"I love working on the house. It's restoring me."

"Can you at least agree to ask for help when you're over your head?" It was a kind request.

"I can try."

The air between them became calm and easy. He reached for her hand as they sat at the kitchen table, "its ok to ask for help, Paige." His blue eyes were so sincere she almost cried.

"Jake, I've always done things my way. I've always had to make due… alone." Paige tried to look strong as she crossed her arms leaning back on the counter.

"I think it's time you relaxed." He sat his plate in the sink and turned to her. One hand on each shoulder he turned her tummy to the counter's edge and massaged her shoulders from behind. The strength in his hands grew warm and healing as he rubbed her knotted neck and shoulders. Paige closed her eyes and allowed the sensation to fill her. His hands relaxed her down through her center, creating dreamy thoughts, the tingling lingered in her head and traveled down through her body pulsing to a throbbing burn in her… holy shit!

Her eyes flew open and she grabbed his hands, "Jake you

need to go."

"Did I hurt you? I'm so sorry..." He looked crushed.

"No," She turned quickly, which put her lips right next to his chin. She looked up into his eyes and swallowed her own gasp before she said, "You really need to go." She guided him toward the kitchen door to the back porch. He was grinning like a fool by the time she threw the door open and stood waiting for him to leave.

"You don't have to do that Paige, I wasn't trying to seduce you." He stopped at the threshold. She refused to meet his gaze and tried to take a deep breath, but her heart became a humming bird in her chest.

Jake's fingers grazed her gently at the jaw and she looked up into the eyes she'd been painfully trying to avoid, "It comes down to trust..." his breath was on her skin creating sparks of electricity.

She gasped out trying to capture a cool edge of indifference, "You need to know, Jake, I'm not interested in dating."

"You've made that crystal clear. I just want you to know me better."

"Why do you want me to know me better?" Her eyes flashed.

"So you can trust."

"Trust is earned... not granted." She pulled away from him.

"Exactly."

"And what makes you want to earn my trust?" she moved towards the fridge to put away the whipped cream and Jake was right behind her.

"You're interesting, beautiful and I believe... trustworthy."

Paige laughed out loud, "How did you come to that conclusion?" She grabbed the pie so she had something to put between them and turned quickly.

Jake shook his head, "Instinct. Anyone who would buy an old house, sight unseen and love it back to life has my vote in the trustworthy department. In my opinion, and it is a humble one, it's easier for you to trust others than to trust yourself. My guess would be you got out of your old business because you wanted to find more meaning in your life. You came here because you were drawn here and now you feel like your home. That has settled in your heart, but not in your head. Once it all has a chance to simmer down I might have a chance at romance. Until then, I'll wait... and be a good friend."

She couldn't speak. He kissed her forehead, which came as a complete surprise. Her eyes went wide in disbelief as he kissed the tip of her nose. "I will wait." His breath buzzed of passion as it grazed her cheek, she tilted her lips higher in anticipation of a forbidden... the cool breeze of a door being gently closed was all that was left of her evening, well that and a raspberry pie in her hand. She felt like an idiot.

~

Blue light from the television flickered against the walls of the living room as Jake entered, "Hey Bro, did you get things right with your Mom?"

"You know I love my Mom, but I think she's going to bust my ass until I'm seventy." Will said flipping mindlessly through the channels on the television

"Beer?" Jake tossed one into the darkness of the living room from the kitchen.

The beer hissed open and Will chugged half of it.

"We need to talk, Will."

"Tonight?" Will chugged the second half, "You know I've had my belly full of es'plainin' myself." His slow and sloppy words let Jake know it wasn't a good time to get things straight.

"What is this brainless swill you're watching?" Jake wrestled the clicker away and it hit the floor. They both tried grabbing for it and ended up with a solid head butt.

Falling back to the sofa, Will rubbed his head, "It's bad."

"What's the matter Suzie, are you bleeding?" Jake was starting to look for dripping blood.

"No, I'm ashamed, I'm worn out and I'm mad as hell" Will blurted out.

"Ahh, you're ready to confess. Ok Buddy let it rip." Jake settled in for the long chat.

CHAPTER 10

Will and Etta

(One year prior)

Parking his newly acquired classic red Alpha Romero Spider and curbing the wheels in front of the flower shop in Nevada City, Will sat for a moment to soak it all in. He had a handful of money in his wallet and whole lotta money in the bank after making it big in the art world. His art captured the heart and energy of his hometown; some saw the images of their own memories, some saw the history of a small town. Everyone saw artistic brilliance. A canvas painted by Will was fresh, ethereal and very expensive. He turned down pearl Jam on his stereo and cut the engine.

Will hopped out and ducked into the flower shop. The cherub-like woman clapped her hands together and flushed when she saw Will burst through the door.

"Oh, my! Look how handsome and grown up you are!" Mrs. Chapel wiped her chubby hands against her apron and rounded the counter to hug him. Her cheeks were glowing like peaches and she always smelled of formaldehyde and carnations.

"I need a bouquet of something spectacular."

"I have some beautiful Argentinean roses..." She wiggled her white eyebrows tempting him.

"Perfect! Can you get them right over to my mom?" He paused at the counter filling out a card while Mrs. Chapel gathered up the roses to show him a sample.

"She's so lucky to have a boy like you. I miss my Terrance something fierce. You give me hope that he'll come back someday."

"Don't we all come back?" He put the money on her counter and charmed her with his best smile.

"Take care Mrs. Chapel. Thanks!"

Etta sat at her desk, thumbing through paint chips she'd selected for her house and watched Will duck in and out of the flower shop. There was something different about him, couldn't quite put her finger on it but she enjoyed watching him, intrigued. He had always been like a brother to her, but the warm tingle she felt as she watched him speed off in his hot new car was not sisterly at all. Perhaps her interest was that Will had actually left Nevada City and *chose* to come home again. It was a luxury she had never allowed herself. Home for Etta was a little house, a few blocks from her office on Broad Street.

There was only a few ways to own property in Nevada City; Inheritance was the first and being independently wealthy was the second. Property wasn't cheap. When Etta inherited her little house she considered it a sign that she was going to stay. She wasn't quite sure why painting the house this summer had become such a nagging issue. The white paint was holding up okay. Glancing at the paint chips in her hand, Etta's niggle of doubt with the choices she held grew into dull disappointment. She stuffed the chips into her hobo bag thinking she'd ask Jake about the colors when she saw him that afternoon.

The town business mixer on the first Thursday of every month was a social event and a high honor among the business community in Nevada City. It was Jake's turn to host and Etta agreed to pick up some appetizers from the café to help out. It always inspired a smirk when Etta saw Jake in a suit. She knew he would rather be in shorts and an aloha shirt hiking or working in the cabinet shop. He'd lost his passion for being a lawyer after his granddad died. They never talked about it, but to everyone in town it was obvious. He spent every spare minute building his business in the cabinet shop and as few as possible in his law office. Her brother owed Nevada City six years of service due to a grant given to him for law school. She admired the way he took care of business and still followed his dream. Jake was one of Etta's favorite people on the planet.

Apples and brie cheese with baby loaves of sour dough bread had been artfully arranged on small cutting boards around the office. Etta lit some candles, and watched their flicker dance on the high sheen of the hardwood floor. The windows ran from floor to high ceiling with carved details in the trim. The city had gone all out to create a grand and beautiful office for Jake when he returned from school as the local council. In the huge mirror over the mantle, she checked her hair and adjusted the straps of her sage green camisole top and smoothed out her flowing gypsy skirt. Etta looked around the office and was satisfied that her job had been well done. She poured two glasses of wine and handed one to Jake.

"Have you seen the boy wonder yet?" Jake asked his sister.

"I saw him in town today. He looks happy. I wonder if he'll let me drive that car!"

Jake laughed, "Yeah, he dropped his stuff at my house and I haven't seen him since."

At exactly Six o'clock, Broad Street merchants piled into the lobby of his office. The sounds of happy chatter, glasses clinking and jazz music played in the background; a monthly ritual that kept them all united. It was the little things that Nevada City merchants were so good at. They kept tabs on each other, they genuinely cared. Occasional peals of laughter rang out in the lobby as someone told a story, and then it lulled to a hush.

Etta looked over as the door opened and Will escorted his mother into the lobby as if she were royalty. Will's suit was a shade between purple and charcoal grey, beautifully cut silk with a lavender shirt. He filled every inch of it with elegance and the self assuredness of success. Mim was beaming, wearing a turquoise halter dress and a light shawl over her tanned shoulders holding onto her son's arm. His wild curling dark hair lent to the illusion that his polished good looks came straight from the pages of GQ Magazine. It wasn't until he made eye contact with Etta that his boyish charm busted out into a smile that spread across his face and lit up every corner of the room. Everything was right in the world.

~

"This place is wrecked!" Will announced after the merchants had dwindled down to the three of them.

"It'll only take a few minutes to clean it up." Etta said, beginning to gather all the dishes lying around.

"No way... not tonight." Jake said, "This mess will wait. Tonight we party!"

"To O'Doul's!" Will announced, holding out a chivalrous arm to Etta.

O'Doul's was only a block away. They walked, arms interlinked, Etta sandwiched between them, laughing in the moonlight, paying no attention to the grate on the pavement which her heel slipped through and stuck desperately into. She fell forward twisting her ankle and let out a squeal of pain.

"Whoa there..." Will's arms slipped around her completely engulfing her waist. The heat of his skin penetrated into her side.

Etta's squinting eyes looked into Will's face, "Shit that hurts!"

Jake had to use both hands and all his body weight to pull the shoe free. He handed the strappy backless sandal to her, which she examined for damage, "Thanks, that was my best Jimmi Chu knock off!" She placed the shoe on her foot and began walking with a limp. Will swept her up and carried her over his shoulder into O'Doul's, fanny first.

"Are you crazy?" Etta slapped at him. Inside it was occupied by only a few patrons, who turned at the ruckus. The oak bar which spanned over 30 feet in length had the polished shine of hardy's relentless rag. His great grandfather had brought it from Ireland over a hundred and fifty years prior. Patrons lazed comfortably in booths as if O'douls was their second home. Ernie sat on his favorite stool, leaned heavily on the bar and shot the three friends a bear-like toothy grin.

Will gently, smacking her behind with a smirk, "There. Now I feel better." He stood her back onto her heels and she narrowed her gaze at him.

"Ah the gruesome threesome!" Hardy, a portly Irishman

came around the bar to embrace them, paying special attention to the new celebrity, "AH the famous Will! I saw your mum driving that little red car, good luck gettin' it back. Darned if it's not nice for a home town boy!" He slapped Will's back, "What are you scallywags havin'?"

"I'll have Makers straight up... You guys, it's on me," Will waved his hand as if the world was his to offer. He slipped off his jacket and loosened his tie.

"I'll have the same," Jake said.

"Me too." Etta added.

"Got to love a woman who drinks Whiskey," Will placed his arm loosely over Etta's shoulder.

He gave her a mischievous look that generated unnerving chemistry. Will had always been an annoying prankster who prayed on her trusting nature like it was his job. He had been her stead-fast life-long friend. Now he felt different. Etta was attracted to him so quickly it was frightening. She passed it off as the whiskey creating naughty thoughts and slid away to the ladies room.

Washing her hands for the cool refreshment, she looked in the mirror, she was radiant. She hadn't called in the "glamour", she was completely herself! There was something going on between her and Will that had never been there and it was certainly the perfect way to end a lifetime of friendship. *Don't be an idiot Etta...* she whispered to herself, *Get a grip and stop this!*

~

Behind a white picket fence, elbows resting on clear plastic table clothes, Will and Etta shared a chicken salad and a Cajun BBQ sandwich. Etta closed her eyes to envision what he was telling her about the city and the people he met there. The fascinating picture of his adventures unfolded like a movie in her mind. Etta and Will never had any trouble expressing their adventures to each other. Things felt normal in the sunshine as she sharked French fries from his plate. There had been no twinges of desire or impure thoughts during lunch, Etta felt sure that avoiding Will after dark and wine would be the key to her survival.

"What are you doing this weekend?" Will asked around his bite of sandwich.

"Painting my house, I am not sure about the colors though," she pulled the chips out of her hobo bag and laid them on the table.

Studying the colors, he ran his fingers through brown floppy curls which slipped down over his furrowed brow, "You puzzle me."

"Do you have a better suggestion? I'm not married to those colors."

"Why would you choose such ordinary colors?"

"I didn't give it much thought I guess." She pursed her lips and looked at the chips again.

"You have an excellent eye for design Etta, just look at your gallery! I'll go back to the hardware store and bring the colors I think will make that little house completely you. You're making dinner and I'm getting lunch," he waved the bill in the air. "I'll bring the wine."

"Deal!" She was so excited to have help with her daunting paint issue that she forgot about her new 'no Will after dark' revelation, until she was halfway home.

She may have ignored the white exterior of her house but the inside was decorated completely in Etta style. Beaded burgundy curtains in her living room, an antique fainting sofa sat in the bay window covered in colorful pillows. The whole space was lit by a perfectly restored carnival glass chandelier and art nouveau antique lamps. Her pieces had been carefully selected and everything she displayed had its own story. In her kitchen she had a pie safe for storage and open shelves displayed fiestaware in bright yellow, turquoise and persimmon. Her Hoosier cabinet sat dignified and filled; used everyday just as it had been durring the turn of the century. A small wooden table covered in Battenberg lace and two chairs sat in the middle of the large room.

Her bedroom was wrapped in purple velvet. A gold and creamy coverlet adorned her bed which was littered with pretty pillows in all shades of velvet and satin, beaded and heavily trimmed. A threefold screen placed in the corner concealed the connection to the bath. Fringed shawls, feather fans, beads and crystal lamps were artfully placed on art deco waterfall furniture. The vanity with a large round mirror amplified the opulence of Etta's treasures. She had created all of this with a deep desire to invite romance into her life.

Herb had been her only real relationship, and that ended as soon as his job was complete after only a couple of years. He wasn't cut out for a small town and had begged her to come back to Los Angeles. It felt like the war of the worlds in her heart trying to decide which way to go. Etta wanted children and a happy home but the only place she wanted that life was in Nevada City. In the end, she had inherited her little house from a client who adored her. That was the deciding factor. She stayed, Herb left. They never spoke again. Nothing in her life reminded her of Him, he was just gone. It was probably best that way.

The aroma of baking lasagna burst from the oven and filled the house. She was putting fresh parmesan cheese on the bread when she heard Will come through the door. He had sterling roses in one hand, a pink box in the other and wine tucked under his arm. Etta immediately stiffened in defense. He was incredibly sexy in his jeans and collared shirt, tucked in but collar unbuttoned at the neck. She could feel his electricity the moment she saw him, but the smell of him dipped into her gut and created a slow brew of wanting.

He kissed her cheek and handed her the flowers, "You better beware, you'll have a line around the corner! What are you cooking?" He opened the oven, bent over and took a huge whiff, "Amazing!"

Etta's gaze was on the curve of his waist slipping into his jeans. She jumped the instant she realized her disobedient wandering eyes had a mind of their own. She handed him the wine glasses and he poured while she kept herself as far away from him as possible, fussing with the roses and preparing the salad.

"What's up buttercup?" He came up behind her with a hand on her shoulder. He'd used that phrase with her since they were teenagers together.

She slowly turned, meeting his look with hesitation.

"Did I make you mad?" Will asked, his dark eyes filled with concern.

"Oh God, no... it's just... I'm getting used to having you around again."

"We've been around each other our whole lives... tell me what's wrong." He stroked her bare arm. Goosebumps crept out and she mustered up the strength to look him square in the eyes. His look intensified and then softened as he leaned closer to her feeling the electricity himself, "Well, that's new." His smile widened, head fell back and his toothy grin crept into a big lazy laugh.

"Yeah... that's new. Laugh it up, Chuckles... not comfortable!" Her eyes were wild with uncertainty.

Will stepped back a bit and handed her a glass of wine. They clinked the crystal together as Will said seriously, "Here's to interesting reunions."

Etta looked at the wine in her glass, "Yes."

"How long until dinner," he asked.

"Whenever you like, lasagna can sit for a while and it just gets better."

"I'll show you the colors for the house."

What Will saw as he looked around her house was genuine Etta. He was charmed by her choices in every corner. But it was the glance into the bedroom where he stopped and stared trying to take it all in.

"Wow, were you going for vintage bordello?"

"Yeah, pretty much. How'd I do?" She cut her eyes around at him which was interpreted by Will as flirting.

"I'd say you hit the mark right on. This is so cool," he walked into her sacred space without hesitation and ran his fingers along the fringed curtains. Again, Etta thought, not comfortable!

"Well if you want romance in your life, you've got to create a place for it. At least that's what I tell my clients." As she leaned through the doorway watching him touch her bed pillows.

"Romance... is that what you want?" Will gravitated back to Etta, and stood so close she could smell the soap on his skin.

"It's what every woman wants, Will."

"What happened to that guy... you know the banker..."

"Herby."

"Yeah, I didn't like him."

"He wanted to move me to LA. He hated small town life. Once he got the Bank up and running, he asked to be transferred."

"Jerk."

Etta shrugged, carefree.

She turned and walked into the living room, setting her wine on an old trunk that served as a coffee table. "Not really, Will, he just knew what he wanted and having kids in a small town with a psychic wasn't in his plan. I challenged his balance." She said without bitterness.

"I'm glad he's gone. You're too good for him."

"Well, that leads to a lot of lonely night."

"Yeah, I know about that..." He sat a respectable distance from her on the couch.

"Common Will, you've had more than your share of love."

"I've had sex, that doesn't mean love or romance."

"I didn't think men cared much for romance."

"You've been talking to the wrong men."

"What about Jenny? I think you loved her."

"I was in lust with her...I thought she broke my heart, but

really she broke my wallet."

"Bitch!"

His smile deepened, "It was worth it."

Etta laughed for the first time that night, took a deep drink of wine "Honesty," She flopped back with the glass in her hand, "God I love our friendship."

"Want to see the colors of your house?"

"Yeah... show me the colors." The wine was settling in her skin, and she felt her body relax for the first time since he'd walked through the door.

Methodically, he placed paint chips together on the coffee table. Etta watched as a brilliant rainbow of colors took flight in her imagination. Will grouped four or five colors together and placed them in separate piles.

"Look at the colors in this pile and tell me how you feel." He said filling her wine glass, then handed a fan of colors to her.

Etta looked at the color combination of dusty dark blue, dull gold and pale terra cotta and closed her eyes, "I feel deep and melancholy. It's beautiful but sad." Will threw the colors on the floor.

"Now these..." She took the brilliant yellow, burgundy and royal blue. She closed her eyes, "This is so weird! I feel exposed and vulnerable."

"Not so good... how about this." He handed her five colors." Interestingly they were not colors Etta would have picked on their own, but together they created a wrapping; a promise of the wonderful story told under the cover of her book.

"They make me happy, and I feel safe. Why did you put these

colors together?"

"This color," Will held up cornflower blue, "represents your spirit. It's clean and vibrant and feminine. This should be the body color."

"This peachy color represents your warmth of character. Paint the shutters this color. They are your arms extended out into the world."

Etta sat back and listened to him continue to explain her in the color world.

"This pale green is stunning, it represents the healing that you do in the world…so subtle and sincere, yet unmistakably your vibe." Will's voice was soft and soothing. She couldn't believe he had given the task so much thought.

"This color of raspberry represents the passion in everything you do. It doesn't rule you, it adds flavor to your deeds. This will be your trim." He pulled out a chip of indigo, "because some of your gifts are mysterious use this on the gingerbread in the eves and on the porch floor." Etta had been smiling for so long her face ached.

"Finally, this white will be used on the railings of your porch and to accent the edges of your fancy trim. It's the purity in which your ideas are conceived…without limits, without judgment." She felt the pulse in his hand as he slipped it into hers, "How'd I do?"

"How did you learn so much about the spiritual properties of color?" She quizzed him.

"Color has a life of its own. I've been around women who use it, manipulate it and heal with it my whole life. What else was left to me than to become an artist?" He rubbed the back of her hand.

"You need to know I'm having very impure thoughts right

now." She couldn't believe she just said it.

"Good," he leaned forward and stopped short of touching noses, "Etta, you are amazing." With his fingers against the side of her face, his kiss was light and lingering. The feeling of his breath in her own lungs kept her mesmerized as she felt the slightest touch of his tongue against her bottom lip and she gasped inviting him in. They looked at each other absolutely caught up in the longing. The next kiss was deep and needy. Etta's hands were underneath his shirt feeling the warm pleasure of his skin. He kissed her neck, brushing his lips to her ears and scraping his teeth along the edge of her jaw which brought out a throaty moan of delight. She unbuttoned his shirt leaving a trail of soft kisses down his fit, tanned stomach. She stopped at his belly button, which gave her an excuse to play with her tongue. His moans increased her pulse as he raised her on top of him and met her mouth with anxious craving. She felt his hands slip underneath her skirt. She lifted her top off revealing herself. Etta opened up her bra from the front he nuzzled into her cleavage. They rolled onto the floor in a wild fit of laughing and various stages of undress. Etta reached for his waist but he just shook his head no and began kissing along her collar bone to her shoulders and down to tease her breasts. She grabbed his hair and pulled him closer, harder until he devoured her nakedness. Etta lost all knowing of where she was. The only thing she could feel was the fire building with every touch, every kiss. Fingertips ran down her sides and over her legs, sweeping her knee and up to the tenderness of her inner thigh. She writhed with anticipation as he lightly touched her most womanly flesh. His kisses trailing down painfully slow, methodically driving her to squirm, his tongue ran across her hip bone, he teased her with gentle bites on her lower stomach and then he did it. His nose rooting lower until she opened herself fully to him and he took what she didn't know she was capable of giving. He made love to her in the most intimate way she had ever experienced. With his mouth he circled her again and again until she felt the sweet flow of release building. He increased the tempo painfully slow, but it was his fingers that drove her over the edge and exhausted every bit of energy from her body. She grabbed frantically at his hair and uttered, "Sweet Jesus, what have I been missing?" He came up smiling to lie next to her and kissed her fingers, her arms and then her trembling lips.

"You taste like peaches... sweet and soft." He kissed her again letting her taste herself in his mouth.

"I think you should follow me..." Etta stood bare and exposed in front of him. Feeling radiant but wobbly, she held out her hand and led him to the room she designed for romance.

He fell onto her bed and she took charge as they pleasured each other. The last time they made love that night, it was full of tenderness. Their eyelids were heavy and stomachs empty. Etta went to the kitchen and returned with one plate of cold lasagna.

"Oh I love you woman..." Will said as she shoveled a heap into his mouth.

"Really..." She laughed.

"Really Etta, I have always loved you, but now it's much more."

Tummies full and physically exhausted, her head relaxed on his shoulder and they fell asleep tangled up in each other's arms.

Will woke to the sound of his cell phone vibrating against the wooden floor. He squinted against the breaking light of morning and reached for the woman behind him. Soft and sweet, she was still sleeping off their night of passion. The fringe hanging down on the drapes over the bed made him smile. Miss Etta got her romance and danged if he wasn't head over heels in love with her. He looked at the sweep of her neck as it connected her shoulders and longing stirred in him again. He snuck out of bed, grabbed his pants and went to make coffee.

The ting against his leg reminded him he'd had a call. It was six in the morning, who calls that early unless it's an emergency? He flipped it open and saw an unfamiliar number from San Francisco. There was no message. He searched the cupboards but found no coffee pot. Sneaking open the pink box he ran his finger across the top of a mini carrot cake and savored the cream cheese icing.

"Hey" Etta's sleepy voice whispered.

"Hey," he looked at her wearing his aloha shirt and a chill ran through him, "No coffee pot?"

"She reached into the Hoosier and handed him the little glass carafe with a funky top.

"Oh, great, something I haven't mastered yet." He took the pot from her and examined it, "Too early for lessons." He kissed her quickly as she took the carafe back and measured coffee into the bottom before clicking the tea kettle on.

"I think the coffee tastes better after it sets in a Jacuzzi of hot water instead of forcing the brew."

"So it's a kinder, gentler coffee?" He said with a smirk.

"Exactly."

"So grind and brew tastes forced?" He was reaching for the carrot cake box when his phone went off again, "Too early for good news. But I don't recognize the number."

"Don't you think you should answer it?" She beat him to the carrot cake pinching an edge off with her fingers.

He flipped open the phone, "This is Will."

"Hello Lover." The voice sounded sharp and mean.

"Who is this?" He walked away from Etta back into the bedroom.

"Who the hell do you THINK this is?" An angry female voice yelled at him.

"Um, well I don't know."

"It's Darla. You knocked me up after that party. Now I've got this screaming shit machine and if you want it, you better come and get it. Or I'm getting rid of the little bastard. Hell if you don't come get it I'll toss it off the Golden Gate Bridge."

"A baby?"

"Yeah, complete with diapers and puke. I'm dead serious Will, come get the little fucker. I don't want it. I got a life to live."

"How do I find you?" He was numb and reeling. The baby was screaming in the background.

"Call this number before noon. Hey, and while you're at it, I could use a few bucks to get myself back on track. I figure it's the least you could do." Will was pacing the floor in Etta's room.

"Ok, give me your address. I'll be there today."

"You must think I'm stupid! Call the number before noon. You don't want the whole world to know your kid bit it off the Golden Gate."

"I'll call you."

He shut the phone, sat on the edge of the bed, running his hands through his hair.

"Oh God, Will, what's wrong?" Etta rushed to him. He put his arms around her middle pulling her close to him. He needed to think. Hell, he needed to get moving. He needed to get a grip and get out of Etta's house.

"You're gonna have to give up the shirt, Love. I gotta go." He was already unbuttoning his aloha shirt, stripping it off of her. She stood naked in front of him. He wasn't even tempted to touch her.

"I've gotta go." He put the shirt on and Etta watched the tails flapping behind him as he walked out.

The little red car hugged the curves and drove like a champ. It only took him an hour to get past Sacramento. He hadn't been able to put things straight in his head since the phone call. He vaguely remembered a Darla; slightly neurotic, beautifully built red headed bartender he met in the City. She'd been one hell of a lot of fun. With a foggy recollection he tried to piece together the dates and times he'd seen her, weighing the possibilities. It didn't really matter if the baby was his or not. There was a kid being threatened and she linked it to him. He grabbed the phone and looked at the time. It was nine thirty in the morning. He searched the phone for his buddy Grant, the cop, who'd have the best advice. Obviously Darla wasn't stable.

"Hey Grant, its Will. I've got a problem and need your help. Are you available, Buddy?"

"What did you do man? I'm on duty." Grant said in a hushed

tone.

"It's a long story. I didn't break any laws... I have a situation and I'm not sure how to handle it."

After meeting with Grant, they determined if Darla was unstable they needed to involve Child Protective Services. Grant agreed to make the calls and followed Will's lead to find out what was really going on. Will made the call to Darla and found out where to go. The baby was still screaming in the background and she warned him to get his ass there quickly before she lost it and drowned the kid.

Will took turns down into what felt like the bowels of San Francisco, a part of the city he'd never been. The farther he went the dirtier and more run down it became. He parked in front of a four story brick building with iron rails on the windows. White plastic grocery bags hung in the trees, soda cans and trash had piled where the wind blew it into drifts like ratty snow. His stomach turned as he heard a baby wail somewhere in the building. He hurried to the apartment number she'd given him, answering the door before he had a chance to knock twice.

"Nice car lover." She looked haggard, thin with dark undereyes. Not quite the woman he remembered. He scanned the room. It was dark with an old comforter over the front window. He smelled rotting food and cigarettes. There was no baby crying. He took a few steps into the apartment and stopped short at the realization that one night of reckless sex had ruined someone else's life, maybe two.

"How are you Darla?" He didn't know what else to say.

"I'm fucking great. Look at this place." She grabbed a cigarette and fumbled for a lighter, "Living the life of luxury while you go out and make it big."

Will cringed when she finally lit the cigarette. Wanting to crush it out for the baby's sake, he quickly decided to not upset her any further.

"How was I supposed to...? I didn't know." He moved a blanket over on the sofa to sit down and realized the baby was swaddled in it. Frozen, he looked at the immobile lump in the blanket and held his breath until he saw the gentle movement of the baby's breathing. First it was relief and then he felt a tear working into his eye.

"What is it you want from me?" He watched her pace the floor blowing smoke from her nose as she relentlessly puffed away.

"I want that out of my life." She pointed viciously at the baby next to him.

"I don't know the first thing about how this works. I don't want you to harm the baby."

"Take him then. Get him out of here. You deal with it, crying, eating, shitting, I've had it."

"I need to be sure it's legal." The expression on his face softened and turned painful, "it's, I mean, he's a boy?" He swallowed hard and looked back to the sleeping baby, "I have to be sure it's mine." He said timidly.

"FUCK YOU!" She screamed waking the baby.

The cries could have broken glass but he moved closer to lift up the infant and placed it in the crook of his arm. He didn't know the first thing about handling a baby but his instincts told him to sway and comfort him. He looked into the angry wrinkled face and felt a rush of deep unexpected emotion. "Shhhhhhh," he cooed rocking it back and forth. When the crying stopped the baby examined him with bright watery eyes.

"Isn't that a pretty picture?" Darla crushed out her cigarette on a paper plate next to a piece of pizza, "What's in it for me, Papa?"

Will found it impossible to respond to the question, shaking his head he asked, "What do you want?"

"That car's real pretty. That'll do for a start."

"So you're going to sell your child for that car down there?"

"Consider it child support." She reached for another cigarette, "He's your kid."

"Please don't smoke while the baby's here." He said quickly.

She threw the pack down on the table and leveled off an incinerating stare, "Look, you handsome piece of shit. Take your kid, give me your car and some money to fix my life and I'll never bother you again."

"Darla, this has to be done legally. I don't want to break any laws…"

"Jesus Christ! You amaze me. Take him now. I can't stand to look at him."

Will looked down at the quiet baby in his arms and smiled, "A boy. What's his name?"

"I put Jon on the birth certificate. I just call him a pain in my ass. That little parasite ruined my body. I'll never dance again. You wanna see my stitches?" she pulled down her sweat pants but Will looked back to the baby's face.

"We'll do it legal, we'll do it right. I will compensate you for the inconvenience."

There was a rap on the door, "Police. Open up."

"You righteous shit!" she looked sharply at Will and snatched the baby away from him. Will didn't protest, not wanting to hurt the baby.

"Come in, Grant."

Darla stormed out of the room shrieking, "Mother Fuckin' son of a bitch!"

"I've got CPS coming up the stairs right now." Grant said looking at Will's empty arms.

"She's got him in the bathroom."

"They'll make sure he's taken from her until she gets her act together."

"She doesn't want him." Will said exasperated, "What if I want to take him?"

"Well that will be determined in family court, Sir." A woman said standing in the door of the apartment, "I'm Amanda Jones. I'll need to speak to the mother of the child. Is she here?" The baby was screaming again. Amanda looked around like the living conditions were something she saw everyday. Maybe they were.

"She took the baby into the bathroom." Grant pointed to the closed door.

Will didn't care if he was the biological father of the baby or not, now he was desperately concerned about the welfare of the child.

"What does she want from you Will?" Grant asked quietly.

"My car and some money. But I want all of this to be legal; I don't want to be dealing with this drama forever. I want Jon to have a good life."

"You want the baby?"

"He's my son. Of course I want him."

Chapter 11

(Present day)

The mood in Jakes house was somber. Will cracked another beer when he continued the story, "I'll tell you what bro. He stole my heart in just those few minutes. Handing him over to that case worker was the hardest thing I've ever done. You know, you hear the horror stories of kids in the system and you can't get them out. I thought a thousand times in the last year that I should have just tossed her the keys and ran with him. It would have been easier. The paternity test only took a few days, but the results to appear in court took three months. All the time I can't see him and he's in foster care."

"Where is he now?" Jake's concern was genuine.

"With foster parents. I am trying to make this as healthy for him as possible. Darla took the car and pawned it for dope. I paid for rehab and she'll be out tomorrow. After all the papers are signed I'll sleep a lot easier."

"We grew up in a safe world." Jake said thoughtfully, "Sometimes I think we haven't been prepared for the real world. How old is the baby?"

"15 months. He just learned to walk. I was there when he took his first step. It was pretty awesome."

"So he's ok, having a druggie for a mom didn't affect him?"

"He's been tested for everything and he's great."

"And you're ready for this?"

"Are you kidding? Where do you think I've been for the last year? I've been taking parenting classes, fighting a legal battle with the state, dealing with case workers and foster families, visitations, first regulated and then those Nazi bastards let me have him for a weekend at a time. I had to get a place down there and prove that I can financially care for him. I've had to play the game."

"And you couldn't let us know what was going on?" Jake was brewing up a case of righteous indignation.

"Jake, I couldn't break my Mom's heart until I knew this was all over and I could bring him home. Nevada City is our safe cocoon from a hateful world. I couldn't stomach the thought of dragging her into a battle. I told her the story in her office yesterday. She was so pissed off at me. First she pouted then this peculiar look spread across her face and she started crying and laughing at the same time. She's probably buying baby furniture right now, creating fung shui for baby development".

"What about Etta? Where does she fit into this?"

"Where ever she wants to. I can be honest with her and see what happens."

Jake laughed, "Way to go Will. You're a dad. That's going to take some getting used to."

"I can't wait to finally bring him home where he belongs."

"Well, you've got some explaining to do."

"Yeah I was going to let Etta cool off for a couple of days..."

"And then spring a baby on her? Think it through, Buddy. She needs to know NOW."

"Shit. I can't stand to hurt her. I love her, you know. It's not that brother love we've all shared Jake, this is the soul-mate love of my life kind."

"Well sober up and take care of business man. I expect to see you kissing her ass for the rest of her life."

"Let me have this night... let me drink this shitty feeling away. Tomorrow I'll come clean and hope for the best."

Etta looked perfectly placed in her white and red polka dotted apron, "The key to great
pie crust is making sure the water is really cold and so is the butter."

Paige had worked the flour and butter into pea sized pieces with some funky shaped pastry cutter, "I think it's easier to let Georgia make pies."

"Phantom pie makers are rarely dependable." Etta laughed.

The kitchen door creaked, and they both looked up. "Good morning ladies." Will said looking nervous, staring straight at Etta. "Paige, if it's alright with you I'd like a minute with Etta."

"Just what makes you..." Etta was fired up looking scared.

"Please, Paige." He shot her a mournful look.

"Sure." She looked at Etta, "You ok?"

"Yeah," She wiped her hands on her apron, eyes filled with fire.

"So you have a baby, a son... and he's coming to live with you next month...for good. And you didn't tell any of us here because what... we would have supported you through it all?" She was pissed off, nerve wracked and overwhelmed.

"I was an ass for not telling you but I didn't want to drag you into the ugliness. And believe me it was ugly." He took her hand.

"No faith." Etta said it straight into his eyes, pulling her hands away from him.

"What are you talking about?"

"We grew up together. You wouldn't have hesitated for a minute to tell your 'friend' Etta about what was going on. But we have sex and magically you need to protect me from ugliness? Do you have any idea how many nights I sat here wondering what happened? Do you have the foggiest idea how it felt to be made love to and left, no call, no letter, not a fucking word. It was the sweetest night of my life and you walked away. I hummed and cleaned my house all that day, thinking you'd pop in at any minute. Do you know what it feels like to be disposable? Have you ever been dismissed? I'm still mad as hell, Will. I have known you my whole life and I adore everything about you. I spent months being sad and then angry and then finally I got to a place where I felt nothing. I found a new friend, I've been helping her with the B&B and now you come in here and drop this bomb on me."

"I'm so sorry…"

"I would have been there with you."

"I didn't tell anyone about this Etta, not Jake or my Mom. I am asking you to be here with me now." He moved forward and embraced her. A year of uncertainty melted away as her head snuggled up on his shoulder and he held her tight against him. She balled up a fist and whacked him square on the shoulder.

"Will's been over there for two days." Paige pulled the

kitchen curtains back looking across the yard at Etta's house.

"That's a good sign," Jake said taking a tentative bite of pie, "What is this again?"

"It's caramel cream." Disgusted with Jake's lack of enthusiasm for her culinary pie making skills, Paige picked up his plate and plopped it into the sink. "You know, I was thinking that I should probably rely on Addy's desserts for the B&B."

"I think that's a solid decision on your part." He smiled apologetically.

"Well, Will walked in before Etta taught me about the filling. How was the crust... was *it* good at least?"

"It's legendary!" He grinned widely at her never quizzing her on the goodness of the Raspberry pie.

"I've got a lot of work to do out there, if you don't mind." Paige walked to the kitchen door and headed straight to the unfinished side of her house. She eyed the power washer, grabbed onto the pull cord, put her foot against the edge of the tool and was relieved that it started right away. She didn't look to see if Jake had followed, she could feel him behind her.

Paige tackled the power washing with all the enthusiasm of a failed pie maker. Jake told her the story of Will's last year in San Francisco. When he finished the story she flopped down on her front porch steps looking at him in disbelief, "You're telling me that a woman who had a one night stand with Will, had his baby, didn't tell him and then asked him to take the baby and give her money?"

"Pretty much..."

"Well, what did he do about it? Sounds like blackmail to me... I mean I know he is fighting for legal custody... but what did Darla get out of it? Women like her just piss me off." She pulled off her gloves, slapped them against her leg and looked at Jake for the answer.

"Well she got a vintage Alpha Romero, which she pawned for drugs. About a month ago Will sent her to rehab."

"So she's still a part of his life?"

"Well, I wouldn't call it a pleasant part. She never asks about the baby, she just wanted more and more from Will."

"What a nightmare. You know, she'll follow the gravy train forever."

"I think things will come to a halt after he signs the papers."

Paige felt the cool prickle of Georgia close by, "take him upstairs!" the ghostly voice instructed. Paige mentally scanned what on earth Georgia would want Jake to see upstairs, then jumped up with the spark of inspiration, "Hey help me with something!" Jake happily followed her up the stairs and into the attic.

She walked to the middle door in the attic and opened it up for Jake to see the beautiful carved bedroom furniture all in small scale for a child. The set had birds and tree branches intricately carved into the headboard and drawers of the dresser, "what do you think?"

"I didn't know you had this stuff up here," He ran his hands over the wood, inspecting the craftsmanship.

"I think we should refinish it." She said proudly, "I mean the baby is coming home to stay, right?"

"We?" Jake grinned hopefully. "Yes, the baby is coming home to stay."

CHAPTER 12

She found him in a gilded frame. In his dark blue suit and white hair, he looked down at her with sharp eyes. Until Paige had arrived in Nevada City her lineage hadn't interested her for a second. Once there, it was all she felt; the desire to know and connect with her roots which apparently, were firmly planted in the red dirt of Nevada County. In her moments standing there looking into the eyes of Judge Matheson, she felt the deep pangs of guilt and then anger. Her gut twisted up and wanted to start screaming, "I hate you". Rattled to the core, Paige felt the chill of rejection hanging over her. She rubbed her bare arms and looked away from the harsh accusing face of her great-great Grandfather, the judge.

Black marble floors reflected light in spite of the cracks that aged the architecture. Paige's heels echoed in the cold hallway to the door that read "Business License Department." She pushed through the door and stood at the ancient counter waiting for the woman behind the desk to respond.

Without looking up, she raised her pen to point at the wall covered in pamphlets. "Applications are on the wall." The woman stated. Her unspoken message was very clear, "You are an unwanted interruption." Paige looked at the name plate on her desk which read, "Blanch Blossom".

"Thank you." Paige thumbed through until she found the right application and took it without bothering the woman again. The courthouse was the only unfriendly place she'd been so far.

The walk home started out leisurely. It was late on Friday afternoon. She'd left Jake in her attic putting the finishing touches on the baby furniture. He paid attention to the tiniest details, even created a guard railing that looked like a tree branch so the baby wouldn't roll out of bed. Most of her free time was consumed with thoughts of Jake. During the day he was at his law office fulfilling his obligation to the city. The last two nights he'd been working on the furniture in her attic. His intangible drive was directed at a little boy he'd never met.

She felt her hesitation to become involved with him crumbling away. He was a big part of her life, just as he said he wanted to be. It had taken little to no effort on her part. Paige replayed his words from their day together and realized she trusted him. Now she needed to trust herself. How in the world was she going to trust herself when she'd made a mess of her life every chance she'd been given? It had only been a few weeks since she met him, but he felt solid. Her appreciation for him had grown into something with foundation, not like her other relationships that started with sex and ended in disillusion. Quickening her steps she hoped to catch him in the attic.

"It's the weirdest thing, Paige," he said as she walked over to look at the finished project in the corner of her attic, "The first door over there," he pointed at the door standing wide open, "I keep shutting it. I mean really shut it, I walk over and make sure the latch catches in the lock and everything. I'll be working over here, then I see it just creak open again."

Wondering if it was a good idea to announce to him that she'd been talking to a pie baking, advice giving ghost for weeks, she just nodded and watched the expression on his face. Jake looked at the door and then back to Paige, "You're not going to tell me that you've got ghosts are you?"

"What do you think?"

"I think there must be an explanation."

"And yet you're sure that you close the door and it latches..." she tilted her head giving him a sideways grin.

"That's what I'm saying."

"This whole town is over a hundred and seventy years old. Are you telling me you've never met a ghost?"

"Well, I sometimes hear my granddad talking in my head, but it's not his ghost, they are just memories coming back to me."

"So you don't believe in ghosts?"

"No, I don't."

The attic door into the main house slammed shut and they both jumped.

"Perhaps you should be open minded," Paige suggested.

"It's a draft," Jake said stubbornly.

The door creaked and slammed shut again. He was watching the top of the stair case like someone was going to come in the room at any moment.

"Jake this house in haunted."

His gaze went straight to her face, "Can't be."

"Believe what you will! I had tangible proof that this house is haunted, but you ate it."

"You're not making any sense."

"That incredible raspberry pie you ate the other night? Well, I didn't bake it."

His eyes narrowed at her in confusion, "So you got it at Addy's?"

"Nope. I didn't get it anywhere. I came downstairs and found it cooling in the window sill."

"You let me eat a paranormal pie?"

"Looked pretty good to me," she looked directly into his eyes.

"Let's go down stairs, I'm getting creeped out."

The mysteriously opening door closed right in front of him and he heard the latch click into place, "Let's go, NOW."

Paige laughed out loud at the way they bounded down the stairs together. He was pale and breathless when they landed in the foyer, "That was just weird."

"Yep, but I'm used to them now."

"Them?"

"Georgia. Etta says there are others. It's Georgia's house and she's always talking to me about silly things like forgiveness and having an open heart."

"Paige, you're a sensible woman. I know Etta dabbles in the paranormal, but this may take some getting used to."

"Etta thinks she's upset about the condition of the house. She's reading up on how we can help Georgia to the other side before we open the Bed and Breakfast."

"So there is a plan."

"Of course, don't be silly."

"Let's go out for pizza, I'm not sure I wanna' hang around for the second show tonight."

Friday nights were always crazy at Louie's pizzeria. The buzz inside was friendly and loud. The juke box was playing Elvis. Louie's voice on the loud speaker announced another finished pizza. Jake found a table next to the front window and they sat down with beers in hand. Paige took a long drink and let the bubbles work their way into her stomach.

"Hey I got the Business License paperwork today!"

"Great! So it's full steam forward."

"Time is passing so quick, I thought I should start everything rolling in the right direction."

"The house is amazing. I've seen your drawings. I snuck down into your library and looked at them on the wall. I must have sounded like a doubting Thomas when I was preaching to you about menus and marketing the other night. The room plans are incredible. You didn't miss a thing Paige. You're a talented woman."

"It feels like the house is talking to me." She put her beer down and rubbed her cold hand against her pants. Jake took it as an invitation to open his hand on top of the table. She hesitated but couldn't help slipping her hand into his. "I instinctively know what to do in each room. I'm seeing it vividly in my mind and then sketch it out. Sometimes I even dream about it. I've got an old Grand piano coming for the turreted window in the parlor. It feels crazy and I love every minute of it!"

"Are you an interior decorator?"

"In my previous life I was a business consultant. All suits and board room meetings... I did refurbish a little cottage in Sisters... but that's another story. I've come to enjoy overalls and dirty fingernails."

"I think both suits you well. Do you believe in reincarnation?"

"I've had some pretty weird dreams of another time period since I've been here… so I'm not ruling out anything… but it's a weird notion."

"How does it feel to be here?"

"It feels right, even Georgia talking to me feels normal and that scares me. This is the time when everything usually falls apart for me, the moment I trust it's going to stay good."

"Because you're finally here, where you belong, Paige." a quick squeeze of his hand brought a round of chills from her shoulders to her feet.

"I'm happy Jake. I don't want anything to mess this up. I'm talented at messing things up."

"I don't think you give yourself enough credit. You've been successful in business, obviously."

"It doesn't take a rocket scientist to analyze numbers and improve market share."

"Well, you've got the funds," He stopped short, "Sorry that was presumptuous."

"I had help, and I'm not proud of how I got it." She looked out the window.

"You want to talk about it?"

Paige shook her head no.

"Nothing in the past can be changed, Paige. But you can make the best of the opportunities and relationships that come to you now." He poured her another beer.

"Thanks." Her smile was weak but it widened as she watched a little boy try to cram a whole piece of pizza into his mouth. "I can't wait to see this all play out with Will. I've become quite fond of him."

"Big stuff coming his way," Jake nodded and raised his glass.

"I can't imagine growing up in a better place than this! It must be every kid's dream."

"Actually, if you talked to any one of the teenagers here tonight they would tell you different. It falls under the category of you don't know what you have until it's gone. Look at those faces." Jake motioned to the noisy corner of the parlor, "dying to get out of here...to drive, to leave, to experience the world out there... anywhere but here."

Paige, remembering her teenage years, looked at the restlessness emanating from the group in the corner; Heavy make-up, piercings, long hair covering eyes, "The thought of them leaving here must drive their parents crazy."

"I know some of those parents and right now they aren't sure how they feel. Apparently raising teenagers feels like nailing Jello to a tree."

"I always thought I was too selfish to have kids. I'm probably right. Anyway, it's a little late for that now. I'll be forty in a few months."

"There's no sin in knowing you don't want them. I like kids okay, I just never saw myself being a dad," Jake said quietly.

"Are you just saying that to make me feel better?" Paige leveled off a look at him.

"Nope, not for a minute. I think I'll be an incredible Uncle to

Will's little boy. I've got my Law Office, cabinet shop and hopefully the chance at a relationship with this woman who came home to save an old house and let her roots dig in."

"There is a lot you don't know about me Jake." She slipped her hands away from him.

He pulled them back, "Everything I need to know is sitting here in front of me. Everything else is what brought you here. How could I not be thankful for it?"

"You make me feel..." She looked away trying to hide the emotional wave.

"Precious," he finished her sentence and kissed her hands. Betty was the farthest thing from her mind in that moment.

They walked holding hands, the satisfaction of full bellies and a three beer buzz. The warm earthy air of newly watered lawns surrounded them on the way home. He walked her up the front steps to the mansion and leaned on the doorway alcove, "it's getting harder to go home at night, Paige." His face looked genuinely pained.

"I dream about you." She said putting her hands on his shoulders, ashamed of herself but the attraction had become too powerful to resist, easily falling into her old ways of seduction.

"You have no idea what I'm dreaming...." He brushed a rouge lock of hair out of her face and let his hand linger on her neck, behind her ear. She was malleable putty, thrilled with each new position of his hand.

"Please let me..." he brought his face closer to her and waited for her response. Paige lost every ounce of hesitation and met his mouth with a warm welcome. He responded softly to her urges, she drew him deeper. He slowed the pace. She reached for the door knob and stumbled backward into the foyer never loosing contact with Jakes lips. She was tugging at everything that was a barrier to their skin touching. His shirt lay crumpled on wooden floor at the base of the stairs. He didn't take anything from her, he let her take. She was panting against the skin of his neck and nipping softly as she kissed his warmth and ran her hands up his bare back. He smelled like something she couldn't wait to eat, warm and musky. Tugging at his waist band, she unbuttoned his pants and pulled hard while she kissed her way down his stomach. Her hands found his backside firm and warm. A moan of deep pleasure came from both of them as she squeezed and kneaded him. His pants fell to his ankles and he stepped out of them revealing his admiration and need for her. Paige reached down to touch him. He was hard and thick and beautiful. Her stomach fell 10 stories and landed with a pounding need in her belly.

"God Jake, You're so beautiful." She said wide eyed and unashamed, his warm, firm flesh filling her hands.

"I wish you could see through my eyes, Paige..." He kissed her neck softly and sweetly, finding all the tenderness he could muster up with the raging need urging him to plunge into her at that very moment and beg forgiveness later.

"You are amazing." He kissed her hard on the mouth, her hands were in his hair but she felt him burrowing into her leg, "Let's go where it's not so hard and cold." He took the first step up the sweeping staircase, reached for her hand and she stopped short, "This way... I'm down here." They made it through the hallway and into the bedroom in a tangled of arms and passionate kisses.

CHAPTER 13

San Francisco

Will's pride showed in his swagger towards the main door of the CPS office. He knew his son waited for him inside the rundown single story stucco building. Though he'd been here dozens of times before, this time it felt different. With no anger or frustration on the horizon he pushed through the doors. The only emotion was the anticipation of bringing his son home where he belonged. The loving arms of family waited for his little boy and nothing in the world would ever be more precious than that.

He'd passed the paternity test, the parenting classes and he made a home in the city that wildly exceeded the criteria of the state. His humanity had been questioned, challenged and tested. This was graduation day. The sweet little baby that held his heart was waiting for him now, deserving of the life Will had promised to him with every visit. In preparation for this day, Will told Jon all about Grandmamma Mim, Uncle Jake and Etta. There were pictures of them all and Jon knew them by name. Will did it with faith they would all be together.

Past the check in desk, he walked down the hallway, two doors to Amanda's office. He knocked lightly and entered. Quickly, he looked around the room but there was no baby.

"Where's Jon?" He asked feeling too chipper to assess the

change in the air.

"There's been a development." Amanda said calmly.

Sheer panic hit him. "WHERE IS JON?" Will placed his hands firmly on the edge of her desk, ready to rip it up by the roots and fling it across the room, he leaning in to get close to her emotionless face.

"William, please sit down. Jon is in the nursery with our caregiver. He's fine." She said, rising to close the door to her tiny office.

The smell of pine sol accosted him, sucking the air out of the room, it left him feeling light headed. A thousand things crossed his mind but Jon was fine. Jon was fine. He repeated it like a mantra in his mind.

"We received a call from the San Francisco Police yesterday. It seems that Darla..."

Will's heart stopped beating as the institutional green walls closed in on him. Shooting out of his seat he slapped his hands on Amanda's desk, "She can't have him now! She's just out of rehab. She's not stable! Darla cannot have my son!"

Nevada City

"He may have been born in February, but we'll always celebrate this homecoming day." Mim's face flushed with excitement. Dressed in faded jeans, a pale yellow sweater set and petite daisy jewelry, she fussed with every little detail in the room she had created for baby Jon. Pale green, beige and peach created a cocoon of warmth, soft and cuddly for a baby to feel welcome and safe.

"Auntie Mim, I thought you'd have the whole crew here, Patti,

Della and Addy… where are they?" Jake asked.

"That baby is making big changes. He's had to adjust to so much. I just wanted it to be us today…" Her open hand reached the side of his face and she flashed him one of her adoring smiles, "Just family." Then she turned her attention back to the nursery.

"You know Will never liked the bright colors that most parents were using at the time to 'stimulate intelligence' in their infants. So I used the same muted colors in his room. I want our boy to feel safe, he's been through a lot." She fluffed a bunny wearing a jean vest clinging to a bundle of carrots.

"These things were Will's?" Etta touched the bedding thinking of how he'd left her with sweet kisses and warm promises.

"I got a few new things, but most of it is Will's."

"I wanted to go with him today. It killed me to watch him leave… again." Etta commented quietly.

"Bless your heart, Etta, I had no idea what was happening between you two. I can't think of a woman I'd rather have with my son, or my grandson." Mim reached out and took her hand, "Really, I'm so happy. Can you imagine what a precious package he's bringing home? Come on out here and help me get the party ready. Keeping your hands busy will help."

A knot of fear turned in Etta's stomach, not a good sign for a psychic woman. But she rationalized it as being overwhelmed. Mim's enthusiasm was contagious. Etta brushed away her feelings of impending doom and concentrated on the preparations. She forced a smile as Mim tied a yellow balloon to a brown bear with a peach colored ribbon. The table outside was set with linens, bears and balloons. It was a tea party setting with all the trimmings, enchanting even to someone not accustom to such things.

"Mim," Etta said, her voice breaking, "Something's not right." Etta's hands grasped the table for balance and she melted into the nearest chair.

"What is it Honey?" Mim was at her side immediately.

"I have a sick feeling in my stomach." Etta could hardly breathe, "My heart hurts."

"Shit. I hate it when this happens." Mim held her hand and sat right next to her, she was used to Etta's ways. She trusted her instincts totally, "What can we do?"

"Well I don't think Will's safety is the issue. I can see Will and he's fine. The baby is ok. Something's wrong though, I feel it."

"Let's not worry until we have something to worry about." Mim was patting her hand, "come on, and let's get you something to eat."

Jake appeared with a crystal goblet of water. Paige sat down next to her and put a hand on her arm. They waited for Will's return with the baby in a brood, full of expectation and now worry.

Mim checked the time again, "That damn clocks' moving like molasses in January."

Her hair swung wildly as they heard a car come into the drive. Excitement sparked as Will's Cherokee pulled into the drive. Will walked around to the back door and opened it up. Reaching inside he brought out a munchkin, wearing overalls, flannel shirt and a baseball cap slightly crooked from the road trip. Etta was too frozen to move, Paige and Jake were standing behind Mim who had placed her hands over her heart, looking wide eyed at the face of her grand baby, "OH My," the tears rolled, "Jon Jon." She spoke softly to not scare him.

Jon blinked his dark brown eyes, wiping them with chubby fists, he looked at his grandmamma and smiled, "Ma." Then he reached for her.

Mims arms were full of happy baby boy and she rocked instinctively side to side holding him close, nuzzling into Jon's neck like a mother bear programming the scent to memory. Then she held him away from her for just a moment and said, "Welcome home." There wasn't a dry eye in the driveway as they headed for the back yard party.

Etta put her arm around Will and said, "God, I'm so happy to see you. I had the worst feeling while you were gone. I'm glad you're okay."

Will pulled her close with an urgency that alerted her, "It's not over, Etta."

Her eyes burrowed into his, "What's happened?" The sick feeling washed over her again.

"We'll talk about it later. I think things will be fine. Come and meet Jon Jon..."

"Could he look any more like Will?" Paige was watching the baby run through the lawn in Mim's back yard. He was chasing balloons, laughing and playing. He tripped in a gopher hole and landed on a balloon that popped. A startled round of crying began. Etta was the first one to him. He threw his arms around her neck and put his head on her shoulder.

"I think its nap time for this little dude." Etta whispered to

Will.

"I'll help." The three of them went into the house and put the sleepy baby into the crib.

"He's so easy." Etta whispered as she covered him up.

"He's easy to love. It's not always this smooth." Will whispered back.

"Well honey," Will said, squeezing Etta's hand, "Here we go.... I only want to tell this story one time... so let's get out there."

The five of them huddled for conversation on the patio. Mim refused to set the baby monitor down and clipped it to her jeans waistband.

"When I picked up Jon this morning, I got some bad news." Will said cutting straight to the point, "I probably didn't do Darla any favors by helping her out financially."

"Damn it Will, You gave her the Alpha, you sent her to rehab. What more does she want from you?" Jake said.

"Well, I did it to get Jon away from that lifestyle. She was very clear that she didn't want the baby. Your right Jake, I gave her the car. She pawned it for drug money."

"Oh my God," Mim whispered, "what a life."

"Then she asked me for more money. I told her the only way I would help her was if she got straight. I didn't send her to rehab once or twice, I sent her three times in the last year. Every time she came out she seemed better. Darla never wavered on wanting the baby, she didn't want him. Her dream was to dance again and I offered to help her get on her feet. It became a sickening cycle. Every time my phone rang I wanted to throw it out the window, but I knew

I had to deal with her. So, the last time I sent her to rehab, I set up an account for her. When she got out I told her I didn't want to talk to her again, I got the Alpha out of hock and left it at her apartment. I knew I was bringing Jon Jon back here. I wanted to be done with her. I wanted to know I'd done everything I could to help her."

"Well, I think you went above and beyond with her, Bro." Jake said.

Will cleared his throat and looked at Jake, "She got out of rehab on Tuesday and on Thursday morning the cops found her OD'd in the Alpha right in front of her apartment."

"Over dosed?" Etta processed the words, "She's dead?"

"Yes." Will said softly, "I'll be living with *that* for the rest of my life. But there's more." He stood and started pacing the patio, "When the next of kin, who is her dad was contacted, the state let him know he had a grandson and that Jon was being placed into the custody of his father…" a gasp went through the group.

"Darla's Father, Miles Callahan, wants to see his grandson."

"And that could lead to all new court battles…" Mim said quietly as she stood and placed her hands on the arm of her son.

"Yes," Will answered flatly.

The hush that hung over them was broken by Mim, "I don't blame him for wanting to see his Grandson. He's lost his daughter and…" Mim's face was wet with tears and pinched with painful emotion… she sniffed and shook her head, "Well, that beautiful gift from God is here now. We're gonna' love him like he's the only baby on the planet. I for one am not going to let this cloud hang over my head. God would simply not be that cruel. I've missed my son for a year. I've missed the first year of my grandson's life. I won't be robbed of another minute." Mim raised her head defiantly, "Now, let's eat.

CHAPTER 14

Dressed in overalls, Paige danced to a Dave Mathews tune while she painted the largest upstairs bedroom peaceful sea foam. Everything got easy the minute she let Jake into her life. She blushed remembering how brazen she was with him. He stayed most nights with her, she couldn't help herself and he couldn't refuse. Working around the antique furniture piled into the middle of the room, covered in a drop cloth, she hummed and painted. Jake crept in the doorway watching her wiggle and hum, a grin spread from ear to ear. In his hands were the unmistakable boxes of Mr. Chan's Chinese food.

"Hey!" she said happy to see him and going in for a kiss.

He wore a silk 'all business' suite and stopped short, "You've been working hard!" He kissed the end of her nose to avoid the paint on almost every part of her.

"OH wow, how did you know I was starving?"

"Anytime you get into a creative whirl, you don't eat. So here I am to feed your starving body." He handed her the bags and looked around for something to set dinner on. He lifted up the edge of the tarp and saw an antique canopy bed, an armoire and an old trunk he recognized from their local flea market. "You're a tornado!"

"Yep, and you thought I was giving all my time to you..." she giggled at him. It was an exhilarating high when she found the perfect piece for one of the theme rooms. Her flare for decorating had taken on a life of its own and was now an obsession.

"This is quite a talent you have. You were made to do this, Paige."

"I'll tell you what I was made for..." she said slyly, taking a piece of General chicken with her painted fingers and popping it into her mouth, "Fortune cookie nookie!"

"You're a monster!" He laughed, "I'll be right back. I have something to tell you."

She laid out the boxes and paper plates and dug in before he was back in the room with his briefcase in hand.

"All business!" She said around a mouth full of chow mien, "I waited for you... like one pig waits for another. Sorry, I was hungry!"

"I'm not. I'm here for the nookie fest..." He crouched down behind her and nuzzled her neck, "You make me crazy!" he whispered against her ear until a twinge of need prickled deep inside. "Paint covered..." He kissed her shoulder, "hair all wild," he kissed the top of her head, "dancing and working," he nibbled her ear, "You are the sexiest woman in the world."

Paige turned and kissed his lips quickly, then pecked him again and again and again.

"You should stop that Paige,"

"Never! I'm going to kiss you forever." She said sweetly, without thinking.

"That's it!" He said, "Now you've done it." She pulled away and pouted a puzzling frown at him.

"Now I have to... and I was waiting..." He said it quick, like pulling off a band aid "I love you."

Then he pulled her close. Paige was stiff as a board and stunned silent. She felt it too, but love came with so many, many ideas and plans and then she realized that she had waited to long to respond. She was paralyzed by a fear so deep she couldn't feel the end of it.

"I've got a meeting at the office tonight." He mumbled into her hair, "Sweet dreams Beautiful, I'll see you tomorrow." He was gone before Paige had a moment to take a breath and respond.

"You didn't even eat dinner," She called down the stairs to him.

"Not hungry." And he was gone.

~

She'd been alone in her own world since the day Jake dropped the 'love you' bomb on her. She did love him. She just didn't know what love meant to him. They hadn't talked about Betty. Had Jake broken up with her? The last thing in the world she wanted to talk about when they were alone together was another woman. After three days of no contact with him, the conclusion was, she did not know a thing about love. Maybe he'd been with Betty. A cold chill ran through her with that thought and then she started imagining all kinds of things. Not even Georgia made a sound as Paige's misery and uncertainty about love swirled around the edges of her focus. Even Wally avoided her, walking around the edges of the rooms and slinking outdoors when she approached.

Falling prey to her old failures and misgivings about how her new life was taking shape, Paige dug out the blue velvet jewelry box the size of a paperback book from the back of the closet. Inside the velvet exterior with a tuft of cat fur stuck to it were years of broken dreams. Hers or theirs, it went both ways. No wonder she couldn't say the words to Jake, she was scared stupid. In her life love had only led to undeniable disaster. She ran her fingers over the latch and popped it open. Seven. There were seven rings in the box. Shame washed over her as she picked up the most humble, the most heartfelt of the rings. A gift on her 21st birthday when she got her first marriage proposal from a sweet handsome young man she didn't love. Diamonds so tiny they were almost undetectable with filigree hearts and flowers on a gold band. She held it in her hand and felt the gold warm with her memories of Tony. His face, excited and expectant as he opened the peach colored box and fell to his knee, Paige set it down quickly before the guilt made her cry, again. Blinking away the tears of young love, she reached for the sapphire surrounded by diamonds in a platinum setting. Gregory had placed the ostentatious gems in a glass of Champaign grandstanding in front of his friends on a yacht off the coast of Florence. She'd been thirty two. The relationship ended when Paige caught him in the sack with a twenty year old version of herself just days after his proposal.

Each ring had a story Paige wasn't proud to remember. They laid in the velvet mocking her every attempt at creating a long lasting relationship. Sorry that she started the exorcise in self pity, the box sat open and Paige ran her finger over the jewels she would never wear.

"A guilty past is a miserable companion, especially in times of uncertainty" Georgia said breaking her week long silence.

"There are a lot of heartbreaks in this box."

"What can you do about it now?"

"Not a damn thing."

"Exactly! Now, tell me, why do you hang on to them?"

"What else am I going to do with them?"

"Liberate your sorrow." Georgia shouted excitedly.

Paige smiled for the first time that day. What a character Georgia was. How in the hell was she going to liberate her sorrow?

"Sell them. Put the money to good use."

The thought of selling the rings had never occurred to her. What use are they in the box, taking up space in her regret filled heart?

"Do it, Paige. Free your conscience. Do you think any one of those men is keeping your love hostage? Still crying over you?"

"No, I'm pretty sure they are not thinking about me for a minute."

"Why marinate in misery? Let them all go. Nothing you can do except forgiving yourself will release the energy you've got in your heart. How do you think you're going to fit a love as big as Jake's into your heart when it's so full of past nastiness?"

Georgia's words sunk in after a couple of minutes. Paige opened the box and looked at the rings again. There was not one thing left for her in that box.

Paige tucked her straying wild hair under the red bandanna and padded down the back stairs to the kitchen for something to drink. She poured iced tea into a huge plastic tumbler and was buried head first in the fridge looking for a lemon when she heard his truck rolling down the drive. Her first thought was to duck into the bedroom and put something presentable on. Then she figured, he hadn't called, it was a drop-in and he'd have to deal with what he saw. She looked at her reflection in the window and fluffed the bandanna ends on top of her head, brushed away some stray hairs and wiped away the smears of mascara under her eyes. He was in his suit, coming up the stairs quickly, knocking on the door with sharp raps. She jumped even though she saw him coming.

"Come in!" She said all smiles.

"I've got to talk to you Paige. And we have to think quickly."

"What's going on?"

"I saw the master plan of our redevelopment downtown. They have taken some old properties and repurposed them as parking, future building sites and renovation."

"You mean the mansion is in the redevelopment area?"

"The property is...what I'm telling you is your property is scheduled for repurposing as a parking lot."

"Oh that's just silly, Jake. We'll straighten this out." Paige smiled, "It's just a misunderstanding."

"Well, that would be fine if we were in Mayberry, but Jed Grisworth is not what I would call an open minded man."

"What are you trying to tell me, Jake? Are you saying that even though I have submitted my business License application, I'm making renovations to improve the property, and in turn improve the City...I own the damn property Jake, they can't take it from me!" Paige was shaking and trying to breathe.

"Have you ever heard the term imminent domain?" Jake took her hand to steady her.

"Of course I have." Cold blades of fear stirred up the past. She started to shake and back away from him, "There has to be a mistake. I have a title company and a deed of trust..." She looked at him for an answer, "This house has intrinsic value to the City. Isn't it registered as a historic place in Nevada County?"

"It's worth checking into, but as soon as I saw the plan at the court house, I wanted to let you know. We need to be prepared for this."

"They don't know who their messing with! I've fought City Hall before!" Paige remembered her loss in Oregon and demanded with a crackling voice, "Who is in charge of the legal city stuff down there anyway…" There was a long pause between them.

"I am," He answered softly.

"What? And you're just finding out about this?" Paige looked confused.

"I've been busy with other things and probably haven't been as available as I should have been to city projects."

"So this could really happen?" She felt small and insignificant as the demons of her past started gnawing at her future, "They could take my house and turn it into a parking lot?"

"It's possible. But the City Council has a soft spot for its past. If you can prove that this house in some way is part of Nevada City's history, then that's in your favor." He stood and put his hands into his pockets, "I'm so sorry, Paige. I haven't had any court cases in a while, and I've ducked out of the City Council meetings to work at the cabinet shop for the last couple of months. This got past me. I've got no one to blame but myself. I remember about six months ago when there was talk about repurposing some of the old run down properties next to Broad Street. Before you were here, this place was a pretty big wreck, ready to be torn down."

"Well, it's not now." She stood and put her hands on her hips,

"So Councilman, are you with me or against me?"

"Do you even have to ask?" He frowned.

"Apparently I do." Her voice was curt, "How much time do I have to make a case?"

"The next City Council meeting is a week from Tuesday.

~

It was almost three in the morning by the time Paige managed to fall into fitful dreams.

She looked out the big turreted window from the main bedroom, the room reserved for her infrequent visits. Wearing a lavender silk robe, trimmed in the finest French lace, she fluffed her bosoms up in the corset and fiddled with the tiny ivory satin rose in the middle. She'd cancelled her engagements and traveled three hellish days from San Francisco to see him. Of course, being famous, she would never admit to anything as common as... love. The feelings she shared with Reece were otherworldly, rare and obscure.

The long auburn hair fell across her shoulders and down below her waist. It was how he liked it best, free and wild. Reece was going to make her an honest woman, or she'd die trying. She'd all but given up her dancing and had enough money to start a good life with the man she was hopelessly drawn to. She ordered up some whiskey and a bottle of champagne. Perched on the edge of the delicately carved loveseat by the window she watched for him. And she waited... for hours. The feeling of abandonment and desperation felt like a fist in her chest. The Champagne was empty, but she wouldn't sleep. Uncorking the whiskey bottle, the pungent aroma caught in her throat but she poured a glass and sprawled on the end of the bed to watch the naked cherubs painted on the ceiling. She would not cry.

The whole house was quiet. With ears perked and eyes unfocused, she detected the sound of boots in the hall. Her heart jerked to attention. She snuck to the door and locked it tight just as she heard him say, "Eden, Honey, it's me, let me in."

"Shhhhh" she slurred, "you'll wake the dragon down the hall... you don't want trouble."

"Then let me in! I've got something for you." Her smile was immediate. Yes, he had something she couldn't live without!

The door clicked open and he burst through all shaved and shining like a preacher on Sunday Morning. His arms slipped around her waist twirling her around the room and raising her up by the fanny. Her giddy breathing came quickly and she was going to burst if she didn't get him inside of her. Eden began kissing his neck and his face and landed on his lips with a tenderness that surprised both of them. He pulled back and looked into her eyes. His pircing silver-blue eyes... something in his eyes.

"You're the prettiest, sassiest, most infuriating woman I've ever seen, Sugar Pie, and I'm damn sure gonna miss you." Reece let her go and reached for her whiskey glass, draining the remnants.

"Miss me?" She smiled sweetly, "But, I'm right here... and

this time, Reece, you are going to make me an honest woman. Or I'm going to know why! I've quit my dancing, cancelled all of my engagements, even the invitation of the King!"

"I thought you we're comin' to say goodbye." He looked at the floor.

"I am here to stay!" She said pulling her robe snugly around her tiny middle feeling very uneasy.

"That is going to be troublesome..." he said hedging for the door.

"Troublesome for whom?" Eden picked up the whiskey bottle and took a swig.

"My wife." Reece said, "I married Mary Ellen Mathews this morning."

"Get out." Eden threw the bottle at his head which grazed him on the chin, "You're wife will have to get used to having me in town. I'm not leaving. And don't you ever step into my path again or I will murder you with my bare hands."

CHAPTER 15

Jake stood in the office of the City manager, Jed Grisworth pleading the case he never wanted to take on. "Come on Jed, you should see the plans for the mansion. It's going to be the premier Bed and Breakfast in Nevada City. She's really pulling it all together, and a ton of money she's already invested."

Jed was a tall lean man wearing a bright green golf shirt and plaid pants. His hair was thinning and grey, heavily sprayed to stay in place. "It's been in the redevelopment plan for over six months. It's how we promised the tax payers we would fix the parking problem down town. I personally don't give a rat's ass if it's a magnificent work of art. If I don't fix the parking down town, I won't have a job next term."

"There has to be another way. She's pouring herself into that mansion."

"Sounds like she's pouring sugar on you, Jake... There are a hundred old houses she can turn into a bed and breakfast around here. We'll give her fair market value for it. She can just relocate." Jed was thumbing through the newspaper instead of giving Jake his full attention. Finally he looked over the top of his reading glasses and asked, "Is that all?"

Jake slammed his hands on the edge of Jed's desk and said, "Jesus, Jed, is there a heart inside that chest of yours?"

Jed's smile was condescending at best, showing perfectly straight, white teeth, "I was there on the board when they decided to grant you the law school education your family couldn't afford. Should I remind you what that education cost the City and how much longer you've got on your contract with us?" Jed stood and moseyed across the room to his bar, pouring brown liquid into a rocks glass, "Care to join me?" Jed held the glass up.

"No." Jake's face went hot with rage at being reminded of his place and his debt, "thank you".

Jed laughed, "One more thing, Jake." He slipped back into an overstuffed leather desk chair, "I've seen you around town with that pretty girl. She looks like she's thick with your crowd. I'm going to give you some advice since your Dad's not here to do it, or your granddad." He took a long drink from his glass and then tilted his head to see the pain in Jake's face, "Keep your pecker in your pants, son and get your job done."

"Yes sir." Jake pressed his lips firmly together, afraid to say another word. He turned to leave and summoned the strength to prevent ripping the door off its hinges. The door knob was firm in his hand as he closed it behind him, solid and slow.

Fuming through the front door of his house, the furious slam rattled the windows. He flipped on the air conditioning, he pulled off his suit and left it rumpled on the floor of his bedroom. Once he was in his boxer shorts and socks, he rubbed his head for some great ideas. There was nothing. Pacing the house, he walked to the fridge for a beer, reached in for a coke classic instead, struggling to keep his head clear. He popped the top and slammed half of the can, felt the burn of carbonated sugar goodness rush through his body.

He studied the can and had a quick flashback of sitting on the porch of the cabinet shop with his granddad, sharing cokes in glass bottles. It was one of the sweet, simple things that reminded him of his childhood. He missed his Granddad, who would know how to handle the situation. With only a sixth grade education Jake's Granddad had more intelligence than anyone he'd ever known. The cheap shot about Jake's dad not being in his life just reminded him what an asshole Jed really was. Jed should lose the next election; it would be the best thing for Nevada City. If they only knew half of the sleazy underhanded things he'd done to keep face in his office. He closed his eyes and imagined that his granddad was sitting on the sofa next to him with some words of wisdom. Jake made a mental note to buy coke in glass bottles, damn the expense.

How had his life focus changed so much in just a few years? Even in the heat of the day the leather sofa felt chilly against his bare legs. Rolling his socks off with his toes, he stared at the thermometer outside his window. It was 97 degrees at six thirty. Begrudgingly doing his time for the city was no way to serve them well. He loved Nevada City but longed to be free of the encumbrances of his debt. Jake's head fell to the back of the sofa and he studied the pattern on the ceiling. This is when he did his best planning.

Paige was clearly not in love with him. Jake recalled the frozen solid look she gave him when he let it just fall out of his face that he loved her. Stupid, stupid, he knocked his head against the back of the sofa. She looked so happy until he dropped the bomb on her. His job was to demo her house and provide a parking lot, remedying the City's most pressing issue of the last two decades.

Images of her sketches flashed through his head. Her artistic nature was a pleasure to watch as it budded and then fully bloomed. She was growing into herself, the self she'd been hiding from her whole life. His smile went painfully lopsided as he recalled her standing in her kitchen wearing those ratty overalls, covered in paint, with that wild beautiful auburn hair all over the place. He wanted to reach over and grab the bandanna bunny ears and pull her close to him. Shake it out of your head he thought. It broke his heart to tell her what the city was planning. It broke it even further that she didn't return his feelings. He felt dead inside.

~

One minute Paige was closing up her paint cans and the next she was in the shower, cleaning up, dressing and then walking across Broad Street staring at Jake's front door. Not realizing she'd walked through Nevada City with any purpose at all. The last thing she remembered, was dressing in her bedroom. Finding herself at Jake's was like an out of body experience. She had to look into his eyes. The dream was haunting her with a thousand unanswered questions. Who was Reece and why did he have Jake's eyes.

The persistent chimes of his doorbell snapped him out of the misery he'd been wallowing in. Jake looked at his bare chest and boxers and decided to ignore it. Whoever it was would eventually go away. Flopping his head back against the sofa, he waited for the intruder to leave.

Paige leaned heavily on the bell for the third time and started to feel foolish. What on earth was she going to say to him? How would she explain her wild imagination creating a dream in another time period with them staring in Nevada City history?

He tip toed to the side window to see who was so nervy. Paige stood on his porch looking sun kissed. She rang the door bell a fourth time and realized that if he was home he certainly didn't want to see her and she beat cheeks off the porch.

He dashed to the bedroom for some pants and hopped back to the front door pulling them up. The only thing left on his porch by the time he got there was her unmistakable scent; like grapefruit and violets it wafted into the entry and tormented him.

Keeping Paige at arm's length was something he hadn't planned. He tossed the coke can into the trash and grabbed a beer, falling back into the sofa for a nice long sulk.

The heat of the sidewalk penetrated through her sandaled feet as she wandered aimlessly down Broad Street reading each business sign. She'd barely got away from his house before he opened the door. What an idiot! There was nothing to be said. Her head was buzzing from the news Jake dumped on her. It was happening all over again. Where was the lesson in this for her. She'd read that if you encounter the same problem repeatedly in your life, you're missing the lesson. The possibility that her dreams were showing her just how reoccurring this theme with Jake was, was ridiculous. How appropriate she thought, just as she got her life together and it felt good, everything should fall apart. It always did. Apparently through the annals of time this had happened to her. Why should now be any different?

Paige walked passed an old gentleman in a pale blue polo shirt smoking a cigarette outside of his jewelry store. She hesitated for a moment remembering the box of rocks in her purse. Reaching into her leather satchel, she pulled out the velvet box, turned and asked the man, "Do you have a minute?"

One of his eyes squatted down as he took a final drag from the filter-less stub held tightly between his thumb and forefinger. Throwing the smoking butt into an overflowing can, he opened the door and waved her into his business without a word. He slowly shuffled through to the back counter of his store and ambled behind the glass case. Placing both hands gently on a piece of black velvet he coughed once and then cleared his throat. From under a wild bush of white eyebrows his dark eyes made contact with her for the first time, "What do you have there?"

She raised her head, leveled off a look and handed the box over into his shaky yellowed fingers. He took the treasures from her and popped the lid. Blindly reaching for his jewelers loop, he gave each ring a quick look through the contraption. He took the gaudy sapphire over to his microscope and looked in three positions through the lens. "Hmmm," he muttered.

"Quite a collection," He dead panned. Pursing his fleshy lips in contemplation, he breathed out a long sigh, "Listen, I'm Samson." He held out his wobbly hand.

"Paige Hamilton." They shook firmly.

"What do you want to do with your collection, Miss Hamilton?"

"I'd like to sell them."

One of his eyebrows rose dramatically and his sharp dark eyes looked over the rim of his glasses directly into hers waiting for more information.

"I've bought an old house off Broad Street and I could use the money."

"That old rat-trap at the top of the hill?" Paige nodded numbly. He frowned and shook his head as if no one in their right mind would attempt such a feat.

Paige stuffed her angry pride, "Now, I've got to convince the city it's worth saving. I need a lawyer."

"You're going to need more than a lawyer!" his whole body vibrated with a chuckle that worked its way into a coughing fit. He collected himself, took a drink of Pepsi from a can and said quite strongly, "I thought you were seeing a lawyer." He raised his head and squinted at her face through bifocal lenses.

Paige felt the pain of the small town sting her, "I don't mix business with pleasure." Defiantly, she reached for the box.

"Just a minute, there..." He softened his voice, "don't get your panties in a bunch."

Paige was furious but she perked an ear, "You have a couple of beautiful pieces there. I'd be happy to offer you a fair wholesale price if you can wait a few minutes for me to calculate."

Paige heard Georgia's voice in her head and swallowed her resistance to doing business with one of the 'crusty old dudes' of Nevada City. She nodded to Samson and sat firmly onto a green vinyl chair with chrome legs. Time was on her side and she'd wait to see what he was offering.

She watched him deftly weigh each ring for gold or platinum content then measure each stone and calculate its worth. He kept coming back to the sapphire, squinting through the microscope nodding his head. Samson disappeared behind a burgundy curtain and returned to the counter, handing her both the box of rings and an appraisal of its contents in a sealed envelope, "Here you go. I'll get a cashier's check if you want to sell."

Paige took the box and the envelope and slipped them into her satchel. "I'll be back tomorrow. I want to sell."

"Fair enough." He called as the door slipped silently closed behind her.

Paige just started walking. The whole move, the mansion, the relationship with Jake, was history repeating itself. Red dirt had only given her the sense of false security. Etta's presence had been scarce since Will had returned and her only other friend, Jake, had become a double agent for the enemy. The uneasy feeling in her chest lurched until she felt like she was going to be sick. She walked past the fire station where she'd attended the barn dance and just past Louie's Pizzeria she ran smack into Addy as she was closing her bakery for the day.

"Paige," Addy's hand was on her arm, her earth mother eyes full of concern, "Honey, you're crying!"

Paige reached up to her rolling eyes, "I guess I am."

"You look like a woman who could use some girl chat."

"I don't think that's going to fix what's gone wrong, Addy."

"Oh dear," Addy threw her huge leather purse over her shoulder and linked her arm through Paige's. "Never underestimate the power of good Vodka," strange advice coming from the baker of gluten free breads and sugar free pies.

Addy led her across the street and straight into O'doul's, "You get us a table and I'll get the remedy."

Paige wandered through the darkness of the pub and found a table against the wall. It was a pretty quiet Monday night. She slid into the booth and realized the uneasy thrumming in her chest was her heart aching. Pulling a few napkins out of the holder she dabbed the tears from her eyes and folded her hands on the table top. Studying her fingers, she noticing sea foam green paint under her nails; another round of sobs bubbled up.

"Okay, now drink. I've got Hardy making more as we speak. He's under strict orders to keep it coming." Addy settled in to her side of the booth and looked across the table, "Paige, sometimes you just have to talk to someone. You're a member of the sisterhood now which means I'm legally required to buy you drinks until you start talking." Addy emptied her glass and quickly looked toward the bar to see if Hardy was making his way over yet.

"It's such a mess… I don't know where to start." Paige was picking at the paint around her fingernails.

Addy nudged the martini glass closer to Paige, "I'm telling you, it's practically the cure for a bad day."

The pink drink went down easily, "Thanks, that's really good."

"M Hmmm… now… what's up?"

"Well, you know I bought my house from an internet auction site."

"Yes, I think you mentioned it."

"The city has plans to tear it down for parking."

"That's ridiculous." Addy waved her unmanicured hand dismissively.

"According to Jake, I've got to make a good case to the City Council a week from tomorrow. They have slotted it for imminent domain and then demolition by next summer."

"Holy shit." Addy said, "Who's responsible for selling you a house that was ear marked for the city?"

"I haven't gotten that far yet. I had a title company, I have the deed of trust, I don't know what I can do at this point if the city really wants to tear it down. I know the house has been there for over a hundred and thirty years, it must have some intrinsic value to the city."

"The only history I can remember was a pot bust back in the nineties." Addy laughed but Paige didn't find humor in it, "Sorry Honey, I'm not very good at making jokes."

"It's not you; I'm really pissed off at myself that I may have missed a vital step in buying the property. It just doesn't matter, Addy. I love that house, I feel like I was born to live there and create this Bed and Breakfast. I'm so passionate about it! I just can't believe that this can be taken away."

"There's a whole bunch of us here who care about you and that house, Paige. I'll put the word out and we'll help you find the way. Wednesday night we usually play games. This week we'll meet at your house and strategize."

"Everyone is so busy with their own lives now, I can't ask them to come to my rescue."

"You need us and we'll be there.."

"Just like that?"

"Yep. Just like that. I'm going to give you some advice," Addy started her third drink, "Do not, under any circumstances stop working on that house. You're restoring her and you're both absolutely glowing. It's like you're spirits are linked together."

Paige looked into the bare, beautiful face of Addy the strange little earth mother baker who tonight, had chosen Vodka as the remedy. For a moment, Paige felt hopeful.

CHAPTER 16

Paige turned Nora Jones on for background music. Georgia remained mysteriously and supportively quiet while Paige continued to work on the house. One more bedroom and the guest quarters would be completed. She looked up into the foyer to admire her handiwork and felt comforted by the warm Tuscan gold of the walls. Light danced through the stained glass windows, creating Monet color splashes along the curved wall. As Nora sang in her carefree sultry tones, Paige swayed to the music, closed her eyes and absorbed the moment. The knowing in her heart said all would be well, logic told her otherwise, she'd had her beautiful creations stripped away before and it almost killed her. The faint recollection of Jakes advice, "when you start thinking with your heart and loving with your brain..." It was a battle she was not familiar with.

Etta opened the door without knocking, carrying a wooden box the size of a loaf of bread like a precious relic, its contents unknown to Paige. She kissed Paige on the cheek and said, "We're finally here!" Mim followed Etta, dragging a second box prepared with volumes of old binders. Addy appeared behind them with dinner. Della and Patti came with drinks and a huge dry erase board.

Paige watched in amazement as the women set up command central in her library. Dinner was served on paper plates but Mim refused to have cocktails out of paper cups and rummaged through the kitchen until she emerged with crystal stemware. "It's absolutely barbaric that we would be reduced to paper cups."

"Well, your highness, I was only thinking of clean up." Della shot toward her friend.

"I'll wash the crystal." Mim said indignantly.

"Okay, for starters," Mim said around a bite of Chicken Primavera, "We've got to know exactly what the city has planned. I brought a copy of the proposal." She laid it out on a large antique library table in the middle of the room. "Jake's right, they want to use this property as a parking lot." Everyone gathered around the table to look at the master plan of Nevada City. There was universal grumbling and heads shaking in disgust.

"I think we should get the best history and lineage of the house for our presentation." Addy said, handing out pink cocktails in glimmering crystal. Paige looked around at the faces; everyone one of them radiant in their own right. Addy's fresh face, straight hair pulled back to a pony tail, wearing jeans and a white shirt un-tucked and naturally casual. Mim's magical essence was focused to a fine point. Della, flowing and fluid, Etta, her hippy happy self, and finally Patti who looked like he just walked out of a board room, threw his jacket onto a chair.

"I hope everything we need is here in the boxes. Don't any of you ask me how I got them!" Mim announce trying to hide a conspiratorial smile.

"Did you steal them?" Etta's eyes stirred with wonder.

"Of course not Darlin', I merely borrowed them for a bit. That old Blanch in the main office wouldn't let me into the archives because it was too close to closin' time. I just waited until dark and used my old key to get into the basement. Easy as pie..."

"Easy for you to say." Paige thought.

Mim was quiet for a moment, dark reflection in her eyes. She wore a flowing dark blue gypsy dress with no shoes. Her signature jewelry was absent, her eyes looked tired but her presence was strong. When she finally spoke she did so with a tone Paige didn't recognize. What she said drew the undivided attention in the room, "Paige, Darlin', I want you to know that Jake really has nothing to do with the city's ambition to destroy your house. He's bound by law to uphold the best interests of Nevada City as their sole counsel for another year and a half." She looked thoughtfully out the float glass bay windows onto Broad Street and continued, "When Jake needed money for Law School and I couldn't help him..." Addy noticed tears working the corners of her eyes and scooted closer to put a hand on Mim's shoulder. "When the City offered him the grant for school with the condition of public service his love of Nevada City was foremost in his mind. Not bein' able to help that boy is one of my deepest regrets. Our leadership was trustworthy and well respected at the time." Her lips went tight and her eyes narrowed as she continued, "Since then, Jed has become a festering boil on the butt of this community. Sorry if that offends you Addy, I know he's your uncle."

"Not by blood, thank God!" Addy patted her hand.

Mim continued, "He's got everyone so wound up around here the city council can't find their asses with both hands and a compass. We should have known if he wasn't born here, he wouldn't have our best interests at heart."

"Not being of Red Dirt and all..." Della said curtly with a pout of her pretty pink lips. Everyone nodded in agreement.

"Jed Grisworth doesn't have the good sense God gave a piss ant." Mim said with contempt, "And I for one, am going to make it damned difficult for him to be re-elected City manager again." They all shook their heads and breathed out a sigh of disgust. "Now let's fry his chicken..." Mim said sweetly, "so to speak."

"Paige, your drawings for the place are amazing." Della said, running her bright red manicured fingers flashing with rings over the lines of her drawings. "With your permission I'll have copies made and then mount them on presentation boards for the Council meeting." Paige looked closely at Della. A Botticelli work of art, her dark hair streaked and tossed into a style carefree and wild. She wore a golden duster over a shirt that exposed her ample bosoms and snug Capri pants. Her tiny feet were adorned in shimmering gold sandals. Della was an artist of sensual perfection and wore her essence well. Her dramatic eyes flashed to Paige, "Well, I think it will make a huge impact. Do you trust me with the presentation?"

Paige said, "Of course! We can use the original sketches. Time is short. Wouldn't the real thing be better than sketches?" Della cocked her head to one side in question. Paige jumped up and said, "Come with me, I've been working reletlessly!"

As the group climbed the grand staircase, Patti cooed, "What a grand color Paige, so warm and unassuming at the same time. It's like this color has been on the walls for hundreds of years, but it's fresh."

"That's the point." She led them through her haunted hallway to the first bedroom and opened the double doors with a flourish. Revealing to them, a color of sea blue that felt like a mist of ocean. The bed was massive and draped around all sides with filmy shimmering fabric. Pillows of all shapes, sizes and textures created the desire to run and jump into the pile of down. It was elegantly unique yet luxuriously comfortable. A gold brocade chase lounge sat in the bay window overlooking the city streets. The women were speechless as they touched and walked around wide eyed through the room and finally peeked into the bathroom.

Della sighed, "Absolutely amazing, Paige, you have kept the originality of the house and made it new. I just want to crawl up onto that bed and melt into it."

"Go ahead!" Paige waved her hand inviting them to jump in.

A spark of delight crossed Addy's face as all the women crawled up onto the bed and with moans of pleasure they snuggled into the massive king sized down filled mounds of colored sand and ocean. Patti, who had been looking out the window, slipped out of his expensive leather loafers, revealing French manicured toenails and seized the opportunity to make a leap into the middle of the bed prompting squeals of juvenile laughter from the women. He sat smugly in the middle and rolled up his black silk sleeves, loosening his lavender tie.

Mim said with a giggle, "I do believe we have a thorn among the roses."

"Paige this is glorious!" Patti gushed running his hands over the textures of the bedding.

"I'm going to send over the photographer from the paper and get a piece put in the Union. We'll get the community interest, with your permission of course." Addy was fluffing a beautiful gold pillow as she climbed down from the bed. She looked back at the rag-tagged bunch billowing with satin and smiles, "Well that would be a pretty picture for the front page!"

"The Goddesses of Broad Street," Paige smiled.

After another moment of pleasure, Mim jumped off the bed and clapped her hands, taking charge of the situation, "Okay chickens, let's get movin'," she led the group back to the Library so they could get to work.

"What's in the books, Mim?" Patti pulled a down feather from his spiky hair.

"County records for properties." Mim gently took the book from Patti and placed it on the far end of the large table. "If I recall correctly, the house was built in the 1860's. We need to have names and dates, and anything else interesting that happened here, especially something that ties into the history of Nevada City and the gold rush." Mim handed out white gloves.

"Gloves for stolen ledgers?" Addy asked with humor.

"We're just borrowin' them. Gloves keep the oils on our skin from breaking down the documents. Don't you all look at me like I'm crazy, old historians die hard, you know. I spent the first half of my life in the archives preserving them."

White gloved, the dedicated committee searched. Patti occasionally made notes on the yellow legal pad next to his volume. Della had been collecting the notes and marking dates on the dry erase board, creating a time line. When all the volumes had been gone through, they sat in silence, looking at the dates, digesting the information.

"Something's missing," Etta said looking perplexed.

"The dates between owners are too long." Patti noted.

"It has to be right under our noses." Della said.

"Wait a minute!" Mim stood and started to pace with a scowl, "We need old newspaper articles that coincide with the dates we have. Things were recorded like a diary in the newspapers back then." She sat in contemplation tapping her nails against the wooden table, "Time is short, I hope we're on the right track."

Etta stood and walked to the middle of the room, her pale blue and lavender tie died skirt moving gracefully around her legs. "I feel it." The women all looked at Etta. She felt energy in the room that wasn't there hours ago when they'd gathered. It was an electricity of discovery, something that was not of them, but created for them, "She's here." Etta's eyes transformed from pale hazel to dark green, her gaze focused on the air in the room. Not looking at anything in particular.

"Who's here?" Della whispered.

"Can you hear her Etta?" Paige asked softly, "I can't hear her."

"Okay Ladies ... this is getting weirder by the minute." Patti said in a hushed tone. Instinctively they had migrated to a huddle. The music suddenly stopped. A door upstairs slammed twice. They all jerked in unison looking to one another for an answer as a chill pricked unanimous skin.

"Georgia?" Paige called out, looking towards the stairs in the foyer. The door slammed again, "That's not nice. If you have something to say... then say it." Paige had a furrowed brow.

"Jesus, I never get used to this!" Patti threw his hands up in a huff and waved them around, strutting like a bird, "I don't know how you do it Etta... it scares me stupid." His hands went quickly into his pant pockets as his eyes darted nervously around the room, blond spikes flopping.

"How delicious," Della whispered, her little heels clicking off towards the foyer. The squeak of the upstairs attic door was magnified through the quiet house; visibly it stood open at the top of the stairs in welcome. Della continued to the bottom of the stairs and started her ascent to the open door.

"Della," Etta put her hand on her arm, "Come back into the library." Della's large brown eyes made slow motion contact with Etta, "That's it, Honey, come back in here for a minute." Etta guided her back into the library where every face looked on in horror. She kept Della's hand in hers as she began to give instructions very slowly with an even tone to keep everyone's mind easy. "Paige, please get me the box I brought. Addy, come and hold on to Della. She's a little distracted right now and I don't want her wandering off without us. Mim, the candles and the lighter, Patti, please join us." Patti was frozen watching the attic door and began to wander to the foyer. Etta went after Patti and brought him back to the room guiding his hand to Addy. She then closed the heavy double doors connecting the library to the foyer.

Paige handed over the box as they waited for direction. Lifting the wooden lid, Etta removed a bundle of sage, a brilliantly clear crystal as big as her hand, a stone bowl, and a feather. She arranged the sage into the bowl and lit it. With the feather she fanned the purification of the sage to herself and then passed it around. She moved to the center of the circle and placed the crystal on the floor. Etta closed her eyes and took in three deep breaths, letting her shoulders relax.

"I draw up from the mother of red dirt my strength. I draw

down from the heavens of these foothills my vision, I breathe in clarity of thought and intention, and I exhale my inhibitions and fears asking that they be transformed into guidance and light." Etta opened her eyes, "Ladies, please join me in this. I draw up from the mother of Red Dirt my strength," she nodded at Patti who was hesitating. He blinked hard and joined in, "I draw down from the heavens of these foothills my vision, I breathe in clarity of thought and intention, and I exhale my inhibitions and fears asking that they be transformed into guidance and light." All together, holding hands the chanting grew in strength and volume.

"And so it is..." Etta bowed her head.

"And so it is..." the group followed.

"I now ask that whatever message this house has for us that it be made clear tonight. We are here to help Paige follow her dream of returning this mansion to its former grandeur. We are here in an effort to preserve this house and its heritage in Nevada City." Around the circle eyes were closed and they nodded in agreement as Etta spoke, "Georgia, we want you to know we are fighting to save this great mansion. We want you to know that your history is important. The city is trying to tear this house down. What can you tell us that may help..."

One deep breath, nothing. Two deep breaths, stillness. On the third breath the double doors of the library blew open with a rage of wind, cold and chilling. A wrath of fury assaulted Paige as her hair filled with a storm of electricity flew out around her face. They grabbed her hands, desperate to hold her as if she might be blown away. The lights flickered, Georgia's voiced boomed with a ferociousness that was new to her. "THIS IS MY HOUSE! This is all I have... everything you need is here! I am all you need...." There was a quiet sob in Georgia's voice, "I've always been here... but I was never enough." A sudden stillness filled in the air with calm they all felt. Like a thick blanket of snow on the room, sound was muffled, the room was peaceful. Georgia dissipated.

"Did you hear that?" Paige asked tentatively, "She sounded so sad. Like a little girl."

"They heard that in Auburn," Patti said shaking. Wiping his sweaty palms on his pants, he studied the other's faces.

Etta broke the circle, walked to the foyer and stared up at the attic door, "Della, you and Patti were both drawn to the stairs, any idea what that's all about?"

"I was?" Della asked.

"We were?" Patti worried.

"There is something in the attic that Georgia wants us to have. She's not showing me what it is," Etta said.

"The other day when Jake and I were up there, one door kept opening. When we closed it, it crept open again. Then it slammed."

"What's in there? That's a whole lotta guidance if you ask me..." Mim said.

"Well, trunks and boxes and books." Paige answered, "I've been so focused on the restoration projects, I thought I'd go through the room next year when I have some down time. It looks like boxes of books, possibly from the library."

"Georgia has other ideas and we'll find our answer in that room." Etta led the five of them through the foyer. As they climbed the stairs they stuck close to one another.

"How exciting," Della's voice filled with adventure.

"It's creepy," Patti grumbled. "Why did she say MINE? Paige I don't like that... like she's possessed you."

"Oh stop it Patti," Mim scolded, "you'll scare us all stupid."

Up the staircase like the keystone cops in a haunted house they ascended. Trying to stay close, bumping and jumpy with one another they stopped short outside the attic door as it creaked open. They exchanged looks in the silence, each hoping the other would run for the light. Patti widened his eyes at Etta and shrugged his shoulders. Rolling her eyes, Etta made one big jump for the light cord. Dull vacilating light pulsed out of the single bulb hanging from the ceiling. Paige grabbed Etta's hand and fearlessly they climbed the attic stairs together.

They gathered outside the door Paige pointed to. From the middle of a very small huddle, came Patti's voice, "so this is the slamming, opening door?" His eyes bugged out.

"This is the one," Paige said. Stepping forward she grabbed the handle, determined and flung it open. The smell of old books and a hundred years of dust swirled out in a smothering cloud. It was dark inside the room; the only sound in the attic was of their own heavy breathing.

"Hello dark scary room... what do you have for us?" Patti found a new wave of bravery as he flipped the light switch. The bulb exploded with a loud pop.

Etta stepped forward, touching Patti's sleeve, "its ok. Georgia's very active, but she's not controlling her energy well. She's not trying to scare us, she's excited and we must be close. We all need to take a moment and calm down."

Mim located a lantern. As she lit it, the glow illuminated

their faces, creating dancing shadows on the walls. She stood outside the door waiting for focus. "We are all ok... let's just take a moment to remember what we're here for."

They nodded in unison as they approached the room. Paige entered first. She turned around in the tiny space, neatly stacked trunks and wooden boxes stood in rows nearly filling the room to the rafters. Answers were everywhere, illusive and right there in front of them, if they just knew where to look. Piling in behind her, crowding the space even more, they shuffled in, stuffing the room with butts, boobs and arms. "It will take us months to read through all of this." Paige whispered.

"Oh look, that one's been moved!" Della pointed her finger to a box at the very top of a stack in the farthest corner. She squeezed past Patti, who lifted his arms and rolled his eyes as her pudgy bosoms squished past his waist. Maneuvering her way through the rows to the corner, Della moved a box to use as a step. Her bejeweled foot landed with purpose on top of the box and as she hefted herself up it collapsed in a choking cloud of dust, throwing her back against Patti again.

"Oh Honey, you have clearly exceeded the weight limit for that old thing... here, let me help you." Patti linked his fingers together and created a step for Della.

"Oh you've got to be kidding, I could crush you!" Della gasped.

"Just do it," Patti shook his hands impatiently.

Della stepped up quickly and reached for the box. She caught one corner of the box but flopped back down to the floor. Patti nudged her to step up again, which she did, this time she grabbed,

"Got it." Something fluttered out of the corner and landed in her hair.

"Holy Mother of..." She threw her arms around Patti's head, "Get it out! Get it out!" But it was flapping in her hair. She threw a leg around his middle. They lost balance and fell to the floor in a tangled heap; the rest of the group tumbled and splayed out on their fannies. Addy pushed against the wall behind Patti's butt. Della was squealing, swinging at her head as a tiny bat released her hair and flew out the door, followed by at least half a dozen of his friends who rushed down from the corner. Della blinked down into her cleavage and saw Patti's eyes staring straight up at her. She jumped up to release him.

"We shall not speak of this again." Patti jumped up, smoothing out his pants, "Well, my heart rate's up girls, nice rack Della," he gave her a wicked smile, "And you smell divine."

Addy had fallen against the boxes. Paige and Etta laughed hysterically, clinging to each other as they lay on the dusty floor.

"Oh my god, I'm going to PUKE! I've had the wings of Satan in my hair!" Della was out of breath. Her hair was wrapped around from one side and standing straight out on the other. "Am I going to have to have Rabies shots?"

"I think we have what we need." Mim's motherly voice was hushed; everyone turned to see her face in shock, holding the box that fell down from Della's whirl.

"I think we should take this down stairs," Etta said, "into better light."

What no one noticed was what Georgia had intended them to find and it was hidden in plain site.

It was after one in the morning. Papers littered the room. Books, brittle and darkened by age were piled into organized stacks.

"It's all so convoluted," Addy sighed.

"There has to be answers, but all I'm finding are receipts and ledgers for boarding." Patti said, his sweaty hair completely flattened against his head.

"Do we just keep bringing boxes down?" Paige asked, "What we need has to be up there… Georgia says so!"

"We're only half way through this one." Etta said, "And we need answers fast."

"Wait a minute," paige said, "I have had some very bizarre dreams about this place."

"Go on…" Etta urged.

"It's not from our current time it's like before the turn of the century. And I'm a…" she stopped talking weighing if she could say it out loud. "I'm entertaining gentlemen in this house."

The silence was defining.

"I was thinking if there are boarding receipts… those may have been working girls renting a room from, well, a Madam?"

"Well," said Della, "There have certainly been a lot of rumors over the years. But Nevada City isn't really proud of its salty history. I'd bet my last dollar that's what this house was used for, but we can hardly convince our city council that's a good reason to save the property. I say we get some pictures, start the community buzz about what's going on here and get some clout behind us. Concentrating on Jed is only going to make us crazy. He has no soul."

"Hell no, Jed will never make a decision in our favor without the pressure of the community. We'll hit it hard." Mim paced as she talked, "Paige... with our help, do you think we could organize a public tour of the mansion, complete with the sketches and the finished rooms? Let's focus on the future instead of the past. We'll have a wine tour. I bet Hardy and the winery will help us out."

"When?" Paige asked.

"As soon as possible. Before the city council meeting next week." Mim looked at her friends, "If you all think we can pull it off..."

"I'll call my cousin at the paper and have him come over tomorrow." Della looked at her watch, "well, today actually. We'll have a piece in the paper by Wednesday announcing our open house on Sunday. We'll plan it for after church hours and hopefully we'll have a bunch coming to the town meeting on Tuesday."

"Great planning," Paige said, "whatever you think we need to do. I'll work around the clock."

Patti stood throwing his hands into the air, "I'm having a total recall of Mickey Rooney and Judy Garland having a show in Uncle Bucks barn! How fun!"

CHAPTER 17

It was surreal and thrilling as everyone in Paige's circle of friends pitched in to create the vision that spread out over her lawn. Linen covered tables under white tents surrounded the wine barrel bar. Thousands of tiny white Christmas lights glimmered. The only thing missing was Jake. He hadn't set foot on her property and she'd been too consumed to think much about it. He was free to be with Betty and she couldn't interfere. She deserved the anxiety she was feeling, it kept her honest. It was probably best that way, Paige justified.

"Are you ok?" Etta asked softly.

"Yeah...."

"He'll come around Paige. He's feeling guilty and horrid. I know my brother. He is racking his brain to come up with a way to save the day. It's his way you know."

"Yes, the messiah complex." Paige smiled weakly. "Etta, this isn't the first time this insanity has consumed my life... and last time..." Her breath stuck in a panic and she began to tear, "It's a reoccurring theme in my past lives apparently too."

Etta put her hand on Paige's shoulder and spoke softly, feeling Paige's uncertainty, "But, now you're here and you're not alone. Let's get ready for this open house, It's the perfect time to wear your Donna Karin black dress." Etta led her into the house and to the closet.

The Goddesses had gathered by the time Paige was dressed. High heels, hair up, sparkling dangly earrings she was ready for the tours and talking and showing off her creation. Mim was heading up the coalition of women, supplying clip boards and paper for note taking, giving everyone last minute instructions. They stood in the foyer in a circle of flowing garments and glimmering jewelry.

"Y'all look like a million bucks." Mim smiled broadly at her dearest friends. She draped a brilliant green shawl over Paige's shoulders and winked, "for color, Darlin'."

"It's how we take on the world." Della said as a matter of fact. "Anything worth doing is worth looking good for."

The tone of highly polished Italian leather shoes on the wooden floor caused all the women to turn, "Amen, Sister!" Patti whooshed through the front doors with his long charcoal tails flying behind him. He placed his sunglasses on top of his freshly spiked hair and said, "Now, let's do this thing." He reached for Mim's hand.

"I hope at least a few people show up." Paige sighed.

"Honey, look!" Patti pointed to the front yard.

From the front porch they looked out over Broad Street. It looked like metal to a magnet. From every angle people were walking towards the mansion.

"Oh...." Paige wiped at an unexpected tear working down her cheek.

"It's show time," Della said as she walked halfway down the porch steps and stopped, waiting for the stragglers to come close.

"May I have your attention?" Her voice was like a soft boom among the crowd and the rustling quieted down. You could tell theater was her life. "I want to thank you all so much for coming out today. As you know, our dear Paige purchased this mansion a few months back and has returned to the city of her birth to renovate and open a beautiful new addition to our community." Della motioned for Paige to join her. "So far she's done an amazing job; you will be stunned when you see the completed rooms, and the renderings for the rest of the place. Right now, we'd like to invite you back to the event lawn where Hardy has set up the wine bar. We'll show you a potential wedding site and then we'll open up the house for tours. Mim, Addy, Paige, Pat, Etta and I will all be here to answer questions but mostly we want information. If you know anyone who has interesting knowledge about this place, please share it with us. The city council has this magnificent piece of our history on its roster for demolition and we'd like your support on Tuesday night if you feel you'd like to see the mansion stay with us another hundred years or so."

Paige looked at the bare wood on the side of the house and then out to the gathering crowd, "This mansion is so dear to me. If you can ignore our projects and look at the renderings inside I will show you the final project." Samson, the jeweler nodded a greeting from the crowd, "In the meantime, please join us out back for a glass of wine and something to nibble on. And we'll get the tours started!"

The women led the way down the stairs. Each one wearing her signature color created a flow of violet, green, fuscia, gold and black flowing behind them as they led the crowd down the walk way to the event lawn. Hundred year old oak trees fingering across the yard created patches of cool shade. Delightfully dressed with floating candles, bouquets of peonies and sweet peas in cut crystal vases graced the top of each spring green table cloths. From behind the wine bar Paige looked out over the crowd of at least one hundred faces, familiar and happy. Etta squeezed Paige's hand.

Sixty minutes into the evening, Paige questioned the wisdom of her shoe choice. With each step in the softened ground her three inch spiky heels dug in, creating a sharp pain in the ball of her foot and a dull burning ache in her ankle. She hobbled to a chair close to the back edge of the yard and flopped down, disheartened by the pain. The yard vibrated with conversation, tinkling wine glasses all aglow with candles and little white lights. Ernie, having turned in his overalls for a banana yellow bowling shirt and Levis, leaned on the bar while pouring wine as he told stories and laughed with the guests.

Eyes dancing and arms spread wide, Mim lead another tour from the side of the house. No doubt she was spinning a stunning visual of what was to come at the mansion. Paige put her elbow on the table and allowed her head to rest into her hand. She absorbed the scene as a snapshot memory in her mind. She was loved, appreciated and more than anything, she didn't want to lose it. The thought brought on an inconsolable wave of anger and resentment.

Reaching down to rub the back of her leg she heard a voice that stopped the breath in her lungs. Slowly, she turned in her chair to see Jake talking to a small group across the yard from her. She continued to rub her calf. Seeing his crisp white shirt tucked into his jeans, sleeves rolled up with his hair neatly combed back was a sharp jab. She looked back to him and noticed his hands on a clipboard. She blushed at the memory of where those hands had touched her body, where she had demanded they go. Determined to stay focused, the pout fell away and she sniffed up the courage to abandon the shoes and start another round of socializing.

With naked feet she resolved to ignore Jake Jenkins and his perfect mouth, and his beautiful strong hands. She made a B-line to the front of the house, smiling and nodding at everyone in her path. Patti and Della were standing by the stairs talking to someone Paige didn't recognize. As she approached the front porch, Paige slipped into a lopsided embrace from Patti. He gave her a squeeze and a loud smacking kiss on top of her curly head. She smiled at the small elderly woman sitting on the porch steps.

"Paige, this is Betty." Della gave her a quick look out the side of her dramatically lined eyes and reached out a hand to help Betty stand. "Betty, this is our dear Paige." Betty bounced up like a cork in water.

Paige made a quick assessment of Jake's sweetheart, wearing a red dress with white polka dots the size of nickels. She was slight in build, white cotton candy hair styled to high perfection, pulled back to show off her yellow button earrings that matched the wide patent leather belt around her petite waist. A black sweater slung over her shoulders with a clasp of enameled lady bugs connected with a silver chain. White pointy shoes with a slight heel gave her the look of a 50's actress.

"What a pleasure to meet you," Paige softly squeezed the hand Betty held out. Betty wasn't quite five feet tall, and appeared to Paige to be at least eighty years old.

"I wouldn't have missed this for anything." Betty said.

Paige instantly recognized the voice as the angel who turned her power on when she'd arrived unprepared and overtired, "Betty I haven't had the chance to thank you for…"

Betty cut her off holding up a hand jingling with bangle bracelets, "No need to thank me, Doll. I have information that will save your house. I've been here since Jesus was a baby, you know." Her eyes were full of mischief, "I think my ancestors and yours must've had quite a time in our Nevada City."

Betty's brightly painted red lips curved into a crooked smile. She was a Goddess too. In her day, Paige imagined, Betty could have easily been a pin up girl. No wonder Jake had fallen in love with her when he was five years old. She was femininity incarnate at eighty plus years old. A rush of pure relief opened up and washed over Paige.

She couldn't help but smile and be warmed by Betty, "I can't wait to hear what you have to say." She looked at Betty with solid concentration. Attention shifted over Paige's shoulder to someone approaching. Della rolled her eyes, Patti stood aside and Betty lit up like a Christmas tree as Jake stepped toward the group. Paige's heels dangled from his finger and he held a clipboard to his chest. Everything in Paige's mind screeched to a halt and a dull buzz rang in her ears.

Betty reached out for the clipboard, "How many do we have now?"

"Close to two fifty," Jake said releasing the bundle to Betty.

"Great." She turned the clipboard and examined its contents, "Paige, Doll, we'll have lunch on Tuesday, before the council meeting." She never looked up, "eleven, at the Diner. I've got work to do." Paige watched, mesmerized by the motion of Betty's skirts as she click-clacked on her way out the gate and down the walk.

"Wow. So that's Betty." Paige was smiling. Before she knew

it Della and Patti had slipped away leaving her alone with Jake, standing in front of her steps.

"I think you shed these out of self defense." Jake held out the strappy spiked heels.

"Thanks." Paige set her shoes on the steps, avoiding Jake's eyes.

"They looked amazing… if it's any consolation" Jake was shuffling his feet, "I don't know how you women do it… but I'm thankful." He looked at her feet in avoidance, "Paige…"

"Jake, I can't do this right now…"

CHAPTER 18

Despite her strongest efforts to ward off the tears, Paige had been crying quietly in bed, cursing the puffy eyes that would follow. If she didn't cry she would explode. Wally wandered through the room, jumped up to the bed, assessed the situation and then sat, looking at her square in the eye as if she was inconveniencing him with the noise she was making.

"Oh what is it?" she said through her sobs, reaching for his furry head.

Wally blinked in slow motion and lazily walked over her arm to lie on her heart. His purr started as a stutter and then went steady, loud and constant. Amazing love vibrated from him. She tried to make eye contact to thank him. He refused her gratitude. It was the warm and fuzzy lullaby that Paige drifted off to.

A monstrous red wrecking ball towered over the mansion. She was helpless, feeling stuck in very deep mud. People were passing by unconcerned with her personal horror. She desperately attempted to scream out. Panic ridden, she fell to her knees and watched as Jake pointed to the top turreted roofline yelling, "Start there..."

Shock consumed her as a tiny squeal broke free, but no one came to help her. She rolled onto her belly and looked up from behind the house. She covered her head trying to shield herself from shards of wood and roof pounding down all around her. That's when she saw at least a dozen women with horrified howls of panic in the upstairs windows.

"NO NO NO NO NO," she cried, "Stop!" A curious crowd gathered around to watch as the house was demolished before them. Cheers rang out as all of Paige's dreams came down in slow motion surrounding the unsympathetic mob.

Paige woke up panting, soaked in sweat. Wally was nowhere to be seen. Sitting up, she swallowed the urge to scream just to feel the relief of actually being able to do it, but she pulled in a ragged breath instead. If you scream in a huge old mansion and only the cat hears it, did you really scream at all? She wobbled to the bathroom and sat down hard on the toilet. Cold and shivering she tried to shake off the night terror. Turning on the hot water in the tub, Paige thought it might be a better way to start the day. After 45 minutes the chill had been chased away. It took hours to conquer the feeling that she was a helpless observer in a series of events destroying her future.

"I have heard the call and I'm answering!" Etta yelled through the kitchen door.

"I'm in here," Paige called from the bathroom.

"Hey, what's up?" Etta flopped down on the freshly made bed. "The urge to come over here was so strong I couldn't go to the office without checking in with you."

"I had a nightmare last night and now I can't get over the feeling that this fight is a lost cause." Paige twisted her lipstick back into the tube and took a quick look at Etta. "I also think there are a few more spirits trapped her than we know about."

"I have it on high authority that it's not a lost cause, but the meeting tonight will tell us what road we take. You're meeting with Betty today, yes? Spirits, yes, but they are fading."

"In about 30 minutes." Paige looked at her watch, "it's more like they're dying, Etta. There is something I can do to set them free."

Etta's face looked tired, and worried. Paige was sure it wasn't about her mansion. Etta's mind had been whirling about a child's future, her relationship with Will and things that transcended the material world. Suddenly Paige's worries didn't seem that significant.

"Thank you for answering the call," Paige said softly to Etta who was now looking out the window. "How is Will doing with all this hanging over his head?"

"Well, he's doing okay. Mim has been talking to him about the importance of family and how Jon's grandfather has the right to be part of his life... he owes it to Jon-Jon." She hesitated, "Will's dead set against it... says if he'd been a decent father his kid wouldn't have become a stripper and drug addict." Etta took in a breath and smiled at Paige, "Family drama... gotta love it."

"Jon Jon is lucky to have so many people who care about his future. You're the psychic, what do you see when you look into the future?" Paige asked.

"Funny thing is, I'm so deeply entrenched in the situation, that I can't see the forest through the trees so to speak... psychic work is like that. It works for anyone but me." Etta glanced at Paige, "You look great! Go meet Betty and get her story before we march into the foundry and take this situation by the short hairs."

"Right," Paige looked at her watch, "Oh, Got to run. I'll see you tonight."

Betty was perched on a chrome stool at the counter, looking sharp in yellow Capri pants, an oversized white shirt belted at the waste and white flats. She was deep in conversation with the waitress who lazed on the edge of the counter tapping her order pad on the Formica edge. The waitress gave Paige a curious look, "I think your girl is here, Bet."

"Hi there, shall I take a booth or do you want to sit at the counter, Betty?" Paige realized immediately that she sounded 'all business' by the look the two women gave her. The waitress bugged her eyes out and turned to look at Betty shrugging her shoulders.

Betty's bracelets jingled as she hopped down from the stool and said sweetly, "How about right here," and led her to the corner booth tucked behind the juke box. The waitress looked disappointed that they didn't stay at the counter.

"I didn't mean to barge in Betty," Paige said softly sliding onto the turquoise vinyl seat.

"Oh don't worry about that old sour puss, she's just nosey and she won't be able to hear us talking over here..." Betty wiggled into her seat and slid her little beaded bag toward the wall. "I don't mean to be right to the point Doll, but I have a date in a few minutes and there is so much I want to say to you."

"Of course," Paige was fascinated with Betty's every move, "I'm all ears. I even brought a pad to write notes."

"No need for that." Betty looked around to make sure no one was eavesdropping. "Jake has it all under control." She reached across the table to pat Paige on the hand.

"What?" Paige said more harshly than she intended, "I mean, he hasn't said much to me in over two weeks. Why should I believe that he has everything under control?" Paige felt her face getting hot and her ears starting to ring, "Oh Betty, there is so much at stake!"

"Jakes hands are very capable." Betty scanned the diner again before continuing, "Don't worry Paige. I know for a fact that Jed can't tear your house down," she winked.

Paige was having a hard time holding back the tears of disappointment. Leaning back against the booth, she closed her eyes. When she opened them a moment later, Betty was studying her face intently.

"Paige, you are going to have to trust. Now I want to tell you something more..."

Paige leaned in.

"I know you and Jake got off to a rocky start, but he's a good boy. He's one of my favorite people. And believe me I've known them all comin' and going through here. He's got a heart of gold and I am asking you to trust him. He's got the whole town behind you now. Jed doesn't stand a snowball's chance in hell tonight."

"Well, I would feel a lot better if I knew what everyone else suddenly knows!" Paige was finding it hard to hide her frustration.

"Shhhh...." Betty looked around and slid out of the booth. Her flats tap tap tapped all the way out the door. Paige sat in a stunned stupor. Not knowing if she should be relieved or start packing. Relieved for what reason? Because Jake had it all taken care of? Because some retired pin up model says so? Her head flopped into her hands, but she refused to cry. Her eyes had been so puffy that morning her vision had been distorted. She didn't want to go into the meeting tonight with her eyes swollen shut.

"Can I bring you something?" the waitress asked. It was

lunchtime and people were waiting for a table. Paige grabbed her purse, fished around for a tip and putting it on the table, shook her head no and headed out.

~

Paige and Etta had walked toward the foundry together in silence. Etta didn't look concerned and reminded Paige to keep the faith. The large crowd approaching the meeting looked solemn. Once inside, they took their seats in the second row beside Mim, Addy, Patti and Della. Betty sat in the front row on the other side from them in a hazel blue pant suit, a brief case on the floor next to her. With a look of confidence, she shot a smug wink at Paige. Jake sat on the stage behind the table and podium. He looked haggard. His sleeves were rolled up with his jacket on the back of his seat. The head chair was empty.

Mim leaned in close to Paige, "Don't worry Darlin', Della's got the slid show and we've got all of our information lined out. It's a knock out presentation."

"Thank you for everything you've done, Mim..." Paiges voice cracked. "You've got so much going on and you've..."

"Don't.... don't you dare get emotional right now. You stay strong with us. This is going to be settled once and for all."

The humming of people gathering around her and the shuffling of chairs echoed in the enormous room. Looking around the old building, the stone floors were unevenly worn smooth with one hundred sixty years of use. Paige felt that the old building would vibrate a story to her if she would just put her hands against the walls and listen.

Jed walked into the building and the energy in the room changed. The air became heavy as attendees settled into their seats.

Jed strutted to the podium, "'E'venin' everyone. Let's start by saying the pledge."

Local Boy Scout troop 139, which consisted of seven boys aged eight to twelve, brought out the California and United States flags and the building echoed with the pledge of allegiance. It brought goose bumps to her arms when she listened to the words. A promise that justice would be served.

"Let's all be seated," Jed's voice boomed with squealing feedback from the microphone, "We've got a lot of ground to cover tonight. And I know my Rita's got a chicken in the oven... don't want to be late for that!"

"What an asshole," Della whispered loud enough to be heard two rows away. Snickers moved through the crowd, stifled the minute Jed looked in her direction. It was just like being in school. Della sweetly blew a kiss to Jed.

"Jake," Jed huffed, "why don't you get us started with what this meeting is all about."

Jake stood up, walked to the podium and cleared his throat, "As you all know, I've become involved with a project involving the property Ms. Paige Hamilton recently bought *in full.*" He shot a look over his shoulder to Jed. "I believe most of you here tonight were present for a tour a few days ago to let you all know what the plans for the property are. Let the record show that Jed Grizwald was not present for the City Tour." Jake cut a quick glance at Paige, "Della has put together a presentation to show you what is in store for that piece of property. Now before we watch the slides it must be said that the problem that plagues our city is parking. Every visitor or local for that matter can't find a damn place to park. It's infuriating. Even disabled people can't find a spot to park here in the heart of town. How many of you had to walk more than four blocks to come here tonight?" At least eighty percent of the attendants held up their hands. "Now, I know it keeps us healthier to walk, but I was on crutches a few weeks back and I'll tell you what... It was hell getting around town. So, I understand the problem. I get it. Every single person in this room gets it. What I am asking is will our City be made better by tearing down a beautiful and historic mansion for parking? Most folks who visit here say it's because of the charm. I am proposing that we come up with a solution that does not rely on demolition as the answer to our parking problem. Della, I think we're ready."

The lights dimmed and Paige watched as her mansion came to life before her eyes. Pictures of the mansion a few years prior were shown. It was a ram shackled wreck by anyone's measure. Della narrated while the pictures clicked through. The pictures progressed from the improvements made so far, to the renderings Paige hand sketched herself. Finally, she saw it on the screen. Complete with her sign out front and guests in the yard.

Jed was at the Podium when the lights came back up, "Heart rendering," he stated flatly, "let's open the floor for comments for 10 minutes, then I have a solution for this .... Problem."

"Let the tourists stay home," Samson shouted from his chair.

General mayhem broke out throughout the meeting until Mim stood, regal and with a raise of her arm, she majestically took control of the room, "My friends, my neighbors, and my goodness," she leveled off a look at the old gentleman. "Listen to yourselves. I've got a longing to see this mansion finished and making money in our community. It's not only an asset but has an immeasurable amount of intrinsic value to Nevada City. As for parking, I have an idea where we can build up instead of tearing down. We can shuttle our visitors in from other locations for the time being. There are alternatives, we've all heard them. Tearing this mansion down is the easy way out." Mim nodded her head back to Jed, content that she'd taken charge.

Jed's chin rested into his open hand listening. He blinked lazily as though the conversation had become a huge bore, "Okay, Ms. Hamilton what do YOU have to say about this project?"

Paige stood and moved to the podium. She waited for the hush to settle and said strongly, "I bought it on the internet, if you can all believe it. I became obsessed with it and clicked that mouse until I owned a mansion in a town I haven't set foot in since I was a toddler. I was born here and this mansion has been the vehicle that brought me home. What I've found since I arrived is so much more than wood and plaster. There is over a century and a half of history in the house. The mansion drew me here, but I didn't fall in love with her until I touched the banister, washed the mermaid wallpaper in the bathroom, painted the walls of the foyer and watched light dance through the stained glass. When I first heard about the city's plans to tear it down I thought 'NO it's mine,'" Paige hesitated, "Today as I sat here watching the slid show, thank you, Della, I realized that my name is on the deed, but this house belongs to Nevada City. I'm just a steward for its survival. Even knowing the complications and now the heartbreak that has arisen for saving this mansion... I would do it again. Mayor Griswold, let it be shown on the record that I object to this threat of immanent domain. I thank all of you who have stood with me and fought to inspire a different way... Thank you." Paige bowed to the crowd in thanks before returned to sit between Etta and Mim.

Jake stood and handed Jed a stack of papers, "Jed, in this you will find over five hundred signatures all asking you to stop the demolition of the mansion on Pine street."

"Impressive, Jake" Jed took the file, "I have the consensus that it is the wishes of this community to preserve this mansion from demolition." Looking smug, he waved the file over his head. "So, my dear Ms. Hamilton, with the power vested in me, by my office and the county I gift you with your mansion at 113 Pine Street. The city will have a cashier's check in the mail to you for your parcel number 34, lot number 433 in the amount of one hundred four thousand dollars. You now have sixty days to show the city a plan on how your mansion will be moved and to what location. This meeting is adjourned." His gavel came down. A stunned moment of silence was followed by loud, righteous indignation. Paige sat anesthetized, trying to let it all register in her head. Move the mansion.

"That pompous ass..." Mim hissed out as a matter of fact. She flew furious towards the stage to have a word with Jed. By the time she navigated through all the people, he was gone.

"Assassination is the only way," Della said holding the pink goddess drink of choice.

Paige sat fuming in the darkest corner of the booth. "How the hell do you move a four story Victorian mansion?" Her finger tapped at the water pooling around her cocktail, "I mean, I know it can be done... but come on."

"Don't be silly Paige, that mansion is not going to be moved. It's going to be open for business next summer," Della said softly reaching across to pat Paige's hand, "And in its current location."

There was a commotion outside as robin egg blue Bentley flew into the parking space in front of O'Doul's, curb feelers grating the sidewalk. The car appeared to be unmanned as it screeched metal on metal smacking into the parking meter. Upon closer inspection Paige caught a glimpse of wispy white hair bobbing from the driver seat. The door swung open and one shapely ankle appeared, then another. Betty, fit to be tied and walking with resounding purpose across on the wooden floor, grabbed the cocktail Hardy handed her, "Thanks, Doll, You know I hate to wait." She winked at Hardy. He blushed and busied himself wiping down the bar top.

"The streets around here are tighter than a cat's ass in a dog kennel." Betty announced to the group beginning to assemble around Paige.

"I thought you retired that car years ago." Della inquired.

"Well, lock your children up, I'm on the prowl. I like the freedom of driving. Besides, I think they've painted over all the places I've run into... time to spread my signature color around again."

In a whirl of indigo tie dye Mim walked in with arms raised to heaven, "That son of a biscuit eatin' rat bastard." Hardy met her half way with the pink cocktail. Mim softened to kiss Hardy's cheek; "Keep 'em comin' Darlin'." Hardy smiled and held up a pitcher of pink liquid which he brought to the women. Mim turned her attention toward the table, "He simply cannot continue to be this cantankerous."

"Alright now," wiggling down into her seat, Betty slung her eyes low and dramatic, "Here's what's going to bury that old monkey in a suit… and save your house Paige."

Eyes and ears turned to Betty. She looked confused suddenly and sat back softly in her seat, "Was I going to say something?"

"Yes, you were going to tell us how to save the house… said you have the secret." Paige felt a wash of déjà vu to the diner that afternoon.

"What secret?" Betty said suddenly full of life, "I love secrets." She leaned forward and put her hands folded on top of the table, eyes bright with anticipation.

Silent looks raced across the table as it dawned on the women that Betty was having memory lapses.

"Are you feeling ok Betty?" Mim's asked.

"Of course, I'm fine."

"I'm not sure a cocktail is a good idea for you." Etta spoke up, "I think I should drive you home. And I can walk back from there."

"Drive me?" Betty looked confused.

"Yes I'll drive your car to your house and walk home from there. It's only a couple of blocks."

"Hogwash Etta, my car is in the garage."

"Oh Betty," Mim said softly, "your car is right out front, you drove it here."

"That's just silly! Jake took my keys months ago." Betty turned in slow motion to see her car parked at the curb.

"Maybe that would be best, Etta."

CHAPTER 19

Pale shadows under Etta's eyes told Paige that a surprise baby, an old love returned, and now the uncertainty of it all had become a terrible strain on her friend. She poured coffee as Etta softly stated what she had been enduring, "Will just loves that baby. The sun rises on his head every morning." Etta wiped a tiny tear.

"That's got to be hard on you Etta. He's just come home and now you not only have to share him with Jon Jon, you've got to share him with everyone else who wants to be part of Jon's life."

"Oh Paige, thanks for saying that, I've been feeling like a wretch. I come home to lick my wounds, but I feel so guilty having those thoughts. I haven't had a night with Will since Jon came home. It's starting to sting. I know there is a lot at stake, I know there are more emotions than I can't possibly imagine from Mim, Will and the baby. My life changed so drastically when Jon Jon arrived."

"I know it's got to be hard. How is Mim holding up?"

"Even with all of the love she's got for him, the practice of feng shui for baby happiness and Tia chi for toddlers... she's wrecked. " Etta thought of her beloved family being torn by losing the baby to his grandfather and the tears started to pour, "Paige, he's Jon's grandfather. He's lost his daughter... I cannot imagine what kind of a father would not know what's going on in his daughter's life until she's dead."

"Sounds like you all need a good break, you're worn slick."

Paige became inspired, "You bring Jon to me. I'll keep him for the weekend. That way everyone gets a rest, recoup and reconnect with one another and I get to do something truly useful to get my mind off of this House."

"Paige, you don't know the first thing about babies. You don't even like them."

"Well, this one is different and he's dear to my heart. Talk it over with Will and let me know. I'll start baby proofing."

"It's a lot more than you can imagine. Bless your heart. I would adore waking up with Will in the morning and spending the day in bed."

"I'll be waiting on Friday afternoon for the little munchkin."

~

It was five thirty in the morning and Jon was banging on his high chair laughing. "Paige doesn't even like children," Mim said in a huff. Her hair was flat on one side and crinkled out in all directions on the other. Her eyes were puffy from lack of sleep. She blinked hard, then squinted to focus and aimed a handful of dry Cheerios to the high chair tray.

"Mom, Paige adores Jon Jon. He's not just any child. She wants to help out and I think it's a great idea. You're not used to this and I owe it to Etta to spend a weekend with her."

"I am totally capable, William, of tending my own grandson," Mim pulled her robe snuggly around her middle and leveled off a stance of defiance at her son.

"Yes, completely capable Mom, but you need a rest too. We've all got to take care of ourselves if we're going to care for Jon. I think it's a great idea. I know you've been dying to go with Della to the farmer's market and to make a dinner for the girls..." Will sent a knowing grin to her, "You do not have to be wonder-granny."

"Dinner for the girls?" Mim's shoulders slumped with a huge sigh, "I would love to stay in bed until nine and have coffee and read my paper. Light some candles in the evening and have a glass of wine. That's what I've been missing."

"Exactly," Will nodded.

"Oh God, Will, we're horrible. We shouldn't look forward to sending Jon Jon away, we should relish every minute that precious child is with us." She placed her hand on top of jon's head.

"Jon is going to spend the weekend with his Auntie Paige." Will said with a hand on his mother's shoulder, "That's the final answer. We're all just one phone call and five minutes away. This is a good thing."

~

Six bags of paraphernalia sat on the kitchen table; safety plugs for all the outlets downstairs, two extra large baby gates, tippy cups, baby bath, baby lotion, powder and a lullaby CD. As an extra reassurance, the woman at the store recommended the barnyard buddies DVD, saying it was the sure fire way to settle down a toddler. Paige started putting cans of chicken and stars soup away, crackers, cheerios and animal cookies now lined the normally empty shelves of her pantry. She placed the milk, juice and fruits into the fridge thinking that it was strangely comforting to have food in the house. It was a luxury she hadn't splurged on since she arrived. There were take out boxes, quick salads and diet sodas, but that was it. She checked the clock and realized she had about twenty minutes before baby Jon arrived for his big weekend with Auntie Paige.

Pulling up her lavender sweat pants and zipping up the jacket with pockets, Paige imagined that she was prepared. She smiled in anticipation of her pint sized house guest.

She opened the door to Will with baby in one arm and a dozen white and yellow roses in the other. Etta was following up the stairs with bags and carriers full of baby things. Jon smiled his three-toothed grin at her and reached for his Auntie. Paige was in love with the wiggling, soft, sweet smelling bundle filling her arms. She couldn't resist the urge to press her lips against his head and inhale the baby scent which filled her up. Something lurched in her gut; a yearning deep and wild and totally unexpected. She looked tenderly at Jon. He whacked her in the face with his stuffed bunny which stung her eyeball to tears. "Thanks, I needed that." Paige whispered to the baby, relieved.

When Paige turned around she assessed the bags and carriers littering her porch and then saw Will and Etta bringing more, "Does a pack mule come optional with these guys? Good grief, he's just one little baby. How in the world am I going to need all of this stuff? I bought everything we need."

"Have one of these?" Etta held up a pacifier with "mute" printed on the stub. "How about one of these?" she pointed to the box with a humidifier in it. "Or one of these?" a pale and ratty blue blanket with failing satin trim was held up.

"Um, nope, But I have blankets".

"Not this blanket..." Etta eyed her suspiciously, "Are you sure you're ready for this?" Paige had to smile.

"Of course I'm ready. We're going to have a grand time, aren't we Jon Jon!" She was bouncing the baby on her hip trying to look like she'd done it before. She felt her back tweak oddly, Jon was really heavy!

"Okay," Will huffed as he brought the final bags into the house, "Bed time is roughly eight, he'll usually go to sleep on his own, just put him down in the pack and play and shut the door. He's an early riser, so I'd go to bed before ten or you'll be dragging your buns in the morning. There's food and juice and snacks in his bag." Will looked nervously at Etta and said, "Well, this is it then." Etta's hand slipped into his and they edged toward the door.

"We're going to Tahoe for the night. Are you sure you'll be okay? We can stay at my house if you're not sure, Paige." Etta offered.

"Nope, I'm completely sure. Your Mom is five minutes away if I have any trouble. Go and stay in bed for a couple of days, you guys need it."

Etta and Will smiled shyly at Paige and then kissed the baby's head goodbye. Paige and Jon waved bye bye at the door until Will and Etta pulled away from the curb.

"Well, Sweet Pea, it's just you and me. What shall we do first?" Jon's eyes were already darting around the room at his new surroundings. "Knock yourself out kiddo, I'm going to go over some book work and you can play here with your busy bee."

Paige handed Jon the stuffed bee with all the activities on its belly. Jon threw the bee.

Immediately toddling around the floor at lightning speed he found a huge glass ball that Etta had gifted her with. A witches ball with strands of glass all though the middle; fragile and very dangerous. She jumped up and took the ball from Jon, which started a round of wailing. No matter what she did, Jon would not stop crying. She patted him and cooed into his hair. She tried handing him some animal cookies which he threw to the ground with furious eyes. Screaming baby noise seared through her body and erased her brain. Jon worked up a cry so hard that he had snot ropes slung from his nose into his mouth. Paige gagged as she wiped his reddened face and then she held him close.

    They rocked together, Jon gasping for air between bellows and then snubbing down until Paige thought he might be sleeping. As soon as she moved, he started crying again. She checked everything in a panic. He wasn't wet, wasn't hungry, he must certainly be tired after thirty minutes of non stop crying. She checked the clock and realized Jon had only been there ten minutes. Why did crying time seem so much longer than real time? She took in a slow deep breath remembering some of the tricks Etta had shared with her, let her core relax, then sat back in the big fluffy chair with Jon's head between her breasts.

    Before she had a clue as to what was happening she let go too. Weeks of tension and anxiety poured out in quiet sobs until Paige's shoulders shook. Jon sat bolt up and studied her tear stained cheeks, putting a chubby hand on the side of her face. Grabbing her by the ears and digging his baby Nike's into her thighs, Jon stood up and threw his head against her shoulder. He gently patted the side of her face. Jon snubbed his sobs into her neck and his body melted back down to her cleavage as he drifted off to sleep. Paige felt her tears fall silently on to his head. She put her arms around the baby and slipped into sweet sleep.

Jon woke up in much better humor and was full of energy. Paige knew she needed to be alert fast as he crawled off of her lap. She watched his gaze go straight to the witches' ball and he frowned, "No No No!" he shook his finger and looked at Paige with a grin.

She looked at the clock and decided it was close to dinner time. Hand in hand they went to the kitchen. Paige sat him in the high chair and gave him a few cheerios while she heated the soup. Jon played happily and Paige breathed a sigh of relief. Crying wasn't her specialty. Chicken and stars swirled in a pan and Paige couldn't remember the last time she had the soup. The phone rang and she balanced it between her shoulder and ear as she poured the soup into a shallow bowl to cool.

"Hi Paige, is everything ok?" It was Will on the other end of the phone.

"Of course it is." Paige smiled at the cherub sitting in the high chair, "we're getting ready to have soup and crackers and then we're going to settle in for some serious television together."

"Etta had a feeling and I'm just checking in...we're only an hour away if you need us." Paige heard the relief in his voice.

"Jon and I are perfectly happy here... alone." Paige said proudly, "Now, go have a great time with your lady."

"Thanks again Paige."

She turned to check on Jon and he was mysteriously gone from the high chair. Shit!

"Jon...." Paige called out. She ran from the kitchen to the dining room, no baby. Her heart was beating rapidly as she saw the baby gate at the bottom of the stairs lying on the floor, looking like

Godzilla had stomped through it. Paige panicked up the stairs, calling for Jon. There were so many places he could be hurt. She couldn't find him.

She grabbed the door jamb to brace herself. She closed her eyes to listen for any detectible noise. Thump, thump thump. He was banging on something, it sounded close.

"Jon," she called out. Thump, thump thump it sounded like a giant running through the house. Sweet Jesus, what was it? Frantic, Paige went from room to room. Jon was nowhere.

She still had the phone in her hand and was dialing the police, when she heard the front door. Thump thump thump the noise was louder.

"Oh noooooo!" she cried heading down the stairs two and three at a time.

Jake was standing in her doorway with Jon on his shoulders, "Is everything ok? This little guy was heading to the bar." He bounced Jon, who giggled, "You look like you've been through the wringer."

Paige sat on the bottom step with a thud staring directly at the two of them. "He was in his high chair." Paige put her hand on her chest to catch her breath, "thirty seconds I looked away and he's gone." Her head fell down between her knees.

"Pulled the old Hudini on her did ya' buddy?" Jake looked at Jon as though they were co-conspirators, "That wasn't very nice". Jon frowned into Jakes face and shook his head. "Why don't you go give Auntie Paige a big hug?" He walked the baby to Paige and Jon fell into her arms. For the second time that day Paige cried with a baby in her arms.

"Thank you," she looked at Jake over the top of Jon's head, "I don't know what happened. Etta had a 'feeling', Will called to be sure everything was ok and then he was GONE!" She felt like an overcooked noodle.

"Being an Auntie isn't all you thought it might be? God Paige, I can see your heart beating in your neck! Are you ok?"

Paige realized what that the thumping in the house had been her heart beating wildly in her ears. Shaking her head in wonder at how a twenty two pound package can consume you, she sat helpless as Jake clicked the dead bolt locked. "I'll check the other doors and then let myself out the kitchen..." Jake said quietly.

Paige thought fast, "We're about to have soup if you want to stay."

"The world traveler must have worked up a powerful appetite." Jake looked at Jon, "I don't want to intrude."

"I would," Paige stumbled and cursed herself, "I'm happy to have another baby wrangler around." She was relieved to say, "I want you to stay."

Jake looked around the foyer and then into the library where the baby station had been set up. He took it all in, "Looks like you're doing a great job!"

Paige assessed the room. Brightly colored blocks were all over the floor, books, discarded, Busy Bee, cookies and the pale blue blanket with the torn trim were strewn with reckless abandon.

They laughed together, "Friends again?" Jake helped her stand up with the baby still in her arms.

"I'm not setting him down again," she stated.

"I'll secure the perimeter and then I think it's safe to set him free."

"Free range baby... doesn't sound safe to me." She narrowed her eyes at Jon, who had her hair twisted in his fist. He was too heavy to pack around for the rest of his stay anyway.

"Four eyeballs are better than two." Jake made his way to the other three doors in the house and locked them inside the fortress.

~

The sounds of barnyard animals singing merrily about the sunshine had faded to blue light from the finished DVD as Jake hit the volume button on the TV remote. "He looks like he's asleep..." he whispered to an exhausted Paige who had the baby on her lap.

"I'm afraid to move." She said softly.

"He's been sleeping for a while, I think its ok." Jake reached for him and Paige cringed at the thought of another round of crying. The baby appeared boneless. Jake picked him up and she dashed for the bedroom, realizing the baby bed that hadn't been set up yet. They made it through dinner with no problems. Bath time was fun and wet. Her bathroom probably had standing water on the floor and would until she got in there to wipe it up. She found the baby bed in a little carrier and flipped it out like a camping chair. Feeling pretty smart, she reached for the blankets and saw the sides had collapsed into the middle. She arranged the sides as the picture on the bottom of the crib indicated but they fell in loose and unstructured. "This is ridiculous!" Paige muttered to herself, looking for further instructions. She folded it up and started again, with two sides catching and two sides folded into the middle.

"Grab it from the middle and shake the sides out..." Jake whispered.

Paige did as instructed and watched the crib magically erect itself. She slanted her eyes at him as she put the baby blankets in the bed. They both held their breaths as Jon was lowered into the bed and lay limp on the pillow. Jake covered him with the old blue blanket and shook his head, "Quite a little man, isn't he?"

Paige stared at Jon resting like a rag doll. She immediately regretted that she let out a deep tired sigh as Jake slipped his hand into hers. He leaned into her hair and whispered, "Betty's dog had puppies. I set up the crib in her nursery." Paige had to smile. They softly walked from the room leaving the door cracked open in case Jon woke up.

In the kitchen Jake searched for something in the cupboards until he turned with a bottle of wine. "I think you need a shower and a big glass of this."

"A shower?" she looked indignant.

His gaze landed in her hair and his smile turned into deep dimples as he pulled a half eaten animal cookie from her wild mane. Paige looked down at the noodle stars buried and dried in the velour, spills of grape juice on her pants.

"I feel like I've been to war!" she said incredulously, "I didn't know how hard this would be!"

"Me either. I guess we can't be upset with Will for being all consumed by this little guy." Jake answered.

Freshly showered, wearing jeans and a sweatshirt with her wet hair pulled into a clip Paige padded her bare feet back into the kitchen. She was too tired to care about vanity. Judging by the look on Jake's face he didn't mind, "You look like a new woman." He stared directly into her eyes. "Paige," he stumbled, "Do you think we can..."

Paige put a finger to his lips, "Shhhh. Can we just talk like old friends tonight?" She assessed his look of trepidation and added, "I don't have the strength to be angry with you. I understand now, Jed is an asshole that you have no control over. Betty keeps telling me she has the secret to the problem, but so far... nothing. I get it Jake, I'm on my own in this."

"That's where you're wrong. The whole city is behind you on this," Jake jammed his hands into his pockets and looked out the window. "Jed is so rattled he doesn't know which way to turn. He made an idiot out of himself. Everyone knows this house can't be moved. He's buried. I want to know if you are ready now." Jake turned to look sternly into her face.

"Ready? Right now I'm ready for that glass of wine and to sit down!"

He handed her a fat glass full of red wine, "Are you ready to ask for help? I'm here, Paige. I've always been on your team."

~

Paige woke up at least a dozen times in the night whenever she heard Jon turn or breath differently. Jake was on the sofa where he'd fallen asleep and Paige had slipped a blanket over him. It was nice the way the night had played out, watching a movie together with her head in his lap. She loved the feeling of his hands in her hair, the way she fit next to him like two puzzle pieces. Thinking back over the past few weeks she realized what a pitiful, prideful idiot she had been. He was sleeping in her front room and she had never felt so safe. He made no move to join her in the bedroom. Jon would have had no objection. For the first time in a long time it felt like everything would turn out alright. She closed her eyes and fell back to sleep with a smile on her face.

The smell of coffee drifted through the bedroom as Paige opened her eyes. Jon, who wasn't in his bed, she assumed was with Jake. She went to the bathroom, took her time putting her clothes on and stumbled out into the kitchen with bare feet.

Jake was leaning against the counter with a mug of coffee in one hand, his smile was radiating joy towards Paige, "Hey my little sleepyheads slept in this morning."

Paige looked to the high chair but Jon was not in it. "Where's Jon, he's not in his bed."

"Sure he is... I just checked on you two, he was snoring like a little puppy."

"Oh no...." Paige and Jake broke into a sprint through the house. Breathlessly they went from room to room. All the doors were still locked. Jon was nowhere to be found. The baby gate was still on the stairs, so they looked through all the rooms again. Jake stopped cold when he went through the foyer for the second time and looked up at the open door at the top of the stairs, "Paige," he called out a little more frantic than he intended.

She dashed into the foyer and immediately saw what Jake was looking at, "That's impossible! The baby gate is up and the attic door is wide open. Have you been up there?" He shook his head no in slow motion.

They broke through the baby gate and bolted up the stairs to the open attic door. Paige was the first one up the stairs. Looking around, her gaze stopped at an old rocking chair which was rocking away while Jon sat on the floor banging something. She ran to him, "Jon... what are you doing?"

The baby didn't look phased by his situation at all. He was playing on the floor and saying, "Gi Gi.... Gi Gi."

Paige nabbed him up in her arms and said loudly, "Georgina, that's not fair! If you want to visit with Jon you have to come down to us."

Jon made a chubby fist and then poked out his index finger, shaking it, "GiGi... NO No no!"

Jake stood pale and helpless at the top of the stairs taking it all in, "So, you want me to believe that a ghost brought Jon up here?"

"You can believe what you like, Jake. That's the only explanation I have for you. The baby gate was up, Jon was up here saying GiGi." She shrugged her shoulders and took the baby back down for breakfast.

The first thing she noticed about the kitchen was the smell of delicious scones on the counter, "How wonderful!" Paige looked to Jake, "You made scones."

"Um... nope. I did not make scones."

"Oh I get it...." Paige looked up as though through the floor to where she left Georgia, "Thank you Georgia."

Jon clapped his hands and said, "GiGi!"

"What's a matter Jake? Never had ghost scones before? You loved the pie!" Paige said with a smirk.

"I thought you were pulling my leg about that raspberry pie. I would've taken that one to the grave with me." He said.

"They're lovely," Paige said with a mouthful, handing a little piece to Jon, "really Jake, you should have one."

"What's that in Jon's hand?" Jake asked.

Paige looked to his chubby fist holding onto something metal and shiny which was now covered in baby slobber and scone scum.

"Jon, can Aunti Paige see?" she pried his fingers away from the skeleton key he held onto.

"Do you feel like we're in an old Nancy Drew story?" Paige asked.

"Well, I was thinking Hardy boys, but hey I'm a guy." Jake examined the key, "It's too small to belong to a door. Have you found anything locked without a key?"

"Not that I can think of. Whatever this key opens I bet we'll find it up in the attic."

"I think it's going to wait until Jon goes home. It's not safe up there for him."

"I'll watch him while you rummage around, but I have to leave at noon." Jake said, "We'll watch Barnyard Buddies" He widened is eyes in faux excitement.

"Ya, that's a good idea," Paige washed the yuck covered brass key and assessed the men in her kitchen. "Ok, you two behave."

CHAPTER 20

Paige searched the attic, making stacks of things she had already gone through. Trying to find anything waiting for the key she had tucked away in her pocket. Georgia was obviously telling her something, but what? Frustration buzzed Paige's brain like a hungry mosquito. Covered in powder fine dust, she checked her watch. It was almost noon and she'd found nothing.

She closed her eyes and shook her hair out. As she watched the dust motes fall into the light streaming through the dirty window, she saw for the first time the turret of a house, a doll house! It was tucked into a corner so tightly it had gone undetected even after all of the rummaging through the attic. She placed her hand on the roof and realized it was much larger than she originally estimated. It stood at least five feet tall. Afraid that she might damage it by pulling or scooting it into the middle of the floor, Paige began moving everything that had been stacked around it. Having entirely forgotten about the time, she grabbed an old curtain and began to swipe away the dust to get a better look.

Jake stood behind her with Jon in his arms, "Wow, that's quite a find!"

"It's an exact replica of this house."

"Let me help you move it..." Jake sat Jon down and together they gently moved the doll house into the middle of the attic floor.

Paige pulled the key out of her pocket and looked for a place to unlock and open the house. There was just a small latch, no lock. Once the house was opened they were staring into a magnificently preserved replica of the house they were standing in. The mermaid wall paper in the bathrooms and bedroom colors were there. Chandelier fixtures and crown moldings were the grandly guilded. Even the carpets and floors were identical miniature recreations.

"Beautiful!" Paige whispered, "Look, it's the table in the library, and look at the tiny books. I feel like I've stepped back in time a hundred years."

"Amazing," Jake responded.

"GiGi.... GiGi," Jon chanted from behind them which made them both jerk around to see Jon rocking in the chair smiling widely.

"Let's go downstairs and get you guys settled, I've got to head out for a Saturday meeting."

~

"Oh I'm eight years old again!" Mim clapped her hands in delight then she fell to her knees to really get a good look inside.

"Are there dolls that go with it?" Della asked. Paige remembered that Della was an avid doll collector.

"I saved these for you to look at first." Paige handed her the box with four pristine dolls inside. Della ran her bright red fingernails gently along their clothes, "I've never seen something this divine! This is real human hair."

"Kinda' creepy if you ask me..." Patti interjected.

There were four fannies up in the air with heads poked inside the dollhouse when the door opened behind them.

"Well, that's a pretty picture," Betty said.

"We didn't hear the screech of the Bentley, Darlin'. Are you stealth again?" Mim flopped over on her butt to look at Betty.

"Jake took my car keys away from me. He said the city didn't have the money for damages." Betty shrugged it off and then came into the room and smiled softly when she caught sight of the doll house. "I haven't seen that since Jesus was a baby! I used to play with that for hours and hours, it was my favorite thing."

"You know about the doll house?" Paige exclaimed.

"Oh Honey, I know about a lot of things. But it seems that these days I mostly forget."

Betty padded further into the foyer wearing a pale blue jogging suit and white keds. Her hair had lost its pouf and was uncombed, but it had a white and blue floral scarf tied in it. Paige watched the exchange of glances regarding Betty's appearance and went to the kitchen to make a pot of earl grey. Etta followed close behind.

"She's never looked like this," Etta whispered close to Paige's head.

"Frail and shaky," Paige added as she poured hot water into the pot. "Can you grab the cups and I'll get the tray and some cookies."

"You've got cookies in the house? My goodness..."

"Animal cookies," Paige said as a matter of fact, "I've grown fond of them." Then she winked and whisked the tray towards the library.

"Have you seen Doc Adams?" Paige heard Mim ask Betty as she walked back into the room with the tea tray.

"Oh yeah, he's sure I'm just old now..." Betty said waving her hand dismissively. "Old and forgetful." Her eyes looked sad.

"There are specialists at UC Davis, Betty. We can arrange for you to see someone there," Della chimed in.

"Nope, I've been seeing Doc Adams for over 50 years. He's the only one that's going to poke around on this old body. If I see anyone else I'll have a lot of explaining to do. I'm lucky my liver's held out this long. Honestly girls, I want to go out authentic. No drugs to prolong the agony. I would have taken better care of myself if I'd known I was going to live this long." She smiled and took the tea cup Paige handed her.

Della, Patti, Etta and Mim all settled in with their tea cups and munched on animal cookies while Betty began, "It's so funny, you know, I can remember things from seventy years ago better than I can remember what I had for breakfast." She glanced off and then announced triumphantly, "Grape nuts and coffee."

"You are going to tell us about the doll house." Etta said.

"What house?" Betty looked confused again.

Paige pointed to the doll house in the middle of the library.

"Oh that house…" Betty thought for a moment, followed by the distinct look of a light bulb over her head, "It's all in the book!"

"The book," Mim asked, "Betty this is a doll house. Is there a book?"

"Oh yes, the book tells everything." Betty's confusion felt hopeless as Paige contemplated the key in her pocket.

Betty perked up in her chair, "I know my mother scribed everything in a book directly from Georgina before she passed. It's all in there. All the gory details of how she came to live in this house and how she was shunned from her family her whole life. She was denied her family name, her heritage and in the end she wanted to make sure this house landed with its rightful owners. Her heirs didn't even know they were part of her family." Betty heaved out a dismissive sigh and shrugged her shoulders.

"Any idea where that book is, Betty?" Patti asked sweetly.

Betty looked around the room and said, "Well, I just know it's here somewhere..." She rose up and began to wander through the room.

"Oh look, the doll house." Betty's face was alight with the wonder and joy of a small child, "I forgot all about it, you know I played with that when I was a little girl. I love this house." Betty looked into the doll house then reached inside. "Look at that," Betty said softly to herself, "It's stuck."

Betty shifted her weight and put a knee up onto the low mahogany table supporting the weight of the five foot tall doll house. Paige thought she was going to crawl inside of it, but Betty started yanking on something. Etta gasped and shot a look of horror at Mim who immediately moved to Betty's side. Patti, Addy and Della joined Paige surrounding the house as curiosity brewed.

"Just a minute... and I'll..." Betty was huffing, working fretfully on the concealed undertaking.

Patti scurried around to the far side of the house, knelt down to peek through one of the turreted windows getting a better view of what Betty was fiddling with. He stood up and shrugged his shoulders, dumbfounded.

A solid click echoed from inside the doll house followed by the sound of a metal release pop open from the base. They all heard the noise, but didn't see the hidden drawer pop open.

"There!" Betty gleefully plunged her tiny hands into the open drawer. Irritation spread across her face as she groped for its hidden contents.

"What happened to my..." Betty put her face down to the edge of the drawer, looking closely, "Dang it all to hell. They're gone." She flopped down onto the closest chair, exhausted by her exploration, "My marbles are gone... who would take my marbles? The only thing in here is this damn book. "

Mim pulled a leather bound book from the secret drawer, "Betty, is this the book that your mother wrote in?"

"I don't know, I'll have to ask her." Betty quietly replied.

"It's locked." Mim went back to the drawer to search, "The key has to be here somewhere..."

Paige had goose bumps all over her body, "Jon found a key..."

"Baby Jon?" Mim asked.

"Yes, it was quite an ordeal, ask Jake about it. But here it is..." Paige pulled the key from her pocket, handing it to Mim.

"This book is intended for you, Paige. You open it." Mim handed the key back to her.

The beautifully tooled leather book felt heavy in her hand. The key slipped into the lock. Her hands shook with the quiver of anticipation as she opened the cover to reveal an inscription. She read out loud:

"This book has been scribed by Mary Bennett, word for word from the recollections of Georgina Thompson-Matheson from Sept 1, 1969 to right before her death in 1971"

I am the bastard child of a famous mother who abandoned me to her wealthy family. My grandmothers, Mimi Matheson and Bridgett Thompson (a cousin Ginny) cared for me and provided me with this home. The house I have lived in all of my life has harbored an aching and captive heart. It has been my protector, my shelter and my friend. This house is as dear to me as I hope it is to the one whose hands it becomes entrusted to. As I approach the end of this life, I have found peace within these walls and the life I was born into.

Paige stopped reading the beautifully scripted handwriting and looked out the window, "What on earth is a Cousin Ginny?" she asked the women surrounding her.

"It was a very derogatory term for the women of England and Ireland who came here during the mining days." Betty said, "When the gold rush started word got to Europe that there was gold in California. Men from England and Ireland came over with hard rock mining experience. They took jobs from the common workers and the local men became bitter. When a hard rock miner started working he would talk to the foreman and say he had a cousin Jack, Jim, or John who would arrive in a month or two and could he have a job. The foremen, needing experienced workers, would save the job for the 'Cousin Jacks'. Local men in need of work were furious that their work had gone to a 'Cousin Jack'. The women, usually sisters or wives coming to the area were called 'Cousin Ginny', and what is now used as a term of endearment was then a dreadful thing to call someone. It started a lot of bar brawls. The phrase also described separation of classes between Nevada City where the well to do lived and the working class of Grass Valley."

"To this day the cities, as closely related as they are cling to the concept that we are better left as separate entities," Patti stated as an authority on the issue.

Betty took a long drink of her tea and said, "Paige, do you know what this means?"

"I'm a little confused actually. I am related to Judge Matheson, so Georgina is my... what?" Paige asked quietly.

"Great-Great Aunt?" Mim answered, wide eyed, "I don't think Georgina had any children or even married."

"It also means, Dear, that you've had a right to this property and this mansion since you were born," Etta said. She stood and placed her hand on Paige's shoulder.

"let's keep reading!" Addy said nesting down in her hair and pulling a pillow to her chest.

"Now let that old salty dog try to stop us." Mim looked like the cat that'd just swallowed the canary, as she curled up in a chair, sipping tea.

CHAPTER 21

Paige lay in bed thinking through the events revealed in the book. The situation with Will's son coming from San Francisco was such a strange coincidence. The baby furniture they had refurbished for Jon Jon had been originally crafted for a baby given away by her mother over a hundred years ago.

Cool air pricked her skin. Georgia was near, she could feel her.

"I wanted you to love me." The voice was timid and hurt. Paige felt guilty and unsettled. She was never going to get to sleep!

Wally stared at the air over the bed as if he were watching something visible only to him. Paige had the sudden desire to have Jake with her. It was almost midnight, but she picked up the phone and dialed anyway, trying to block out a strange unsettling sense of guilt and shame that gnawed around the edges of her mind..

"Hi," she said softly.

"Hi," his voice was husky with sleep.

"Sorry it's so late." she said.

"Paige," He paused, "You can call me anytime... What's up?"

There was a long silence from her end and then it burst out of her all at once, "I miss you, Jake, and I'm such an idiot." Then there were tears. She hated the tears. She sniffled as the uncontrollable wave of emotion took hold of her. "First there was Betty and I can't believe I seduced you knowing about Betty. I'm so ashamed. Then the house drama and now all this truth..."

Ten minutes later Jake walked into her bedroom.

"There you are..." he sat on the edge of the bed and reached for her, "Hi."

She slipped into his arms. He stroked her hair and held her until she started telling him Georgia's story. Jake listened for over three hours until Paige had exhausted every detail.

"Jake, there are some strange coincidences. Georgia alludes to growing up in a boarding house... but..."

"There have always been rumors." He leaned closer, kissing the top of her head.

"Rumors about this being a... a bordello?" She asked quietly. He nodded, yes. "There's more..." Paige flipped through the pages until she found what she was looking for, "I found a name listed during the time that this would have been a bordello." Here it is. She let her finger rest upon the fancy scrolling letters spelling out " Hilda Grizwolden". Her eyes made a quick dart to Jakes face, "Do you think this could be a relative of Jed?"

Jake threw his head back and smiled at the ceiling, "wouldn't that be sweet justice?"

"How do we find out?"

"Just so happens I know someone who's got the records for a few more days. Auntie Mim would love the opportunity to fry his chicken." He paused and took a good look at her face, "How are you doing? This is a lot to digest in one day."

"Well it's close to daybreak and you're here listening to me. I am rambling brainlessly that's how I'm doing." She looked into his eyes, "Jake, there is something else that I want to say to you." She wanted to talk about her dream of being one of the girls in the brothel. It felt so weird, but it was a far memory she couldn't dismiss.

"Don't Paige. I just let those words fall out of my mouth. I knew you weren't ready to hear them."

"It's exactly what I needed to hear." Her hand touched his face. Her confessions from another life would have to wait, "Jake, I love you too."

~

Hammering noises from the side door banged through the house until Paige realized someone was knocking. Washing the paint from her hands, she padded toward the door she never used just in time to see Jed making a quick retreat down the steps, "What can I do for you?" She called toward his back.

He turned slowly looking sheepishly over her shoulder to the edge of the door, "I wanted to save you the embarrassment of having this on the front door."

Paige turned quickly and snatched the "NOTICE OF IMMENENT DOMAIN" from the nail he'd hammered into her siding. "You know, Jed," she said sweetly luring him back to the porch, "There is no need to be so nasty with me. We really have a lot more in common than you know..." She smiled.

Jed sauntered back up to the top and looked down his nose into her smug face, "The only thing we have in common is you're standing on land that's going to belong to the city in less than thirty days."

"Really? I've got some interesting research that says your great grandmother, Hilda Griswolden used to reside in this house... oh well I'm not sure they called it a house back then." Paige winked slowly.

"What do you know about..." Jed stammered, "How the hell did..." He stomped his foot at Paige. The veins in his forehead were pulsing purple.

"Oh, please do be careful." Paige said softly, "this porch hasn't been reinforced yet... not knowing if I was going to move the house or not..."

"You've," Jed pointed a finger and stomped again, against the creek of rotting wood, "You've been nothing but trouble since you sauntered into town and started dripping honey all over Jake. Acting like you own this place."

"You leave Jake out of this, Jed, and I do own this place..."

He grumbled and turned just when the boards cracked under his feet. Paige jumped back into the safety of the door jamb as the porch swallowed him up to his chest in splintered rotting wood.

"Oh, I'll have to call someone to get you out. But it's after hours. You're dinner might be late... what did you say Rita was making tonight?"

Jed grabbed a sideways board and tried hefting himself out of the hole. The old timber snapped, toppling him backward into the hole again. Paige was looking for a step ladder while Wally waltzed past Jed's chest and circled his head. Carefully and thoroughly Wally assessed the situation. Jed, who was apparently allergic to cats, began an uncontrollable sneezing fit.

~

"So what now?" Paige asked Jake as she looked at the letter in her hand.

Jake walked around behind her and read it again over her shoulder, "Jed's such a sneak." Shaking his head, "You know he didn't say a word to me about this letter. It officially releases the city's hold on the property... not just the house but all of it. It's over Paige." He kissed her shoulder, "The skeletons in his closet must have started rattling when his family name was linked to unflattering family history."

"Mim must have made some copies of the records to share with him. Together with the entries in the stories of those women... must have been humbling for him."

"This calls for a celebration!" Paige said joyfully, relieved to have Jed's final word in writing.

"I'll shop and you call the troops... or would you prefer a private party?" Jake puffed his chest out and raised an eyebrow like a cheesy super hero.

"So many of them had a hand in saving this old mansion, I think we should throw a real party." She smirked at his ridiculous pose and rethought her decision, "Tonight you and I celebrate and Friday we party."

"That's my girl," He picked her up in his arms and walked her to the bedroom to ravage her slowly. It was Saturday, they had all day and there was nothing they'd rather be doing.

"No drinks? No flattering? No empty promises?" Paige laughed uncontrollably. It felt good to be joyful.

Jake stopped and looked firmly into her eyes, "Never an empty promise, Paige. But... here's one you can take to the bank."

He kissed her neck and his whiskers bristled against her ear, "You're going to have trouble explaining the smile on your face when I finally let you out of this bed." He tossed her into the down nest of bedding.

"GOD, I love you, Jake."

Landing on top of her, he began a trail of kisses on her hand, "The feeling, my little flower, is most," kiss, "mutual."

Wally strolled off the bed at his leisurely pace, no doubt rolling his eyes like a teenager.

~

Paige gazed out her kitchen window at the mound of rubbish in Etta's yard, "She's working like a logger over there." She yelled to Jake who was coming in from the back porch.

"She's on a mission. I don't think you've ever seen the determined, creation mode of my sister. She's a force to be reckoned with." He joined Paige at the window. "Looks like she's taking a break," Jake said. "Hey, help me make a menu for the party Friday and I'll put the order in at the bakery and the caterer."

"I want it to be fancy and fussy and fabulous!" Paige gushed.

"The big F's, You got it, Babe, I think that's perfect." He was so pleased to see her joy.

"Should we invite Jed?" Paige asked with a wicked smile.

"I think that would be a wonderful step at burying the hatchet... no hard feelings." Jake was proud of her, "Now, what to feed the guests?"

"Let's call Addy and ask her what's good right now," Paige thought for a minute, "Oh Jake, I don't want her to work, I want her to enjoy the party." She said through pursed lips, "I think the only easy way out of this is to ask her advice."

"I'll leave it to you two then... my request is meat, red and a lot of it."

"My request," added Paige, "Champaign! The good stuff... cases of it! If we have any left-over we'll use it when we open the B&B."

"Little bubbles, no troubles."

"What does that mean? I've always wondered," Paige asked as she reached for the phone.

"Great Champaign has tiny bubbles, big bubbles mean big headaches the next day... little bubbles, no troubles," Jake answered.

CHAPTER 22

Having her hands in the earth was one of the best ways Etta knew to ground herself and find center. She had been working in her garden for at least six hours. Her knees ached, her back was throbbing, but her head was starting to clear. Marigolds were planted flanking the long winding walkway. Weeds were discarded and the wisteria trimmed around her porch. The sun was blazing hot on her back as she crawled a couple of feet to the hose bib and turned it on for a drink.

"You know this water is not fit to drink," Addy said leaning on the gate.

"What do you mean? We drank from the hose the whole time we were kids and nobody died."

"That we know of..." Addy widened her eyes and came through the gate carrying a couple of iced coffees.

She sat on the bottom step of the porch in the shade of a peach tree and handed Etta a cup, "You need help getting up here?"

"Nope... just...." Etta crumbled as her back cracked in an unusual place. A twinge of pain froze her movement, she flopped back down with a "woof".

"Do I need to call 911?" Addy asked.

"Don't be a smart ass, Addy, just hand over the goods...caffeine, revive me." Gratefully, Etta sipped the cool liquid through a straw.

"You're doing a lot in one day," Addy stated the obvious.

"I need to see results in at least one area of my life. Nothing says everything's ok like flowers on the walkway." Etta inspected the work of the day.

"Looks great though," Addy tilted her head.

"Will's tied up in all kinds of drama with the baby. I feel helpless." Etta took a long draw from the coffee, "I've been an emotional mess. I'm trying to hide it from him and Mim. They have so much going on, but I'm a wreck."

"Healer, heal thyself." Addy said without hesitation.

"You know how that is... never as easy when it's my own life."

"Makes you a better healer to understand this, Etta..."

"You get all those smarts by shunning the glutens in your diet?"

"Well, partially, yes... keeps my head clear and my body free. The Coffee is sweetened with Stevia. Can you tell?" Addy's constant concern for a healthful diet was endearing to Etta.

"No, my dear friend, I can't tell." Etta smiled, "Thank you for caring about me. You know I'll submerge myself in a vat of chocolate and red wine if not carefully watched."

"Here's the wine and here's the chocolate." Addy lifted a brown all natural gift bag, "The wine is organic and the chocolate is dark with lavender and sea salt." She held out a hand to help Etta stand.

"You're a good friend," Etta said, suddenly tired and sore. "A great friend would invite you in to share with her, but I've got a date with my tub."

"I wouldn't dream of staying, Love. I've got a class in about thirty minutes." Addy kissed Etta's cheeks and whispered, "Call me if you need anything at all."

Once she stripped down exposing the filthy feet and hands she tentatively submerged herself into the deep, wide wonderfulness of her claw footed tub, her muscles began to relax. It was like an old security blanket. Could have been that her sun sign was Aries/ fire, her moon was Leo/fire and her rising was Virgo/earth. Water balanced and soothed.

What in the world was going to happen between her and Will? He had told her repeatedly that she was a permanent part of his life. He was a man of his word. It was tough to feel connected when they didn't see each other for days at a time or spend nights together. The trauma of having him walk away for over a year wasn't helping her heart believe his words of love. Etta could justify Will's current preoccupation; Jon needed consistency in his life. Will and Jon both sleeping at Mim's was the natural way the living arrangements unfolded but Etta's nerves, her heart and her whole being had been deeply rocked by all the changes.

She felt like an outsider in her own life as the drama dug in deeper every day. Etta was certain Will was now keeping things from her to protect her emotionally. It was possibly the reason she was withholding her complete trust from Will. She felt like an intruder in his life! That was the final thought as she forced her relaxation. She closed her eyes and accepted the warmth of water. Her muscles pulsed with appreciation as they warmed and unknotted. The sensation spread deeper to her bones and then she felt the warmth swirling towards her chakras. As she began to feel more centered and peaceful, she drifted off into an altered state.

Brown, no, it was more than brown; she freed her inner vision to see tan and warm auburn shades of fall crept into her view. Leaves floated down from the sky landing on brilliant green grass. The dry, crackling sound of leaves being run through followed by giggling brought a burst of joy to her heart chakra, as the sweet smells of fall twirled around her. Small tennis shoes, black canvas high tops delighted in a leaf dance. Tiny white mary janes with lime green socks appeared jumping in the leaves next to the black tennies. A chorus of laughter filled every space in her body with the purity of a love she'd never experienced before, an emotion so deep she wept in its presence.

The intimacy of the moment was gone in one breath.

~

The thought of lighting up a cigarette drifted through Mim's mind as she watched out her bedroom window for Etta to arrive. Her fingers twitched as she inched closer to the dresser where she kept a secret package of Virginia Slims. The struggle to keep her non-smoking status was strong. Living long enough to see Jon grow and flourish was the most important thing in the world to her. She could feel something bothering Etta, her girl, her precious replica of Henri. It had everything to do with the baby and Will. How could it not? It was certainly a mess. Later in the week, Miles Harper would arrive to meet his grandson, Jon, for the first time. Uncertainty swung wildly over the family like a guillotine. Sitting with Etta would soothe both of their ragged nerves. She jumped up and rummaged through her drawer until she found the sweet small package of cigarettes and ripped open the foil.

Lighting up, Mim sat at the stone patio table in the shade of a mammoth flowering mulberry tree. The first drag of her cigarette penetrated without guilt. She closed her eyes and exhaled into the intermittent breeze. She'd forgotten how much she loved to smoke. She'd been buying packages of cigarettes and then tossing them away for over a decade. This was the first time she'd indulged. Remembering her smoking breaks when the kids were young seemed archaic and self-indulgent when she looked back. She didn't care. Defiantly, she held the slender cigarette between her fingers and took another drag.

"Well, there's a blast from the past," Etta said as the gate clunked shut behind her.

"Caught me." Mim smiled, "Just felt like the right thing to do."

"I bet it does." Etta reached for the contraband and took a deep drag herself.

"Help yourself." Mim pointed to the package of Virginia Slims on the table.

Etta simply shook her head, "Interesting times we live in…"

"Amen, Sweetheart." Mim reached across to touch Etta's hand.

"You know, Mim, I can sit with anyone and talk to them about their future and what direction to take, and how life will unfold for them…" She looked off into the sky and then back into Mim's eyes, "But I've never been able to do it for me. Right now I don't know which end is up."

"I know, Honey, it's hard. It's always been that way with you. It's all about how you can help someone else… never about what's right for you." Mim sat thoughtfully for a moment, "This is a hellava situation we've got here. You're in love with my son and I love you both so much I could just burst with it... then our little baby shows up without warning... a grandson! What a joy, what an adjustment to my life and what a bundle dropped into your lap. Quite honestly, Etta, I don't know how you're dealing with it all. Why, you haven't even had a chance to be pissed off at Will. I know I haven't." She took a final drag and put the cigarette out.

"I love Jon. I know he's going to be a part of my life forever... but I don't know how I fit into everything. It's complicated. I'm confused. I don't know if I am helping the situation or hurting it. I miss being with Will but I feel guilty when I take him away from Jon. I can't be mad at Will right now," Etta sighed.

"He is like a puppy," Mim laughed, "Jake's been saying it forever... like a big floppy dog who can't be trained. You just have to love him and hope for the best."

Etta's eyes misted over, but she was determined not to cry, "Jakes right." Her shoulders fell, "He blew into town for a couple of days a year and a half ago and it was like I saw him for the first time as a man. He wasn't a brother figure... I just felt so different... I fell in love." Etta smile fell, "Sorry, you probably don't want to hear about my love life."

"Don't be ridiculous! You're both my children. He sure does know how to work us." Mim chuckled, "Rolling into town driving that beautiful red alpha and strutting around like the king of the world. I adore that child... man." Mim took a short little breath out, "our boy."

"So... What is your advice to this lovelorn, woman with an uncertain future?"

"Oh Darlin', the only thing uncertain about your future is how you embrace all of these changes."

"I'm not sure what the changes are." Etta's sandal tapped out frustration against the stone bench.

"As far as I can see you've landed in the middle of a life situation. I mean, look at how we all became family. Your parents killed unexpectedly, my return from Texas, your moving here to this house on your 13th birthday. Do you think that was a life we all would have chosen? If I had a perfect life, I would be sitting here with your Mamma and we would be discussing how to raise this beautiful grandbaby. You would have her to lean on..." Mim became quiet.

"You've been more than a mother to me, Mim. You've been a solid touchstone and you've never let me down. You're my best friend. I'd love to be sitting here with my mom talking this out with you both... but here we are just you and me. I think we did a pretty darn good job." Etta thought for a moment, "Whatever happened to Gary? I don't remember Will mentioning his father or you bringing him up at all."

"He was young and wild and wanted to be single. We lived in a decade of free love. It never set well with me. He wasn't sorry to see us go. He sent me the money after he sold the Texas house and that's what bought this pile of rocks."

"This is your heart, Mim. You've made this the place our home."

"It is a home... but my heart is here..." She put her finger to Etta's shoulder.

"If you're asking me what your choices are, I'd say, you've got two. Stick it out and stand by Will no matter how this works out or walk away. Since I know you won't walk away, I think you should be planning an expansion on your house to include a couple of bedrooms and probably a family room in that big empty basement. I can't imagine that Will and Jon will be happy living here with me after we're on the other side of this. Jon loves you, Etta. He needs a mom. I've done my work. I'm a grandmother now. I'm tired. I want to be thrilled to see him coming toward me not happy to see him go. I'm feeling guilty myself. But I've got a huge fear that the moment Miles meets that baby he's going to fall in love with him like I did. Right now, tired as I am I would wrestle a tiger to keep that little cub next to this mamma bear."

"So what your saying is suck it up, quit whining and make some moves in the right direction about how Will and I will live as a family."

"Yep. That's exactly what I would do... well, after a wedding. I'm still a little old fashioned. Make baby steps in the direction you want to be going, it'll get rid of your helpless feeling. Don't let this paralyze you. Make a plan."

"Without talking to Will?"

"Of course. He's my son, but he's still a man. He can't see past this meeting and I guarantee that he'll thank you for doing the thinking right now. He's consumed with fear that Miles will want custody. What's he going to do once this is all settled? If you wait for Will to tell you what he's got planned, you'll be a frustrated wreck and full of resentment. Just do it, Etta. Plan how you're going to house these two men, get moving on it. It will give you something to do while all of this plays out."

"It's all so simple to you."

"Simple as pie..." Mim patted her hand, "now quit fretting and start planning."

Mim stood at the sink in her kitchen and watched the tail of Etta's car disappear down her driveway. Shaking from the core of her bones, she ran water over her hands, then her face. How could she give Etta such bold advice? She had no idea how it would all end. She had to have faith in her son... the same son that disappeared for over a year? No phone calls, just cards telling her to not worry he was fine. All of their lives rested on the outcome of the visit from Miles. She honestly didn't know how Will would handle the situation if he had another fight for custody. Grabbing a dish towel she dried her face, grabbed the pack of smokes and headed back out to the stone table again.

~

Etta pulled into the drive of her little cottage with a new sense of purpose. Faith in the future with Will was rejuvenated by her afternoon with Mim. The sweetness of dancing tennis shoes and mary janes filled her with hope. She walked around the outside of the house scoping a place where an addition would look like it naturally belonged. Once she spotted the space she went inside to think it through. Her bedroom was in the farthest back corner of the house, adjacent to an expanse of property which was level. It was the natural path for an addition. .. If she opened up the walls into both her living room and kitchen her bedroom would become a beautiful formal dining room. The little dinette in the kitchen would never work for a family, the dining room would be perfect.

With a sketch pad, Etta curled up on the chase lounge in the bay window and sketched the new floor plan for the house. Two, no three bedrooms and two bathrooms would be added. The master and a beautiful bath would be upstairs in the attic and the children's' bedrooms would be on the main floor. Children? Jon was just one little baby... Etta was planning for at least one more. She'd drawn it all out before she had a chance to think it away. She then thought about how the basement would make a great family room and remembered that Will would need an artist studio. Etta threw down her pad and scampered happily to the far corner of the back yard to a very large and dilapidated wood shed. She assessed the door that hung crooked in its jam, noticed that two of the little panes in the side window were broken. The building was overgrown with wisteria and Ivy. She'd never contemplated turning it into anything. She'd had enough space for all of her projects between the house and the studio in town. Looking closely, the building had almost completely disappeared beneath the heap of shrubbery. Giddy with inspiration, Etta envisioned a winding stone pathway from the patio to the studio.

What first? She went back to the kitchen and reached for the phone to pull in a favor from an architect client. As it rang, she heard her front door creak open.

"Etta?" Paige called. She had every intention of making an appointment with Etta to try getting to the bottom of her dreams and feelings about Jake.

"In here..." she would have to leave a message with the architect. She hung up the phone when she saw Paige looking at her sketches.

"Wow, what do you have going here?" Paige asked.

"Just dreaming to maintain my sanity." Etta reached for the pad of paper.

"Looks pretty good to me." Paige held fast to the sketches, studying all the details.

"Big changes coming for the Goddess..." Paige smiled at her friend.

She reached for the book again, "Come on, Paige, they're not finished."

Paige released the sketches into Etta's hands, "Sure..." Taking a step back, Paige leveled off a look, "You know, you don't have to hide that from me. We all know how this is going to go. This happily ever after... I have all the faith in the world in you, Etta," her pause was just a little too long.

"But you're not sure about Will." Etta interjected, "I mean, he's disappeared for a year ... made love to me... left me without a word or a thought... I know." She bit down on her lip and said with firm determination, "He's going to come through this. Jon is going to be placed into his care permanently and I'll eventually build onto this house for our family. I'll turn the wood shed into an artist studio for Will. Our children will grow up together Paige, just like Jake and I did with Will. It's the picture perfect ending to this nightmare."

Paige felt sad thinking how much of Etta's heart had gone into the dream, "From your lips to Goddess' ears, my friend." She reached for her hand.

"And so it is." Etta whispered giving her hand a little squeeze.

"Hey, show me what you're planning!" Paige swallowed her fears, forgot about her own issues and looked brightly at the sketch book that Etta still held close to her chest.

CHAPTER 23

Etta had cleared the overgrowth from the shed in the far corner of her yard. It was good to sweat and feel her muscles working. She assessed the huge mound of shrubbery that would need to be hauled off or burned before she could go any further. It had been two days since her chat with Mim. Will had been tied up, stuck in San Francisco meeting with his lawyer. Keeping busy was her only sanity in the waiting. He assured he'd be back in time for the party at the mansion Friday night.

She recounted the conversation she'd had with Jake about their parent's estate. They hadn't left much; being in their thirties when they died. The little remnants of their lives were treasured by Jake and Etta as the most valuable things they owned. The house where Jake now lived, some stocks in TI that Etta had held onto all these years at Mim's insistence. Etta had asked Jake for her father's wedding ring which had a ruby and tiny diamonds on either side. He was very sweet about the whole request. The turquoise velvet box was taken from the safety deposit and placed into her lingerie drawer for just the right moment.

It seemed to Etta that everyone wore the same guarded smile when she talked about Will and her having a normal life. It's what she wanted. She'd seen it. Knew with every fiber of her being it was going to all play out the way she envisioned it. Will had assured her that he wanted to settle down and give Jon the sweet small town life they'd all had. She reached for a glass of tea sweating on the cement ledge and gulped, allowing the chill to fill her belly. She was determined to co-create that life with Will.

The phone rang from the patio. Ed, her architect, was on the other end.

"I've got the renderings all done. You caught me between projects... looks incredible. Once you see the drawings, you'll be floored. It's gonna' be a spendy venture though. When you want to stay true to the period your house was built..." Ed chuckled.

"Do you have time to drop them by this afternoon?" Etta asked. "I'm covered in dirt, greenery and sweat at the moment, but I don't want to wait."

"I'm heading out in about 30 minutes. I'll see you then."

"Great!" Etta clicked the phone off and headed in to clean up.

~

Large blue prints covered the entire surface of the dinette table in Etta's kitchen. As Ed explained each detail, Etta saw it unfolding into reality. Then he showed her the exterior rendering, which included her wood shed turned artist's studio.

"You captured it," Etta said softly. Running her hands over the images, "Just a few tweaks and it's perfect."

"I'm sure there'll be a lot of tweaks."

"Won't be enough time for much tweaking... I'd like to start right away." Etta gave Ed a wide smile, "I'd like to be done before the snow flies... and I am thinking since we're ripping the rear end out of everything I'd like to remodel the kitchen as well."

"Etta, it might be more cost effective to start a house from scratch." He presented her with the estimate for all the work she'd asked for, "The kitchen is going to add at minimum of thirty thousand onto that total."

Etta stared at the number and let the zero's compute in her head, "Okay... wow, that's a lot more than I thought." She set the estimate down like a precious relic.

"I'll call you tomorrow afternoon, Etta. The contractor who worked the estimates is listed there... I'm pretty sure he'll need at least twenty five percent to get started."

"Sure. I'm going to the bank in the morning and see what I can come up with. Thanks Ed, you did a great job."

That night Etta had a bottle of red wine with some pasta and looked over the renderings again. Ed had captured every detail she'd asked him for. In her mind she was already painting the children's rooms. Her vision of little shoes dancing in leaves was burned into her mind. Yes, two bedrooms downstairs. The master suite she'd share with Will would be romantic and wonderful, just like her room now, only bigger. She had some amazing antiques stored at her studio that would make the impact she visualized.

How was she going to fund the project? It was more than triple what she thought it might be. She could always take a loan out on her house. She owned it free and clear. She'd talk to Jake in the morning and see what he had to say about it. He was smart with money... something that had eluded Etta her whole life. Once she had a few dollars they were spent. She loved shopping and spoiling the people in her life. It was her greatest joy. Now she wanted to invest in her future.

Jake held the door for his sister as they entered the bank on Broad Street. It's where their parents had banked, it's where everyone banked. The name had only changed twice in forty years, which was almost unheard of. It was a solid cornerstone of Nevada City history. Etta was nervous as her sandals padded across the marble floor, renderings rolled and tucked under her arm. Jake sat next to her supportively as she presented her project to the loan officer. He looked barely old enough to drive.

After a couple of questions on the part of the loan juvenile, Josh, who showed little interest in helping Etta actualize her dream, Jake cleared his throat and asked, "Josh, we have been generational patrons of this institution. I believe that our roots run back to the foundation of this bank in Nevada City. Do you have any intention of helping us with a loan?"

"Well, I'll refer you to the mortgage department." Josh said flatly.

"That would be *great,* Josh." Jake said squeezing Etta's hand under the desk.

"Actually, Josh, I would like to go to the safety deposit box we have... can you do that for us?" Etta smiled sweetly.

"I'll call someone for you." Josh said curtly.

"Of course you will..." Jake said with an incredulous look on his face.

Margie, the manager of the bank appeared in Josh's cubicle opening, "Hi Jake! Hi Etta," She reached for Jakes hand and then hugged Etta. Josh gaffed quietly behind them as the old friends walked out arm in arm.

Jake gave Margie a quizzical look, "What's with the kid?"

"Corporate sent him in a month ago," she rolled her eyes, "He's a piece of work."

"I just need to get to my box, Margie, and then I need someone to help me with the stocks that my folks left."

"I can do that." Margie led them into a long hallway, "Here you go. Just meet me at my desk when you're ready."

The metal container was crammed with boxes of coins, and odds and ends that neither of them wanted to lose track of through the years. The stocks were in an envelope on the very bottom. Etta hadn't looked at them since she was 18 and given access to everything through a trust.

"Well, I guess if there is a good time to redeem them, this is it."

"They're yours, Sis... I just hope they are worth something. How much money do you actually need? I don't think Josh gave you an opportunity to get that far."

"I need one hundred and fifty thousand dollars."

"No shit?" Jake's eyes widened, "I'm not sure they're worth a fraction of that.

"Jake, do you think I'm being an idiot?" She looked him straight in the eye.

He took in a deep contemplative breath, "You are never an idiot. I think Will has had some idiotic moments in his life. His heart has always been in the right place. Where the hell is he anyway?" He stopped himself short and held up a hand, "Nope. I'm not going there right now. He's got nothing to do with your question. No, Etta, my darling sister, you are never an idiot." He took her hand and kissed it.

"You know, Will has everything to do with this." She clutched the envelope close to her chest, "I love him desperately, Jake. I love Jon. He told me he wants a simple life here at home with Jon and me. I know he's buried with the legalities of Jon's grandfather... he can't think about the future right now. I'm doing it for him... for us, I mean."

"From your lips..." Jake said softly.

"Let's see what this is worth and go from there," Etta said, full of hope.

~

Margie assessing the amount of stocks handed to her, she typed and waited, staring at the screen of her computer. She typed and tapped her fingers against the edge of her keyboard, waiting and clicked again. She squinted at the numbers on the stocks and made sure they were accurate, leaning in close to her computer. She took in a careful breath, "Etta, I'm trying to make sure everything I've entered is correct before I give you this figure. From the dates and numbers on your stocks, what started out as several thousand shares have split over the last 30 years so many times I stopped counting. Looks like... and I'm hesitant to tell you this until I've confirmed it... but it looks like..." Margie wrote the number on a piece of paper and pushed it across the desk into Etta's uncertain hand.

~

Mim ran water over what was left of the package of cigarettes before shredding them into the trash. Sickened by her lapse in good sense, it had taken her thirty years to quit. She sure as hell wasn't going back to that old habit now, regardless of how wonderfully intoxicating it felt. She had things to stay healthy for and she smiled widely as she watched Jon on his jumpy horse in the family room.

"Well, little chicken, are you ready for lunch?"

"Yeah," Jon clapped his hands.

"Good, then we're going to have a nap."

Cheese sticks and applesauce were his favorite lunch. Mim was helpless when it came to refusing him anything. With Jon tucked in and sleepy, Mim went to her room to look for the right outfit to meet Jon's Grandfather, Miles Harper. She had arranged for him to meet here where Jon felt safe at her house. Where Miles could see how happy and settled he was here. She slipped hanger after hanger across the bar in her closet; Suit, too stiff, dresses to fussy, jeans to casual. Finally she pulled out a pale yellow flowing crepe top and a pair of white slacks. Pretty sandals and the right jewelry would make the proper statement; well put together, confident, not overdressed. Mim laid it all out on the bed and studied every detail. She was so nervous about meeting Miles. Miles had the opportunity to rip the whole bottom out of her life. She reached for the phone and dialed Will.

"Hi Mom." He said out of breath.

"Hi... what's the situation down there, Will? I'm absolutely paralyzed with fear up here."

"This is exactly the reason I didn't want to involve any of you in this until it was a done deal."

"William! Stop that and just fill me in. What's happening?"

Mim snipped.

"Well, it's not good... Miles has filed a petition for custody dependent upon his visit inspection of our living arrangements in Nevada City."

"*An inspection?*" Mim was livid, "What a pompous ass, is he bringing a team to check all the closets and the corners of the house?"

"My lawyer needs to be present, Mom... Do you mind?"

"Jesus, Will... this is turning out to be much more than I thought. I wanted Miles to meet his grandson. I thought it was the only fair and human thing to do. I assumed that we were dealing with a human being."

"I've never met Miles, Mom. We'll just have to wait and see what happens on Sunday. I'm playing it safe and want Tony to be there. I promised Etta I would be home for the party on Friday night but I'm not sure I'll make it."

"Oh, Honey... what's left for you to do down there? It's so important to celebrate this milestone for Paige and Jake."

"I've only got one thing on my mind, Mom. That's not allowing anyone or anything take Jon from us now. I can't lose him twice."

Mim took a breath that shuttered her whole body, "I know..." She didn't want him to know she was crying.

"Okay, Mom, I gotta run... Tony's waiting."

In her life, Mim had left the husband who'd cheated her out of a happily ever after with his immaturity and infidelity. She'd moved across the country with her infant son, intimately experienced the grief and sadness of losing her lifelong friend,

Henrietta, and then taken the surviving children into her life as her own. Celebrated as a celebrity with her books and art, she'd traveled the world once she'd felt her adult children were doing well. But she never felt as alone and as helpless as she did in that very moment. She'd never really had a shoulder to cry on. Being strong independent and totally "Mim" had always felt like a good thing, until now.

    She longed for the touch of someone who was there for her and only her. She missed the boat on having a life partner by raising her kids and not allowing anyone to interfere. Her children had been through enough in their young lives. She was completely dedicated to them. What had she taught Will by never allowing a man to get close to her... never showing any of them how to nurture a healthy relationship? Having been so focused on providing a perfect life with no drama, she had given him no example of love between a man and woman. She'd taught Will to be a fierce parent but never taught him how to be partner. Poor Etta would be the guinea pig of Will's inexperience. Mim blamed herself for the breakdown, having been too selfish to share her children with anyone. She wrapped her arms around her middle and sobbed her heart out. What had she done?

CHAPTER 24

Paige stood back from the twenty foot long dinner table in her dining room. Twenty two high backed cream brocade chairs, various height sterling candles sticks with dangling leaded crystals shimmering and shiny reflected the feelings ready to burst from her chest. Rose and wisteria bouquets towered thirty inches from the table top draping down to create romantic drama. She couldn't wait to share it with all of those who had a hand in the creation of her life in Nevada City. Paige couldn't take her eyes off of the beautiful tablescape. Appreciatively, she tilted her head when she turned the dimmer on the chandelier down to the lowest setting. Little thrills of anticipation ran over her bare arms when she heard Jake come in the kitchen door.

"Paige?" He yelled out.

"I'm in the dining room." She pushed through the swinging door to the kitchen.

"Oh my..." Jake whispered when he kissed her cheek.

"Wait until you see the dining room!" Paige said proudly.

"Anything sparkles more than you and I might not be able to take it!"

"Too much?" Like a little girl, she twirled in her new dress covered in pale blue sparkles on the hem and neckline. Her hair was swept up into rhinestone clips, her strappy silver diva shoes tapped out happily when she walked. She shined all over like a new diamond.

"Too beautiful."

"Come on, I want you to be the first to see it." Her hand slipped into his and then she noticed he was wearing a tuxedo. She slid her fingers down his silky lapel, "Rented or owned?"

"Owned...Occupational hazard of the job." Jake nudged toward the dining room, "Show me this masterpiece of entertaining."

Paige pushed on the swinging door and stood back for Jake to see it all. He said nothing, but walked in, putting his hands into his pockets.

"Well?" Paige widened her eyes at him, "Is it too much?"

"Amazing... it's going to impossible for me to wait." He said, "So I'm going to duck out and I'll be right back, I forgot something." Before Paige could form a pout, Jake was gone.

In the kitchen, Addy was going over the final touches for dinner with the chef. Charlie, a round red headed woman had come in from Auburn so Addy could enjoy the celebration with her friends

"It smells amazing in here." Paige commented to the women gathered around her kitchen work island.

"Charlie is the best!" Addy said, "You let us have artistic license and look what happened... Chateaubriand, this amazing rice salad, and look at these vegetables. It's a work of art. Charlie's been working since early this morning and guess what's for dessert Paige... It's tiramisu."

Paige peeked inside the pink bakery boxes, imagining the delight. "It's perfect." Paige flashed them a super charged appreciative smile.

~

Etta primped in front of the mirror. Her peaches and cream dress flowed like a whisper around her legs as she moved about her dressing room looking for the lost earring. She hadn't seen Will in over a week. He'd called one time since he arrived in San Francisco. He sounded harried and emotionally disconnected from her. Rationalizing the situation was getting harder as she whirled on with the renovation. She'd signed off on the architects' renderings, hired the contractor and they would have the okay on her building permit Monday. Soon there would be holes in her wall and the non-stop noise and excitement of change. Change in every area.

She couldn't wait to have Will and Jon Jon with her all the time. To Etta it felt like standing at the starting gate of her life in three feet of mud with no jockey. Determined to finish the project, she envision it to the finish line. She looked at the wall in her bedroom which would be gone in less than a week; the color of butter cream frosting would coat her dining room with warm welcoming and lead down the hall where the children would have their rooms.

She did it again, Children, indicating more than one. She imagined a little girl as well; it was easy to imagine having seen the shoes. Hard conceiving a child when the daddy was never here in her bed... he would be. She could feel it. In the meantime, the sweetness of home would be created for the family of her dreams with the only true love she'd ever had in her heart.

Finding the earring under the edge of her dresser, she

slipped the sparkly vintage button to her ear and smiled at the final result. Seeing Will was going to feel electric. She had so much to tell him about; the house remodel, the stocks… She was keeping the artist cottage a secret for now. She'd surprise him with that as a wedding present. She heard Mim holler into the screen door and come in.

"Precious girl!" Mim reached up to touch the scarf in Etta's hair. Etta immediately noticed the exhaustion in Mim's face.

"Is everything okay?" Etta asked quickly, "Have you seen Will yet?"

"I'm fine, Darlin', you and I have a lot going on." Mim winked in slow motion and moved toward the chair in the bedroom to sit, "I couldn't get Will on his Cell phone. He's probably in a dead zone."

"Yeah, me either…" Etta sighed, "Jon was doing ok with the sitter?"

"He was playing ball when I left… wearing him out is a good thing right before bedtime. He loves Tammy. She'll have him in bed by eight dreaming about puppies, his new favorite thing."

"OH!" Etta turned quickly to face Mim, "I can't believe I haven't told you!" She walked close to Mim and sat on the edge of the bed, "Do you remember when you thought it would be best for Jake to take the house and for me to hold onto the TI stocks when Mom and Dad died?"

"That seems like a million years ago." Mim waved the air as if to fan away the painful memory.

"Well, turns out it was the best advice I could have. I went to the bank yesterday, because I have a project I want to fund and guess what those stocks are worth Just *guess!*" Etta stood boldly.

"I have no idea, Honey..." Mim looked away for a moment. "I can't imagine..."

"Eight hundred and thirty thousand" Etta stated, "Dollars!"

Mim stood up, shaking out her brown skirt then she pulled her glittering velvet wrap around herself, "Well, how fabulous! Shall we?" Arm in arm, flashing like stars in a moonless sky, they walked next door.

Half way to Paige's mansion Mim patted Etta's hand, "Do you know how happy your parent's would be right now? Just knowing what they have given to you?"

"I miss them so much ..." Etta swallowed a lump, "But they did gift me with you..." Etta put her head against Mim's shoulder, "Thank you."

Paige greeted the women in the foyer, kissing each one on the cheek.

"It looks like the Rockefellers are coming for dinner!" Mim went directly into the dining room to get a look at the beautiful table setting leaving Etta and Paige alone.

"I thought you'd be walking in with Will..." Paige whispered, "Have you heard from him?"

"Not in days." Etta said.

"Are you sure..." Paige stopped short. It was a night to celebrate the independence of her mansion, not to talk about the emotional investments Etta was making into a relationship that hadn't had a chance to gel yet.

"He'll be here, Paige. I know what I'm doing." Etta said softly reading her friend perfectly.

"I've brought in Hardy to make the drinks!" Paige said, "You better be the first to have your crystal filled with the Goddess juice."

Betty arrived on Jake's arm wearing a silver ball gown that Paige was sure vintage 1950's. The netting skirt had tiny crystals sewn into the folds of material. The bodice was scrunched and off the shoulder. Her wrap was an amazing burned out velvet of purple. The white cotton candy hair do was perfection with a tiny tiara. Betty looked like a royalty coming to court.

"I feel like I should bow to the queen. Betty, you're a vision." Paige kissed her cheek and grabbed her hand.

"Jake drove me in the Bentley," Betty's eye glistened like a three year old.

"I see that… He's a very chivalrous date!" Paige said sliding a sweet look to Jake who still had hold of Betty.

Della appeared covered in a hot pink cocktail dress which accentuated her voluptuous curves. She sashayed into the foyer and shrugged out of her black faux fur wrap which Patti caught as if the move had been practiced a hundred times. Patti was decked out in monochromatic black with a hot pink rose fully bloomed on his lapel. His blond hair combed back slick against his head created a model handsome look. Paige was mystified by her friends' ability to rise to a black tie affair with only days of notice.

"Della, you look delicious!" Paige stated.

"Well, how often do we get the opportunity to play dress up as adults? I relish an event that allows princess jewels and high heels!" She blinked her long eyelashes and shrugged her shoulders in delight. Della's eyes were lined Egyptian style. She was a knock-out!

The buzz of glitzy guests created the glowing ambiance of a real cultural black tie event. Everyone had arrived by seven thirty and the dinner bell was chimed at eight. Etta never got far from the front door expecting Will to walk in any moment. He didn't.

Once the guests were seated, Paige stood at the head of the table with Jake and made a toast,

"Looking around at your faces in the candlelight and crystal I am surrounded by the inexhaustible beauty, tenacity and sheer determination of precious friends. It was our intention to let you know how cherished each one of you are... how important you've been... how thankful we are that you have opened your lives and your history and welcomed me home. As this journey begins, I express my deepest gratitude to you all... The mansion is safe!" Paige raised her glass but was interrupted by Jake.

Looking flushed, he cleared his throat, "well, hard to follow that statement but I think I can." Jake looked at the faces all intent on what he was about to say, "Paige has only been here a short time, but seems like she's always been here as one of us. I recognized her the moment that I met her as the love of my life. It took considerably longer for her to let me entertain the thought in her presence." The crowd smiled remembering, "Tonight seemed like the perfect night..." He reached into his jacket pocket and pulled out a jewelry box. A whisper of gasps circled the room. "This is the ring my father held in his hands on the day he asked my mother to marry him. It is the most precious thing I have to offer you as a token of my love. Paige, will you marry me?"

Her hands shaking, tears welling, as she reached for him and held him tightly... there wasn't a dry eye in the house.

"Paige..." Jake whispered in her ear, "Is that a yes?"

"YES!" she exclaimed, jumping up and down with excitement. The crowd applauded. He slipped his mother's ring onto her finger as the presence of love surrounded her, healing the past and promising her the future she'd been denied for more than a hundred and fifty years.

Etta smiled brightly and looked at the door, again. Her tears were for Paige and Jake, she couldn't have been happier for them. She wrapped her arms around Paige and welcomed her to the family. When she realized her tears were not going to stop, she quietly slipped out the back door.

Etta honestly believed Will was going to come busting through the door, tux tails flying behind him, looking dashing and handsome and just as in love with her as Jake was with Paige. She'd seen it in her mind like a movie. Prince charming comes in at the last minute and sweeps her into his arms. She wasn't going to give up on that movie yet. After all, she didn't know what it was like to be a parent. She didn't know what that kind of love felt like. From everything she'd read, a parent could perform impossible feats of bravery: lift a car off of their child or heal them with a prayer and a touch. Will was worth waiting it out for. She stood up, fluffed her skirt, wiped her eyes and went back inside to celebrate love.

~

Paige and Jake sat quietly snuggled into the reproduction turn of the century sofa in the parlor.

"Etta went home early," Jake said quietly.

"I'm so worried about her, Jake."

"I want to say she's a big girl. She's always been the rock. Now it seems like she's throwing herself into the renovation for..." He stopped short remembering Etta's rule, "You know I'm going to honor my sister's rule: *when you fear something strongly you are contributing to its creation, say it out loud and it will be so.* They'll be no broken heart for her. I'm going to see the future she wants. Let's be part of that creation." He stroked Paige's hair until the sparkling combs fell out releasing her wild auburn curls over her shoulders.

"That is exactly what Etta would say!"

"That is what I wish for her. It's what we're going to help her create."

Paige closed her eyes, conjuring up the image. "Yes...I can see Jon Jon playing in the yard. Etta with her polka dotted apron in the kitchen cooking dinner for her family. Will, playing with a ..." Paige's eyes flew open and she looked at Jake, "Oh, a little girl, that was weird."

Jake laughed deeply, "Honey, you don't know the half of it..." He smiled to himself feeling for the first time in days that everything was going to be wonderful in Etta's world.

He seized the urge to put his hand in her hair one more time and kissed Paige sweetly, "Now, my red headed visionary, what do you see for us?" He kissed her neck.

"Well..." She pulled him up from the couch, slipped the tuxedo jacket from his shoulders and watched it hit the floor. With a naughty grin, slowly she unbuttoned his shirt, slipped her fingers into his waistband and led him to the bedroom, "It starts in here."

CHAPTER 25

The day had come when the family would meet Miles, Jon's grandfather. Since nine that morning, Jon Jon had been with Tammy, the capable loving nanny that Mim had hired as an act of self preservation. She felt it was the healthiest thing to do in the situation. Mim, on the other hand had nothing but time building pressure in her guts, which were tangled and throbbing. She'd dressed and primped to be sure that she looked the part of dotting grandmother; Fun, casual, capable and loving. Why was she so worried? How much trouble can one man create against a whole family? A whole city of capable adults had come together to raise the child they loved. She swallowed hard realizing she had started to cry, again.

"Damn it," she whispered to herself and dabbed her tears gently with a tissue, "Never let them see you sweat." Crunching gravel announced Etta pulling in the drive. It was one o'clock, almost showtime. Where the hell was Will?

"Well, look at you!" Mim called from the door, "You look beautiful!"

Etta was absolutely glowing, "I just talked to Will, he's about 10 minutes away. Tammy have Jon in the back yard?"

"He's down for a nap. I wanted him well rested for this... whatever it is. Tammy's a jewel. I can't believe I didn't think of hiring a nanny earlier. She's off for the rest of the day."

Will's jeep pulled into the drive and Etta felt her stomach clench when she saw the concern on his face. Etta quickly sized up Will's companion, "That is not what I expected his lawyer to look like. Great energy, I like him."

"Great energy or not," Mim said as a matter of fact, "I don't know why this has to be so stuffy and formal."

"Will says we're too trusting and we don't know what Miles is capable of. I tried to convince him of my *fear it and create it* theory, but he's not buying. He's not willing to leave this to chance." Etta reached for Mim's hand, "I'm nervous."

Mim gave her hand a firm grasp and together they met at the Jeep to welcome him home.

Will stepped out and Etta flopped in front of him waiting for the happy reunion. There was no hug, just an introduction, "Etta, Mom... this is Anthony Leona, the finest custody lawyer in northern California."

Etta looked hard at Will trying to figure out his coolness and decided quickly it wasn't the time or the place. She then turned and shook hands with Anthony projecting a warm welcome.

"Call me Tony, please," he said to both women, never taking his eyes off of Mim, "Miriam, it is an honor to meet you."

Mim felt her forehead rise up in surprise at how attractive Tony was and how delightful it felt to have her hand kissed by his lips.

Etta felt the electricity of Will's hand on her lower back and then the sweetness of his kiss on her cheek, "You have an amazing glow," he whispered in her ear. "Now, I've got to see our little man," he rushed off.

Miles was over thirty minutes late. The tension in the house was so thick it was hard to breathe. Mim busied herself in the kitchen putting finger foods on a silver tray.

"I hoped this day would be friendly, like welcoming family." Mim said to Etta.

"Well, that's your way, Mim. Being late like this is just disrespectful." Etta said curtly.

"It smacks of self importance," Mim said then stopped herself. "I'm not going to get catty. I'm going to be a wonderful hostess, with a warm welcome. This is Jon's grandfather. I think he'll be delightful when he gets here."

A twenty year old pickup truck rattled down the driveway much too fast and stopped in a cloud of dust and gravel sputtering to a pitiful silence. She quickly motioned to Etta and they watched from the kitchen window as a man in his fifties jumped out of the truck and ran around the other side to open the door for a woman. The man, apparently Miles, was wearing jeans, a pale plaid western shirt with the sleeves rolled up to above the elbows. Obviously in need of a haircut, he repeatedly pushed the overgrown salt and pepper hair out of his eyes. The woman accompanying him was dressed as a twenty year old in spite of her fifty year old figure. Her barely contained bosoms jigged while she pranced on the gravel drive. Wearing skin tight stretch jeans and a glittery silver top, a cigarette dangled from her fingertips as she whispered something in Miles' ear that made him nod and smile.

"Not on my walkway..." Mim whispered vehemently as the

woman dropped her cigarette and snuffed it out with her pudgy turquoise pump.

"Wow," Etta said. Looking sadly at Mim, she slid the window open to hear what they were saying as they approached the front door.

"This old babe's got money," Miles said.

"Classy digs. I could get used to this." The woman's eyes darted to every detail of Mim's front yard.

After hearing that, Mim wanted to grab Jon and run far away. These were not people that were going to have in any part in his life. She could easily see how Miles' daughter had turned out the way she had. "Oh Etta, I'm judging," she said ashamed of herself.

"No, you're not Mim, you're seeing the obvious. Goddess help us!" Etta whispered.

Mim dabbed her eyes and opened the door with a bright smile.

The meeting went from uncomfortable to unreal as they could smell sour bourbon on Miles' breath. Will entered the room with Jon, who was rubbing the sleep from his eyes.

"Jon, this is your Grandfather, Miles. Can you say hello?" Will asked softly into Jon's ear.

Jon looked at the strangers in the living room and buried his head against his father's neck. Everyone gasped as Miles jumped up and reached for the baby. Letting out a yowl, Jon clung to Will's shirt collar in protest.

Then Linda, Mile's partner, rose up, "Hey there, Handsome," she cooed in a baby voice, "you wanna' come see... your..." Her shoulders fell and she looked toward Miles, "He's not going to call me

Grandma is he?" Linda asked horrified. Miles shot her a warning look. With her aged cupi-doll face and her bouncing bosoms, Linda smiled, got so close to Will he could smell what she'd had for lunch and went back to baby-talking Jon, "Who's the luckiest baby in the world? You've got Grandpa Miles," She smiled widely at Jon, "Yes you do." Her pony tail was wagging behind her, looking absolutely ridiculous.

Jon scowled and slapped at Linda's face. Mim took in a sharp breath and stood to take control of the situation, "Why don't we all go outside for some refreshments. Jon loves it outside and I think he'll be more at ease out there."

The group migrated toward the French doors leading outside and Mim overheard Linda whisper to Miles, "What are we gonna' do? He doesn't like me."

Apparently Tony heard the comment as well and followed Mim to the kitchen, "I'd love to help."

She turned quickly to hide her fury. "What in the world do they want with that sweet baby?" Mim spat at Tony.

"Opportunists, I'm afraid to say." Tony stated. "Sadly, Mim, this is what we feared."

"I will not have that baby tainted by those... those... people!" Mim smacked the counter with her fist. "Did you smell his breath? He's drunk. I heard them talking on the front porch. They are in this for... for the money!" Mim's eyes stung with righteous indignation.

The look Tony gave her did little to soothe her nerves, "We'll do everything we can to keep him safe and here in Nevada City."

He reached across the island and covered her tight fist with his warm hands, rubbing until his touch eased the tension in her balled up fingers. It had been a long time since she'd needed comforting and even longer since she'd received it.

"Our lives are in your hands." Mim hesitated, "I told Will we didn't need you and now I'm so glad you're here." Something darted across the back yard and caught Mim's attention, "Now what?" She moved to the French doors leading out into the yard, "That son of a biscuit eatin' rat bastard..." Mim howled, creating her own wind tunnel as she flew outside.

Will shot his mother a defeated look as she busted out the door. She stormed into the huddle of adults who were watching in disbelief as Jon gleefully rolled on the ground with a black and white bundle of adorable fur. His giggling was met with a tiny pink tongue licking every inch of exposed skin in a fury of mutual wild excitement.

"What kind of a dog is that?" Mim asked Miles.

"He's just a mutt. My neighbors had a litter and I thought he'd like to have his own dog." Miles squatted down to call the puppy, which ignored him completely.

"So you brought this dog for the baby?" Mim asked, eyes narrowing to slits. She was feeling the urge to start shooting fire lasers at these people who assumed that the easiest way to a baby's heart was through a puppy.

"Who doesn't love a little puppy?" Linda cooed to Miles as she slipped her arm around his waist and shot him a sly wink.

"Babies don't know the first thing about puppies. They can hurt each other." Mim said feeling very tired. As if on cue, the puppy yelped. Jon dangled it by one hind leg clasped in his chubby fist. The puppy twisted and turned. Jon released him and the puppy snapped repeatedly at the child with razor sharp teeth. Blood curdling screams shocked the air as Jon wiggled his hands. The puppy kept snapping at him. Etta scooped Jon up, realized that he was bleeding and ran him straight into the bathroom. Will was right behind her.

Miles reached down for the puppy, "Well, you can't just pick the little guy up by a leg and not have him bite you." He scratched the puppies head while tucking him under his arm. The puppy covered his face with forgiving licks.

"It occurs to me that you have no more concern or forethought to Jon's safety than you do for that puppy's." Mim was looking directly at Miles.

"Well, didn't you turn out to be an uppity bitch?" Miles spat out, and shoved the dog to Linda, "Take him to the truck." Miles stormed back into the house.

Frozen in her place, Mim's eyes stung with the unshed tears of frustration. Tony reached for her, "This is pretty much what I expected from him, Mim," He rubbed her shoulder lightly. "I have a plan."

"Have you met him before?" Mim asked quietly.

"No. But after talking to his lawyer, I knew what to expect."

"How much do you think he wants?"

"I have no idea. If I have my way he'll be lucky to just walk away and not look back."

"I wanted Miles to know his grandson. I thought it was the right thing to do." Mim justified, "I should have listened to Will."

"Will's been through a lot in the last year." Tony turned to look her square in the face, "He started out with a 'full of faith in humanity' attitude, now he's more of a realist. He has worked harder than anyone can imagine making sure Jon grows up surrounded with love. I should know, he hired me the very first day he held Jon in his arms. I've watched his dedication, his strong sense of family. I know that came from you."

"Maybe you know why he didn't tell me about my grandson until recently." Mim said softly, hurt.

"He couldn't stand to break your heart. He knew the odds were stacked against him. He couldn't take on the system alone, so he hired me."

"And here you are..." Mim said thoughtfully, "Thank you, Tony".

"You know, Mim, he thought he was home safe when he brought Jon back to Nevada City. If he'd known that Miles would come crawling out of the woodwork, he'd have stayed in San Francisco."

"I'm glad he's home." She took in a deep breath, "I've got to make sure Jon is okay."

Jon's cries were so shrill they could have broken glass. Mim tore to the bathroom where Etta had Jon on the counter tending to his tears and puncture wounds. She heard Will's voice coming from the kitchen, "Does that dog have shots? Do you even know where he comes from? He could have given him rabies for Christ sakes." The veins in Wills neck and temple were bulging, his hands were in his pockets. It was a trick his mother had taught her hot headed son when he wanted to hit someone.

"Look, you overeducated Mamma's boy," Miles thick finger jabbed into Will's chest, "you're responsible for my Darla's death.

I'm going to get what's coming to me, so you better get ready to pay up."

"You didn't even know where she lived. What kind of a father doesn't know his daughter is pregnant or where she works?" Will spat, "Did you even know she was a stripper or a drug addict?"

"Darla had a mind of her own. She didn't want to talk to me. I didn't follow her." He stated flatly, "Now I've got a grandson and unless you want to hand him over, it's going to cost you," Miles said with a cocky smirk.

"He's not going anywhere. I'll see you dead before that happens," Will hissed.

"Just like you got rid of my Darla?" Miles raised an eyebrow, "How is that going to sound in court?"

"Just one cotton picking minute!" Mim thundered into the room, "Will didn't have anything to do with your…"

"That's enough!" Tony yelled over the arguing, "Stop talking. We're overly emotional and this isn't going to accomplish anything." His common sense took charge, "Now, I'm going to suggest that we continue another day."

Linda had slipped into the kitchen through the patio doors and sidled up to Miles, "What's all this about, Daddy?" she pouted at the raised voices. Miles shrugged her hand off of his arm.

"I think this boy should pull himself off the tit long enough to write me a check and I'll leave your perfect family alone. Otherwise, it's going to get real ugly." Miles poked again at Will.

"Just for the record, Miles, What would that number be?" Tony held up a mini tape recorder, "just for the record…"

"Will!" Etta raised her voice from the kitchen door with Jon in her arms, "He needs stitches!" Her eyes were wild with worry even though her voice was calm for the baby's sake.

"Nice going you two," Will spat at the couple standing in his mother's kitchen. He was at Etta's side immediately with car keys in hand, "Let me see…"

"I can't get the bleeding to stop. I'm afraid to take the pressure off. He's got a really deep gash on the back of his hand."

Mim was furious with herself. How could she have insisted that Miles be given the chance to know his grandson? That perfect little hand, tender baby flesh ripped open and bleeding… all because she believed in the inherent goodness of people. She paced the hallway outside the examination room of the doctor's office. Praying that nothing would be permanently damaged, she wrung her hands. The baby screams were blood curdling. Mim held her breath when she heard him howl with pain and paced when he took another breath.

Etta poked her head out from the examination room and spoke softly to Mim, "Three stitches, all done."

Back at Mim's, the baby, an absolute noodle of exhaustion fell asleep immediately in the car. The adults sprawled out on sofas wishing they could do the same. Tony crept into the house looking like he'd been hit by a truck.

"Good Lord, you look like I feel," Mim remarked.

"I took the puppy to a vet's for observation. I had to chase Miles and Linda down to get him back." He held up his hand to quiet them, not wanting to stir up another hornet's nest of anger. "The vet's going to make sure there's nothing wrong with the dog and then he'll let us know. He'll have to be there for 10 days."

Will reached over and took Etta's hand into his, "Take a walk with me?"

Etta wearily nodded and they headed out the French doors and into the emotional security of the beauty they grew up with. The sun had dipped down behind the trees to cast long shadows over the lawns. Will pulled her close to him, their hips touching and his arms warm around her waist, "I'm so sorry I missed the party. I've been wrapped up in this... this..." He looked close to cracking wide open.

"I know you're working so hard to keep Jon safe, but Will, I've got so much to tell you. I started…"

"Oh, the Baby's up and he's really crying." Will dropped her hand to dangle by her side and ran back into the house.

Etta let out several quick and jerky breaths deciding it was time to head home.

With a kiss to Jon Jon's head and a peck for Will and Mim, she left alone. Again.

CHAPTER 26

Etta contemplated the limp two day old salad in a bowl and cold congealed pizza in her hand. She stuffed the pizza into her mouth and tossed the salad into a compost container. The light was on in Paige's library. Jake's truck was not in the drive. Her gut told her Paige was alone. Wiping the pizza from her mouth, she headed over to the mansion for some girl chat with her soon-to-be sister in law.

Paige's conversation reverberated out to Etta. She stopped short of knocking on the kitchen door and listened. "I'm not kidding Georgia, come on. You gave Jon the key and Betty the journal. Why are you hiding this from me?"

Etta laughed to herself and knocked lightly on the door before she entered, "Roommate quarrel?" Etta called into the kitchen.

"Not exactly." Paige leaned in to Kiss Etta's cheek, "I'm just frustrated. I put things down where I know I'll be able to find them and then they're gone. Georgia is acting like a little child."

"Sounds like she's bored now that the house is safe. Maybe it's time to see if she wants to go." Etta glanced up at the ceiling.

"Oh, I don't know," Paige said softly. "I'm used to having her around. It's not so lonely when I know she's lurking." She shifted in her chair, "I've been fascinated with the journal of her life. Did you know her mother turned out to be a famous dancer? She danced for royalty in England and then she toured the country for decades. No one wanted to talk about it back then, it was scandalous. There were rumors that she was a woman of loose morals… and that she retired to run a brothel!"

"I don't think any city wanted to call attention to scandalous ties. Well, Virginia City pretty much had a devil-may-care attitude, but…"

Something loud slammed in the library. They both jumped and ran through the foyer into the library to find Georgia's journal in the middle of the floor.

"Georgia, you know Paige loves having you here." Etta looked at Paige to chime in, "We understand that you've been here for a long time. I can help you if you'd like to go see your family now. Would you like to move on?"

The air was still. No response. Paige said, "I know how much you love this place, Georgia. I am honestly going to care for it and preserve it for another hundred years. It's okay if you want to move on now." Nothing.

"She'll let us know when she's ready now that we've offered to help her." Etta said.

"You really can guide her to the 'other side'?"

"Yes, of course. It's in the psychic training manual," Etta responded dryly.

"I've had dreams of this house during the gold rush days, Etta. I don't think it was just a boarding house. I don't know what to make of what I've seen. In my dreams, I'm here and…" she searched Etta's face for how much farther to go and realized there was something on her mind that didn't include walking a ghost to the great beyond. "So, tell me about Jon's grandfather."

Etta recounted the meeting of the grandfather and Linda; The puppy bite and finally her disappointment of no time really spent with Will talking about their own relationship.

"There's certainly a lot going on, Etta. Are you okay?"

"Sure, just let down I guess. I wasn't even able to tell him about the money."

"He'll calm down as soon as the dust settles."

"Miles made some pretty disturbing accusations toward Will about his daughter's death." Etta said.

"What do you mean? Will had nothing to do with her death," Paige remarked.

"I mean, he dropped the bomb that he was going to file a civil suit against Will for the unlawful death of his daughter if Will didn't pay up."

"What a mess." Paige finally said.

"Well, Tony's on the ball. He recorded Miles trying to black mail Will in Mim's kitchen."

"Good God," Paige breathed out, "I wish there was something I could do for you two. I'm sure this is not the reunion you expected."

Etta quietly shook her head.

"Tell me about your house!" Paige changed the subject, "What's the progress. I wanted to come over today, but I knew you were tied up with the meeting."

"It's messy. I didn't know I would need to have a mask on just to walk through the place. But it's going to be worth it when it's done. I'm so close to having Will and Jon with me, Paige and then today happened and I'm so deflated. I feel like it's farther away than ever." Her eyes looked dull and drained.

"How is Jon's hand?"

"Three stitches doesn't sound like much until you're looking at a little hand." Etta said sadly, "I think it might scar."

"You'll be amazed how resilient babies are and how quickly they heal."Paige read that somewhere. "You wanna have a coke and play scrabble?" She changed the conversation again.

"Sure. Where's Jake?"

"Busy with finishing touches on a project." Paige smiled slyly, "So when will the downstairs bedrooms be done?"

"Soon." Etta answered, "Can we play dirty word scrabble, I need to do something 'bad'. I'm telling you, Paige if Will doesn't get close to me soon I'm going to explode!"

CHAPTER 27

"I'm going to take Jon and go over to Etta's, Mom." Will called out down the hallway.

"Oh no you're not," Mim sassed him back, "I've got plans. We're going to have our picture taken and then we've got a date with the park." Mim walked out of her room with Jon in tow, "You two have a lot to talk about. Etta hasn't had three minutes with you since you came home. Go see her, alone."

From his perch on Mim's hip, Jon waved happily, "Bye Bye," to his father.

"A conspiracy I see," Will picked up his little mister and kissed the top of his head.

"Bye Bye," Jon repeated.

"Thanks mom, see you tonight."

"We'll be fine if you want to stay longer..." Mim gave her son the 'you know what you need to do look'.

"It's ok, baby boy, let's take a walk and see what's blooming in the back yard." Mim felt the tiny hand grasp hers as they walked slowly though the front room. She didn't have the patience to walk along at Will's pace when he was a baby. She'd picked him up and carry him. Her life was in such a hurry back then. Right now she couldn't think of anything she'd rather do than walk at the pace of Jon Jon.

Mim's rose garden was a carefully crafted winding path of blooms. From stark white blossoms fading into pink and the deepest burgundy, they carved out an enchanting niche in the landscape.

"This is the rose of friendship," Mim said to Jon as they examined a perfect yellow rose of Texas. "It has an entirely different smell from the red rose over here." They moved to the next rose in the garden which was velvet blood red, "This is the Abe Lincoln rose, see how it smells?" She pulled the bloom down to Jon's height and let him sniff the rose. Jon wrinkled up his face and giggled at a large yellow and black caterpillar crawling out of the flower.

"No one answered the door, so I thought I'd come around back," called Tony from the garden gate, "I hope you don't mind."

"Of course not," Mim said, glad to see him, "We're having a lesson on roses."

"Hello, Jon," Tony bent down and held out his hand to the toddler.

"Woses!" Jon pointed to the flowers.

"Aren't they pretty?" Tony turned his undivided attention to Jon and pointed toward the fire and ice rose which had white petals fading into hot pink and burgundy. "These are my personal favorites, they smell like raspberries!"

"berries" Jon clapped his hand.

Mim studied the two of them sniffing flowers together. Tony sat softly on the ground and held the caterpillar. His tenderness when he explained patiently to Jon about being gentle with the caterpillar was unexpected. Her appreciation turned to joy then curled into a great big grin.

Swinging the sledge hammer at the wall of her bedroom gave Etta a rush of adrenaline. Bam, her frustration at being left alone for weeks. Bam, the tension of her unfulfilled desires for the man she loved and couldn't quite seem to be alone with. BAM BAM, the way he didn't confide anything to her. BAM BAM BAM, she hadn't even told him her news yet. She'd become wealthy and focused. Damn, she choked on powdery drywall residue. She could hardly see through her protective goggles. Everything was covered in the dust of destruction. Etta smacked the goggles against the legs of her coveralls. Clouds of chalky dust billowed out from her pant leg. Stepping back, she took a deep breath to clear her lungs. Running her hand over her hair created a whirl of fallout and another round of coughing.

She was laughing out loud to no one but herself, covered in filth when he walked in. Etta's arms chilled even though it was hot outside, her gaze was drawn to see him grinning ear to ear in her foyer.

"That's about the prettiest thing I've ever seen." He was wearing blue jeans and a black t-shirt, "I only have one question, Etta," he smiled like he had a secret, "Need a hand?"

The goggles dropped to the floor in a puff, "Hi," she said, paralyzed at how good it felt to see him standing in her doorway. The heat in her cheeks flushed down to her belly and she still couldn't move. She wasn't expecting to see him. Her whole day was planned out so the demo would be done by Friday. Her feet might as well been nailed to the floor. Hell, yeah she could use a hand.

He shuffled his feet with a look of complete bewilderment, "I would be happy to help," he hesitated and looked around, "if I knew what you were doing."

"Right now I'm demoing the wall between these two rooms." With hands on her hips she shot him a look that must have been received as bitchy.

His ears pinned back a little and he looked weary. "Jon's with Mom and I'm here for the day. You can put me to work or we can talk about what's going on."

"There's not a doubt in my mind that I need both." She was tearing up. That was an unexpected turn in the conversation.

"Don't cry, Honey," Will was at her side immediately, "You'll make mud!"

"Don't be cute when I'm upset with you." She let out great big sobs.

Will took her hand and walked her out back to the patio, "I have a great idea." He guided her to sit and ran back into the house returning with iced tea and a cool wet face cloth for her. "Now, here I am and let's get to the bottom of this."

"Where would you like to start?" She said through a rack of sobbing, "Would you like to know how it felt to be left alone, *again* with no word from you about how it was going in San Francisco?" Her hands were wringing the cloth, "Or we can start with how I ended up with almost a million dollars in my bank account." Her eyes shot sparks at him. Etta stood, because her anger was bigger than her body, "Or how I've started tearing the ass out of my house to accommodate a family."

Will slouched down and threw his head into his hands, "What a mess I've made."

"You are in a shitty situation, Will. You've made the best

decisions for Jon. I *know* he's your first priority. I do think we need to work on our communications though. You could have easily confided in me while you were in San Francisco... let me know how things were going. It's what couples do!" She started to pace. This was her opportunity to tell him everything on her mind. "You did tell me that you wanted a life with me here in Nevada City. You did tell me that I was the love of your life... soul mate stuff. I didn't make this up in my mind, Will... but I'm starting to feel like I did, because soul mates talk to each other." She was flapping her arms around dramatically.

"Wow...Okay," he took in a deep breath and a drink of her tea. "Yes, I want a life with you in Nevada City. This is where I want my family to be raised. I just thought what was going on in San Francisco was all too much to share. I didn't want to drag you into the pain of all of this. I didn't want to hurt you."

"Too late," She said drawing her lips into a thin, strong frown.

"Etta, do you have even the slightest idea what I'm going through here?" He raised his voice.

"Well I can only imagine, Will, because you won't talk about it," she spat back at him.

"You know what?" He stood quickly and started to walk toward the garden gate, "I'll get back to you when it's all over."

"Oh it's over all right..." She stomped her foot so hard that the energy of the vibration rose to her neck.

The gate slammed shut.

"Shit." She flopped down in tears, "That's not how I wanted it to go."

With her anger and sadness channeled, Etta demoed three

walls and was ahead of schedule by a day.

~

Sitting in the shade of the mulberry tree, Tony and Mim were enjoying a simple summer salad.

"I sure do miss my grandchildren," Tony said as he watched Jon Jon play with his apples and yogurt in the high chair. "They're in Pennsylvania with their mom."

"That must be hard. Are the parents divorced?" Mim asked.

"My son screwed up his marriage… literally. He fooled around and I don't blame Gilda for leaving him. Her family is back east, she needed the support."

"Hard to live with the decisions you don't make for yourself when they affect everything you hold dear, I imagine."

"That's why I'm so passionate about this case for Will. I will do whatever it takes to keep that money hungry creep from Jon."

"Oh Tony, I blame myself for this mess. I encouraged Miles to see the baby… if I'd just kept my mouth shut."

"Miles found out about the baby and he wasn't going to be stopped. He knew Will was successful in the art world. But when he arrived and saw this beautiful place, his greed came out full force".

"I'd give it all up to keep Jon with us." Mim misted up.

"Miles is counting on that. But I have a plan," Tony said, his eyes glimmered mischievously as he reached across to pat her hand. Unexpected chemistry jolted them to look into each other's eyes. The gate slammed open and she quickly pulled her hand back.

Will walked over to kiss Jon on the head, "I'm going to grab some gear and then Jon and I are going to go fishing."

"I thought you were going to spend the day with Etta."

"Complications I don't want to talk about." Will said flatly.

Jon, flopped over from his father's hip to kiss his grandmother as Will balanced his pole and baby paraphernalia in the other arm. The gate clunked shut and they were gone.

Tony and Mim looked at each other shocked, but smiling "I wish he wasn't such a hard head," Mim said under her breath.

"Well," Tony started shyly, "I can't imagine a more wonderful companion to spend my day with. I'd love to have a professionally guided tour of the area, if you would do me the honor."

~

After the day she'd had, Etta realized that nothing less than a shower and a wire brush would cut the crud off of her body. Her mind splintered in four different directions while she demolished the walls of her precious house. Why in the world was Will acting like she didn't have the right to know about how things were going in San Francisco? He professed his undying love to her, he'd asked her to have a life with him in Nevada City. He had done everything but apologize and ask her to marry him, which was essentially all she wanted. It wasn't that out of order. Why should her desires be ignored? And now that her future was obviously on the back burner how long would it remain there in William's life? She'd been waiting for well over a year now. Her wandering mind went to the far extreme. She was furious, how dare he just walk out in a huff.

The water blasted down from the shower head as Etta took all of her clothes off then stepped into the tiny shower stall. Stinging needles of hot water stripped away the residue of a truly wretched day. She inhaled the essence of lavender soap waiting for the calmness to sooth her raging emotions. The steam and the delicious scents did nothing to improve her distress. Then she did it; she closed her eyes, placed her palms on the tile walls, planted her feet firmly on the floor on either side of the drain and she opened her mouth under the pounding water and screamed. Her scream turned into a wale as she slid to the bottom of the shower stall racked with emotions that she could not turn off. She looked up at the shower head through her furious wrath and watched it come down to pelt her legs. Etta's butt remained on the tile floor until the hot water turned tepid.

    Wrapped in a towel tucked above her bosoms, Etta, thoroughly drained of all emotion, slipped her feet into flip flops and shuffled out into the kitchen for a glass of wine. The wine opener wasn't in the drawer it was supposed to live in. She looked through two other drawers and then slammed the last one shut out of sheer frustration. The pounding in her head was a sharp reminder of her emotional fit in the shower. She abandoned her search for wine and went for the aspirin on the shelf over the sink.

    With a finger of cranberry juice in a glass, Etta examined what was left in a vodka bottle. Why bother with a wine cork when her vodka had a screw off lid? Perfect. Looking out her kitchen window, Etta gazed at her magnificent garden and then her eyes wandered to the shack that she visualized as Will's art studio. She was creating it… not Will, how could she know what he even wanted when he didn't talk to her about anything. Disgusted with herself, she threw on an old sun dress and put her hair in a clip. Pouring a second drink, she slammed it down quickly which drained her bottle empty.

Flopped on the couch, Etta numbly flipped through the cable television line up. Not one thing worth watching. Pursing her lips, she shook her head and tossed the remote to the floor. A soft wrapping on the door snapped her out of her pity coma. She raised up, it might be Will coming to redeem himself.

Paige stood at her door in khaki shorts and a plain white tank with a bottle of vodka in her hand. Etta opened up the screen door, grabbed the bottle and turned to the kitchen, "Thanks," she called over her shoulder. "I was almost dry."

"You started without me..." Paige said lightly to hide the alarm she felt.

"Well, I couldn't find the damn corkscrew..." Etta slapped the counter with her open hand, "So I found something with a screw lid." She fiddled with the top of Paige's bottle and smiled when she found that the cork came out without a cork screw, "Finally something that makes sense around here..." Etta said as she poured herself another drink.

"Clearly, the cranberry is for color only." Paige was trying to read her friend's face.

"Clearly!" Etta's affirmation was enthusiastic, "Which is the only fucking thing that's clear to me these days."

"How about I make us something for dinner."

"Not hungry." Etta blinked her eyes slowly, shook her head and swayed, trying to focus on Paige.

"Oh, I think it'll do you a world of good. Besides, I'm starving."

Paige opened up the fridge to see what would be quick and

easy. They had an emergency situation on hand. She looked on the shelves. Yogurt, juice boxes, finger cheeses, all baby friendly foods. She flopped a bag of string cheese onto the counter and turned to get some crackers out of the pantry. Then Paige saw for the first time, really understood, what Etta had been doing. Three walls were completely gone, down to the studs, exposing her bedroom to the rest of the house. Etta, with intuition as her guide had ripped her precious house apart to accommodate a man and child that were obviously not here. Paige nodded to herself as if she understood and then turned back to Etta, who was fumbling with the cheese, unable to open it.

"Let's sit down over here and have something to eat." Paige moved to the kitchen table and sat with her friend.

~

"What have you done, Will?" Jake was standing over his friend, his brother on the bank of the creek.

"I took my son fishing. The day got out of control and this, as you well know, where I come to think," Will said. His eyes were straight ahead into the water of the creek. His jaw set in iron.

"Don't you dare ignore me, Bro," Jake shoved his shoulder.

"Come on Jake," Will turned to make eye contact and pointed to Jon playing with rocks along the water's edge, "Not now.... Not cool."

"What I really want to do is beat your self-important ass for what you're doing to the family. Do you think beyond yourself at all? Has it occurred to you to ask Etta why she's tearing her house apart?"

"She's always doing something goofy," Will shrugged and stared back out into the water.

"You sure can be a world class narcissistic ass." Jake jerked his thumb towards town, "She's creating a nest for your family. You know... the instant family that you sprung on her. The reason you left her holding her heart in her hands over a year ago without a word. You know, for the stripper you had a one night stand with and then a kid?"

"You're right." Will looked solemn, "I'm an asshole."

Jake started to pace, "No, no no... That's not going to fly, Will, you agree to just shut me up and then go about your business. I can't believe what you've put those women through because you won't open up and talk to them, tell them what's going on in that self important head of yours."

"Fuck you, Jake," Will was furious, but thoughtful, "I can't stand to see the looks of pain on their faces!"

"So you just don't look at all!" He threw his arms out, "While you're pursuing your martyrdom, we're here trying to make sense out of all of it. I see it all. I'm the one picking up the pieces. Yeah, I'm talking about your mom too. She's been beside herself; Etta could have withered and died for all you cared over the last year. And, here you are... wondering why anyone would be pissed off at you, golden boy."

"Why are you busting my balls?" Will yelled.

"Because I love you, Brother," Jake let his shoulders fall, "I love those women you are torturing. I don't understand it. In your life you've been handed talent, good looks, charm and humor. You got it all. You are adored by everyone. But when things get tough you duck off alone. I'm telling you it leaves the rest of us scratching our heads. You are *always* here for us when we need you." Jake moved around to face Will, "Who was there for me when my granddad died? Who was there for us when our grandmother went into a home and we needed a place to stay? You know better than this! We stand together. What makes this situation any different? Why is it so hard for you to accept help? You're killing us!"

"JON!" Will yelled out staring at the empty bank of the creek where he'd just been playing with rocks.

~

"I thought I saw Will over here this morning," Paige said, as she handed Etta a piece of string cheese.

"He was here for a few..." Etta said around the cheese in her mouth, "He's infuriating!"

"I imagine he can be. Do you want to talk about it?"

"Oh Paige..." Etta started, "I've fucked up my whole life! I should have never let him sleep with me. It seems like another lifetime ago."

"You two had a troubled year or so..."

"I can live without a lover. But I cannot imagine my life without my friend. Will's always been my best friend. He's my life. Now I've gone and turned *woman* on him. Seriously, Paige, I used to laugh when he'd tell me stories about the women in his life getting so emotional on him. It made him crazy! He would describe scenes exactly like the one we had here this morning and tell me he left in a heartbeat, couldn't stand the drama. He'd tell me it just wasn't worth it. Now I've turned into *that* drama." Etta's head fell helplessly to the table top with a thud. Paige winced.

"Well, you know I love your family... and the situation is complicated to say the least. But Etta," Paige reached across the table to stoke her hair, "Have you considered for a moment that if Will's had the same situation over and over, that he is obviously missing something?"

"You mean I am not being a typical woman?" Etta snubbed.

"Of course you're a woman! Will just seems to bring out the worst in our gender at times I would say. It's his pattern to be non-communicative."

"He's not a bad guy, Paige..."

"Of course he's not, Honey! He's in a bad spot and he's overwhelmed. He's hurting you and that's intolerable to me. I have every right to be pissed off at him. Jake's going to come unhinged when he hears about this."

"He already has." Etta looked up through her hands, "He was here earlier. All I have to say is, I hope Will's hiding out somewhere safe, because Jake was fuming when he left."

"He's got every right." Paige hesitated, "But it's not going to help things if he uses Will as a punching bag."

"Oh God, Paige, what have I done?" Etta looked straight up into Paige's eyes, "Something's wrong."

"Yeah, something's wrong..."

"No, I mean really wrong... OH NO! It's a panic." Etta was out the door, mechanically moving down the street. Paige was confused and hoped it was not the alcohol making Etta act crazy. She followed her. Then Etta broke out into a run.

~

Both men set out in different directions. Will sprang over the huge rocks along the edge, searching for his son downstream, yelling for him with every breath. "Oh my God… Jon… JON!" Will frantically scrambled over each rock in his way. Super human strength filled his lungs as he yelled again, "JON!" Buzzing in his head, nothing would come into focus as he scanned the shore and water for his son.

Jake went the opposite direction toward the covered bridge. Dodging trees, rocks and washes in his path, his eyes darted into every crevice as the panic built in his chest. It was close to dusk. He looked out over the water, dreading that he might see Will's tiny little man floating, too late to save him. His heart stopped as his scan caught something bobbing in the water. It was white and red. "No…" he cried out in dread springing out into the chilled flow to find, not a baby, but a fast food bag floating by. He dismissed the pounding he felt in the ground as his own heart beating, but the heavy breathing sounds were not coming from him. He looked up just in time to see Etta fly over the edge of the creek like a wild woman. Jake said, "Jon… we've lost Jon."

"Up this way…" Etta moved quickly through the brush, whacking the weeds away with her hands as she squatted down to see things from Jon's perspective. "He went this way…" She was like a hound dog on the trail weaving side to side. Stopping for a few seconds to fine tune her senses, then she'd push on, "He's up this way, but he didn't take the path." Jake and Paige trailed behind her creating a wild eyed search crew. Light was growing dim. Paige felt the sting of tears working but willed them to stop. Jake pointed to a higher trail and they spread out.

"I can feel him. He's up here," Etta yelled out, "under the

bridge."

They followed the trail and rushed through all the obstacles to find they had risen above the creek by at least twenty five feet. It was a sheer rocky drop to the water from where they stood. Paige held her stomach before she looked over the edge. The water was rushing as it came over the rocks, "Oh no…"

Jake was fast behind her and took her hand into his, "I'll go."

Etta was up ahead about fifty feet at the covered bridge entrance looking down into the gully. She began sliding down the steep trail to the base where she was fixated on something. They followed behind her again.

Will had turned to come upstream, which was against all logic to him. His intuition wouldn't let him ignore the feeling. Darkness was falling. He'd scaled some huge boulders and spotted small little spaces where a baby could navigate through. He followed his heart, which was beating like a homing pigeon in his chest. He whispered to himself, "Home to my boy… where are you Jon?" It felt like a hundred miles when in fact it was only about three hundred yards. He followed the water's edge almost to the covered bridge. He could see movement in the brush and rushed forward.

A huge oak had fallen across the creek creating a solid barrier to where Will knew he'd find Jon. He spotted a crawl space underneath, but he wouldn't fit. He grabbed limbs and scrambled over the top of the humongous tree in his path. What he saw as he landed on the other side of the tree fixed both of his feet to the ground. He was petrified to move an inch. Jon was forty feet ahead, crawling out onto a log in the violently rushing white water. If the baby fell in, he would be swept away and pummeled immediately.

He couldn't take his eyes off of Jon, but he could make out people coming down the trail toward the baby. Will moved forward with mental calculations of how he could walk in the water, up to Jon to prevent him from falling in. He was about thirty feet away when he realized the people coming down the hill were Etta, Jake and Paige. Etta reached the edge of the water first.

Will held his breath that she didn't bump the log or startle the baby. If either happened Jon would fall into the water. He planned for the worst and struggled into the rough and rushing water. He stopped at the path of least resistance, where he imagined Jon would flow if he fell in. He wasn't sure Etta knew he was there, she hadn't looked at him, she wouldn't take her eyes off the baby. He didn't want Jon to turn at his voice, so he stayed quiet.

Gingerly, Etta approached the precariously perched baby on the log. Jon went from crawling to sitting on his padded behind. She didn't make a sound, didn't say a word. She didn't want to startle him in any way. Jon was patting his hands making baby sing-song noises from the barnyard animal movie, oblivious to danger he was in. Her heart rocked at his innocence.

Etta took in a steady breath and reached slowly for the back of his overalls. Jon looked around to see her and he smiled happily, "Ma!" he held up his hands and fell backwards into the rushing water. Etta screamed, "NO... Jon!" he slipped under the water's surface. She dove over the log and into the water, feeling the denim of his overalls brush her hands and then rush away.

Will had prepared a barricade which Jon could not pass through but he jumped out into even deeper water when he realized Jon had taken a different path. Will dove under the water to grab his son. For a moment he was confused and came up empty handed. Then he saw the top of his head bobbing. Jon was stuck in an eddy between himself and where Etta was trying desperately to get to Jon. It was Jake who jumped in and pulled the baby out. He was limp and blue, hanging over Jakes arm like a noodle. A site that paralyzed both Will and Etta.

Paige took the baby from Jake, gently laid him on the ground and began pumping the water out of his lungs.   Life guard certification from high school came back to her in a flash. Jon started to vomit and cough and breathe! When he reached for his father in a frightened cry, Will pulled his son to his heart and held him, crying into his tiny shoulder in a huge gush of relief.

Will opened his eyes and looked at the dripping, frenzied, beautiful bunch of family surrounding him. Paige shaking and covered in baby vomit, Jake looking like a frightened wet dog and Etta, sweet Etta, with her hands over her heart, her eyes closed in a sacred moment of thanks. Instinctively he reached for her and pulled her into a hug with the baby between them. Etta reached for Paige, Paige reached for Jake and soon they were all huddled and shaking together.

CHAPTER 28

"Etta, you've got to put him down. The doctor said he's fine."

Etta rocked Jon mesmerized by his baby soft breathing against her chest. How close they were to losing him in the water. The stone hard panic she felt when her feet started running down the street and then finally getting a clear image of what she had been pulled toward. When her intuition switched on like that there was no way to explain it to another rational human being. Her body just started to move until her mind got a clear picture of where she would be going. It was a nightmare she would never forget. Right now she couldn't imagine anything more precious than holding Jon in her arms and watching the miracle of breath as he slept.

"The crib is in the hall closet... can you set it up?" she whispered to Will.

"It's already done," he motioned to the other room through the bare studs that used to be a wall. He took Jon out of her arms and then placed him in the crib. Etta trailed behind not wanting to let Jon out of her sight.

Will turned and whispered, "All snuggly."

Her head fell against his shoulder and the warmth of his arms pulled her next to him.

"I'm sorry," he said softly against her ear.

"Let's talk in here," She pulled him towards the kitchen.

Trying to keep her hands busy, Etta clicked on the tea kettle and rested at the kitchen table.

Placing her hands in her lap, she looked directly at Will. She'd know him her whole life, but the emotion on his face was a mystery to her. She continued to wait, staring straight into his face.

He looked thoughtful before he spoke, "I'd sure like to know what you're thinking right now."

She let out a snort-laugh, "Honestly?" She shook her head, "I'm thinking you're not likely to bolt out the door and disappear with your son sleeping in the front room." She placed her hands on the table and leaned forward, "So I better say everything now, while I have the opportunity"

"I deserved that," he nodded, tired and waiting for his licks.

"I think we're both raw and exhausted. Maybe this should wait."

"I think you should load up all of your misgivings and let me have it right now." He tried to put on a brave face, "Everyone else has... let her rip." Will sat back in his chair folding his arms defensively, wiggling under the penetrating stare, he then letting his hands fall into the table top and leaned forward, exhausted.

Etta reached across the table. His hands were warm under her cool touch, "I can live without you as my lover, Will, but I cannot live without you as my friend."

Will looked down at the floor and closed his eyes, "Wait..."

"Wait for what Will? What is it that I'm waiting for?" Her voice had the squeal of frustration.

"Let me start by saying that I'm... I'm sorry Etta." His eyes were red rimmed when he looked back to her face, "I'm sorry I didn't tell you about Darla when she called me here." He slid his chair closer, "After the night we had…" He took both of her hands into his, "I mean, it took me a while to realize what happened. It was an amazing night… the best night I've ever had, actually. But you can't even imagine how quick that memory got buried in San Francisco. The baby, then Darla, and then court… I didn't know which end was up."

"Will, do you remember me going to school all those years?" Etta sarcasm bubbled up, "Well, I did graduate with a degree in family counseling. I could have helped. I've got an office and clients and everything. I've come to the harsh reality that you think you're above it all. I would have been there with you every step of the way."

"I've pissed off the people who love me the most." Will hung his head again, "How can I make it up to you, Etta?"

"You can hold your head up and look me in the eye and tell me what we're going to do now." She said, her voice boldly rising, "And then I have a lot to tell you. If you'd stuck around this morning…" She looked back toward the sleeping baby.

Will looked toward the front room, "Jon can sleep through a football game… he can handle a little family chat."

"Ok, it's your turn. I'm planning my life, William."

"Well, first and foremost, Jon's custody needs to be settled. I'm not going to be sorry. It's my priority."

"Understood, and I'm with you."

"Once that's behind us we'll have to talk about…" Will looked at the bare studs that used to be walls, "where we live." It was nice to watch Will squirm. He blinked away his curiosity and then continued, "I… I mean *we* can buy a house together," he stumbled.

Etta tried to keep her polite smile from turning to a full on grin, "Yes?" She batted her eyes at him in anticipation.

"And when you're ready..." He closed his eyes and held his breath before saying, "You are my friend and my lover, but I want you to be my life."

"Your life?" Etta questioned.

"Yes, my life and my wife." He looked relieved to have said it out loud.

"I see..." she looked sharply at him, "any idea why I've ripped the walls out of my house?"

"Jake tried to school me about that earlier today," he answered.

"And how do you feel about living here in this house...our house. I can show you the blue prints. I'm adding kids' rooms down here and a master upstairs with a bathroom, a great big one." She could feel her own excitement surfacing.

"That's it!" Will pushed the table away and fell to his knees between Etta's legs, "I can't take it for another minute." His head fell into her lap and her hand instinctively lifted onto his head and stroked his hair, "Yes, put your hands on me." He looked up into her face, "Love me, heal me," he begged. Etta eased up and led Will to the bed, which was conveniently four feet away in the kitchen.

Waking the baby was not an option. Every sigh and passionate yelp had been tempered to purrs and whispers; a covert mission that was executed to perfection. Will's fingers left a trail of chills as they ran from her shoulder to her elbow. The comfort of his body under her head was something she never wanted to be without again. Her first morning urge was to arouse Will and love him again.

The amorous thought was quickly squelched by the sound of Jon Jon clapping his hands in the early morning dawn. Etta knew they only had moments before the quiet love spell they'd woven through the night would lead into a round of cheerios and bright light in the kitchen.

"He's so good to play by himself." Etta whispered.

"He's only got about three minutes left in his repartee," Will wiggled a little and Etta reluctantly released his shoulder.

"Oh, I don't want to get up yet, Will, bring him in here with us."

"I can do that." It was too dark for Etta to see the amusement on his face as he pulled on his pants and headed for the crib.

She slipped on a shirt and opened up her arms for Jon's running jump onto the bed, "Good morning, little man!" Etta brushed the wild blond hair from his eyes and kissed his scrapes as she tried to snuggled down with him in her arms, "How are you this morning?"

"Ma!" Jon jumped up and jammed his foot into her hip bone and fell onto her chest with a hollow thud. He lurched at Will, "Daddy." Jon's head landed exactly where Etta's had been just moments before. He slapped his father's bare chest then climbed onto his belly with his bare feet firmly in Will's crotch.

"That's not going to work, Buddy." Will lifted him high into the air and jiggled him until he giggled loudly.

"Are you sure we should be so rough with him?" Etta worried.

"He looks okay to me, huh, Buddy? You okay this morning?"

"Ouwie," Jon patted his forehead.

"You're right, Wild Cat, I think yogurt and cereal. No

wrestling."

Jon balled up his chubby fist and pointed one finger at Will, "No, No, NO!"

"He told you!" Etta smiled over her shoulder as she pulled on a robe and headed for the kitchen.

~

"He calls you Ma already?" Paige asked.

"He calls all females Ma." Etta answered humbly, pulling a cherry tomato from Paige's salad and popping it into her mouth.

"He calls *me Annie Paige.* She looked up trying to access the memory, "Or something very close to Paige." She set her fork down and said seriously, "I saw Mim in town yesterday with a man I didn't recognize."

"Isn't small town life wonderful?" Etta smiled brightly, "Well, the way I hear it Tony, Will's lawyer, took her out on the town yesterday."

"I saw her from the other side of the street and I swear she looked like Jackie O with those huge glasses and her hands waving around telling a story. I smiled all the way home just thinking about it."

"As long as I can remember, Auntie Mim has been alone. She's traveled and had flings, I'm sure, but no one ever stuck when she came home... for us."

"Sounds like it's time for Mim to have a companion." Paige looked out the window, "You know, I can't imagine not having a man around. I think the longest dry spell of my adult life was nine weeks." She looked back into Etta's eyes, "Isn't that just awful?"

"Sounds like you should be thankful." Etta chuckled, "I've gone years. Our pool to draw from is a little shallow around here; I mean my brother's quite a catch, but…"

"He is!" Paige looked at her ring shooting rainbows in the sunlight, "I can't believe how happy I am, Etta… really, to the core kind of happy!"

"Yes, Sister, I do see it."

"So, what are you and Will going to do? Did you tell him about your plans for the house and the shack out back?"

"Nope. He said he completely trusts me and to be honest, he's too busy preparing for the court date."

"You guys were busy!"

"It felt good. It's exactly what we needed." Etta said softly, "I don't know when I'm going to see him next. I'm going to relax and wait the nightmare part of this out." Etta looked at her watch and jumped, "Oh I've got a client in five minutes…I've got to run." Paige watched Etta's tied dyed skirt and silver strappy sandals flip flop their way out of the café and down the street to her office.

The titter of familiar laughter drifted out onto the sidewalk where Paige was dining. She strained to see through the reflection of the glass and saw Mim at a table, very cozy with a handsome Italian looking man. He gazed at Mim adoringly. Paige could practically hear the crackle of electricity from where she watched. Who was that man? She closed her eyes and sent a silent blessing for Mim's happiness. Etta had impressed upon her the importance of thoughts as things and she wanted Mim to be the recipient of true love. Blessed be!

~

Tony's dark brown eyes caught the light and reflected flecks of topaz, "Of course we've saved room for dessert!" he said joking to the waitress. "We've been here three hours," he continued with a hearty bear laugh, "It's almost time for dinner." He squeezed Mim's hand and asked, "How do you feel about a triple chocolate cake with an old vine French Bordeaux?"

Mim's mouth watered just thinking about the decadent combination, "Sounds sinfully divine."

"Well, my dear Emily," he addressed the waitress again, "I feel a sin coming on!" he tapped the front of his shirt like WC Fields in an old black and white movie. The humor was not lost on Mim, she was absolutely charmed.

"You're spoiling me," she said, completely enjoying the delightful dance of flirting.

"Miriam, I haven't had anyone to spoil in so long, please allow me this pleasure. And believe me, my dear," he kissed her hand, "it is a pleasure of the highest degree."

"I'm not sure how to act." Mim looked at him through the blur of growing adoration.

"You're doing just fine." He nodded enthusiastically toward the waiter as he tasted the wine to be poured and made a toast, "Here's to bringing the baby home to stay."

"To Jon Jon." Mim said wishfully.

CHAPTER 29

"Okay, so I've been screwing up," Will said as he lifted a beer bottle to his lips. "But I'm trying to make it right." Will shook off a thought, "Have you seen the plans for that house of Etta's?"

"Yes I have. She's not happy unless she's creating something." Jake smiled with love for his sister's antics.

"I know that feeling. I haven't painted in over a year." Will drained the bottle and shook his head no when Hardy offered him another, "Have to stay clear right now. Can you believe my Mom's been out with Tony twice in two days?"

"I hope he's a good guy…" Jake said protectively, "This is new to her."

"I never got it; she's never been in a relationship. She's beautiful and charming and since she left my dad in Texas, there hasn't been another man."

"That *we* know of. Maybe she didn't want any bad influences on you."

"Oh, shit man, don't get deep on me now…" Will shook his head, "I've got barnyard animals singing in my very near future!"

Jake slapped Will's back, "I know that one first hand. He's growing fast. I already see it. Try and let all the bullshit fall away and look at what's real."

Will threw a hug to Jake and then went home to have some playtime with Jon before he went down for the night.

In the car on his way to Jon, Will reflected on what it might feel like to be Etta in the situation. Not once had she asked him when she was going to see him again. She'd bought bedding and toys for Jon's stays and even stocked the fridge for the baby. He hadn't thanked her for all the sweet things she was doing or all the patience she had with him. Jake was right, he really was an asshole.

~

Etta stood in her own rubble assessing the work she'd accomplished. Eight hours of destruction and hours of clean up made for a long and tiring day. The workers took out the walls and put supportive pillars into place. The look was astonishing. In just one short week her tiny rooms, separated by walls had become one large living space. Of course, her bed was in the kitchen, which was going to be a problem. Paige had offered her a room in the mansion until she'd finished the demo but she didn't want to be away from the progress, not even for a night. She didn't want to be at Paige's when Will decided to spend a night with her.

Etta had imagined it exactly as it was turning out, well, without all the dust. Lord, there was a lot of dust. She shook her hair out and spotted another nail on the floor. How was this ever going to be safe for the baby? Falling to her knees, she scoured the bare wood floor for anything that might be harmful if ingested.

"Great angle," Etta jerked up to see Will with Jon in one arm and a pizza box in the other.

"MA!" Jon wiggled out of his father's arms and ran to her.

"Hello, little man." She kissed his forehead, "How are you tonight?"

"Daddy," Jon pointed and clapped his hands, thrilled with both of them.

"You're mighty precious, Jon." Etta stood up to kiss Will, "Food… how did you know I'd be starving?"

"Remember when Mom added the rooms on to the back of the house?"

"Yes," Etta remembered very well when Mim added on to her house to accommodate two teenagers who'd lost their whole world.

"She'd go all day and eat nothing until Addy brought dinner."

Etta nodded, smiling at the memory of feeling so loved. "You know… not once did she make us feel like it was an imposition to bring us into your home. To her it was a great adventure, a wonderful extension of her family. I don't remember her complaining one time."

"You've had a great mentor." Will looked at her knowingly, "And Etta… all of this," he waved his hands around, "is not going unappreciated. I want you to know that."

"I'm doing the same thing, aren't I?" her smile slipped thinking about how much Mim had dedicated to them. How wonderful that they shared the same links to their past.

CHAPTER 30

"Will says you raised Etta and Jake when their parents died."

Tony looked deep into Mim's face for her history.

"One my saddest days was seeing those children lost and alone in the front yard of their grandparent's home, just babies." She looked off into the street as she conjured up the memory, "Then the second saddest moment was realizing that I would never see my best friend again. Those children were the closest thing I was ever going to have to her in my life. I was there when Henri gave birth to Etta and I left for Texas when she was pregnant with Jake. They were so in love. Henri and Bob were the quintessential high school sweethearts."

"Lucky kids to have you remembering their parents' love like that." Tony said. He put his arm around Mim's shoulders as they walked down the street from the studio, "You cold?"

Mim shook her head then shrugged, "I guess so. It always creeps up on me, how much I miss them."

He rubbed on her arm, then took his jacket off and draped it around her shoulders. Comforted by the warmth, she smiled, "That's nice, thank you."

"Where would you like to go, beautiful? I feel a long talk into the night coming on."

"A fire actually sounds nice. People will think I'm crazy

building a fire at my house in the middle of August."

"I have the perfect place." Tony guided her to his car.

"Oh, my goodness." Mim added wickedly, "I can't remember the last time I went to a man's hotel room."

"It's my home away from home. I've got a gas fireplace. No shame in that."

Tony led her across the bridge to a huge Victorian house he'd been renting a room in. Unlocking the door from the patio overlooking the little Deer Creek, he ushered her into his space. Mim immediately slipped her shoes off and slid onto the overstuffed sofa, tucking one foot under her butt. Tony draped a blanket over her lap and went into the kitchenette of his quaint guest suite.

"You'll be warm in no time." He returned handed her a glass of red wine and placing a cheese board on the wooden crate that served as a coffee table.

"This is so nice." She sipped, "I didn't know this place was rented out." She watched him grab another glass and join her on the sofa.

"It normally isn't. Will made the arrangements for me. I've only met the owner of this house one time. She's an odd little woman, I can never remember her name."

"I've seen her a couple of times." Mim said, "She's not very social. I think her name is Fanny or something like that."

"She's a writer." Said Tony, "she doesn't like noise or company and I told her we'd get along just fine."

"I should have been more hospitable and introduced myself a few years back when she moved in…"

"You're absolutely charming and hospitable, Mim, I felt

welcome right away when I met you."

"I think I had plans for you the minute you kissed my hand." Mim said boldly.

"Tell me more..." his deep brown eyes shone with comfortable warmth.

Mim glanced over his face. His dark hair, disheveled by their walk curled to rest on his forehead and she pushed away the desire to reach over and smooth it back. Her eyes went back to Tony's, "what would you like to know?"

"Well, how did someone so sweet and wonderful end up without a man in her life all this time?" He asked tentatively.

"Well, that's the sweetest way of asking me why in the world I left a husband in Texas to come back here alone I've ever heard." She held up a hand to stop his rebuttal.

"It's my fault mostly." She tried to shake off old regrets. They were so much a part of her now it would have been like missing an ear. She breathed in and the reasons for her life choices were crystal clear, "It's a long story..."

"I've waited my whole life to hear it, Miriam." Tony took a deep drink of his wine and settled back for the tale of Mim.

"We were inseparable; Addy, Della, Henri, (that's Etta and Will's mom) and me. By the time we were in high school all we could talk about was getting out of this crummy little town. We heard about the world out there changing in every way. We read magazines and newspapers, so it had to be true, but Nevada City stayed the same. You know, the fifties were ending and the sixties were turbulent with the war... we were so fired up about what was going on. We seemed to be stranded here, suspended in time while the rest of the world kept turning. Our mothers still stayed home and wore aprons in the kitchen, for crying out loud." Mim took another drink and let the memories take her.

"I was fifteen years old when I met him." She closed her eyes and ushered the dreams of a young heart into her mind, "Patrick was the new kid at school. He came from Berkeley, which was the axis of the whole world to us at the time… so close and yet so different. Patrick showed up with a guitar over his shoulder, he was sensitive and poetic. His long hair and love beads made him an alien hippy who landed on the planet 'Leave it to Beaver'. Just his presence seemed to insight a riot with all the girls at high school. I could sit for hours and listen to him talk about the world "out there". I wanted to experience his point of view so badly. I wanted to see what he had seen. All the girls had a huge crush on him. I watched from a distance. He felt dangerous. My mother would have had a stroke if I'd brought him home as a date." Mim laughed at the memory.

"I knew a couple of girls like that…" Tony said slyly.

"I guess it was because I hadn't thrown myself at him that he turned to me as a friend. Our conversations became easy and funny. We spent most days together, after school. The other girls were so jealous even when I assure them we were just friends. Oh, but I did fall in love with him. I could listen to him talk about philosophy and the state of the world for days and never tire of it. He was funny, too. His sense of humor could lift me up on the darkest day. Pretty soon, I tried to get myself into situations where we'd be alone. I manipulated that poor boy into all kinds of situations where he had to kiss me a few times. We'd spend days together just walking and talking and laughing. He'd sing to me and write songs about love.

When he sang to me I felt as if it was only for me. I thought he respected me too much to 'go all the way'. With him I felt cherished. I knew we'd be together forever and have a family and a life." Mim took a big swig of wine.

"He went to college the fall after he graduated. My heart just ached, I missed him so much. I couldn't believe I had to wait another year before I could leave with him. He came home for the holidays and our romance felt stronger than ever or at least I thought it was. He came to our house on Christmas Eve."

"I thought your mom would have hated him?" Tony's smile was wide with anticipation and he ran his fingers down her arm urging her to continue.

Mim felt safe and warm in his company, but let her eyes focus on the fire before she continued... "and we snuggled by the Christmas tree and took a walk in the snow all bundled up. He sat me down on the bench down town, you know the one in the park. He got down on his knees in front of me and I just knew..." Mim closed her eyes and put her hand on her heart, "I knew he was going to ask me to marry him."

She looked back into Tony's eyes, "He said to me, ' Mim, if I was to ever marry a girl it would be you. But you need to know that I've been dating men.' Well, I'll tell you my tongue went numb! When he asked me to say something... anything, I just stared at him. When I finally found my voice I told him that nothing he could ever do would stop me from loving him. My heart fractured into little pieces that night. He kissed me sweetly and then he walked me home." Mim looked to the ceiling to stop the tears that were forming, "And, by the time spring rolled around Gary had asked me to marry him. We waited until I'd graduated high school. He was my ticket out of here. Texas wasn't Berkeley, but it wasn't here."

"So you left with Gary and ..."

"He became well known at the college. While I was studying and being a wife the girls flocked to him. I was pregnant with William before I graduated college, illustrated some books... made some money of my own. Gary was enjoying the days of free love. I was furious at first. It was just my pride." Mim shrugged her shoulders slowly, "I'm sure he felt tied down to a wife that never really loved him and a child that he hadn't planned on. When I got the call about Henri and Bob, I packed up the wagon and left Texas. I never looked back."

"Poor Gary," Tony commented. "So, you lived with your parents?"

"Gary didn't call my mother's to talk me for a week or so. I think it took him that long to figure out I was gone. My parents had a guest house. They were thrilled to have William and me close by. They indulged all of my friends and their children over the years. This truly is the most amazing place to raise kids."

"Jon is lucky." Tony said caressing Mim's hand, "Your stone cottage is your parent's house?"

"Well, no. I bought it for us after Jake and Etta's grandmother had a stroke."

"It's a beautiful home, a touchstone."

There was a long silence between them. Mim felt vulnerable and a little silly for telling him about her secret love.

As if he could read her mind he smiled and leaned forward to touch her face, "You have a beautiful story, Mim." He kissed her softly on the lips, "Thank you for sharing it."

Mim felt safe and adored as the warmth of his hand grazed her neck, "You are a extraordinary woman." His kiss lingered a little longer and Mim was swept up into something that swirled her out of her head leaving the sadness behind. The only thing she felt were lips on her neck. For the first time in her life she wasn't overwhelmed with the desire to strip off all of her clothing and have her needs met immediately. The emotion was serene and grounded, moving rhythmically through her body. Oh, who was she kidding? It felt like the most erotic drug of her life. She couldn't wait to get naked!

~

"Son of a bitch!" Will yelled in his mother's kitchen, slamming down the papers he'd been handed at the door, "Where the hell is everyone?" Jon was safely outside swinging with the nanny.

Tony's car pulled down the drive and Will narrowed his eyes to see who was in the passenger seat. Recognizing his mother, he whispered to himself, "Holy shit."

He bolted out the door waving the papers in his hand, "Nice to see you...Tony."

Mim slipped out of the car, her love hangover bursting the moment she looked at her son's face. "What is it?" She herded everyone into the house.

"That white-trash fuck has filed another motion through his lawyer. They've offered to make a settlement uncontested in court." Will threw the paper bundle toward Tony.

Tony picked up the legal documents and read them over.

Raising one eyebrow he stated, "That's bold, but not unexpected."

He walked around the table and placed a hand on Will's shoulder, "He's aiming high. I know his lawyer, who's actually a moron. This can be used in court to prove he's just gold digging."

Will folded into the kitchen chair. His head hit the slate top of the table, "I'm so damned tired of this. Let's give him what he wants. It's basically all I have left. I don't want to fight anymore. I don't think anyone realizes how exhausted I really am."

Mim was behind her son, hands on his shoulders, "What is it he wants?"

"One Million five hundred thousand dollars, as part of a civil case in Darla's unlawful death." Tony said flatly. "It's not necessary. Any judge will see that this man doesn't care about Jon's welfare. You have provided exemplary care of Jon. He's safe and well adjusted."

"Keep reading," Will said from beneath his collapsed head.

"What is he talking about... an incident at the creek?" Tony said and fell into the chair across from Will.

"What?" Mim looked from one man to the other as Will told them the story of losing Jon at the creek.

Mim was emotional as Will ended his tale, "Well, my first question is how he would know where Jon sleeps at night and what happened at the creek? Have you noticed anyone lurking you don't recognize? Do you think he's got a private detective on your trail?" Mim was pacing the floor.

"It's none of his business where Jon and I spend the night!" Will stated.

"His lawyer is trying to prove that Jon is in an unstable

environment. Not that Miles would know the first thing about how to create a stable one... but that's beside the point," Tony said.

"Oh, my God!" Mim flopped down next to the men, "What do we do, Tony? We're not terrible people. We love that child. We're where he needs to be. There are eyes on our every move?" She shot a look to Tony's stern face, "What have we done?"

"First of all," Tony said with his chest puffed out, "This is a thinly veiled attempt at blackmail. No family is above reproach in court. You can take the best parent in the world and put them under a magnifying glass and find flaws. That's what his lawyer is trying to do. No one is perfect."

Mim stared down to the floor. Will stood up and paced, "I'll get the money."

"That's ridiculous! Even if we take this to court, I believe we can convince a judge that Miles is not only in this for the money, but he's no more concerned with his grandson's welfare than he was with his own daughter's."

"I'm not willing to take that chance." Mim said boldly, "I've got money..."

"No way, Mom, this is my mess." Will said and he stormed out of the house.

"I never spanked him..." Mim said as a matter of fact, "I believe I may have to start."

~

"And he's gone again?" Paige asked Etta.

"Yes, he was furious! Hardly said a word about what he's doing. Same old situation, for me. But he and Tony took off this morning in a whirl of dust. Mim's got to be heartbroken. Jon's with her and the nanny. She's had one over night date with Tony and now he's gone. Boy, do I know *that* one. Will wants to write that son of a bitch a check for one point five million dollars to get him to go away. I don't even know if that will work. It didn't for Darla. She'd still be bleeding him dry if she hadn't killed herself." Etta looked off, remorseful. "That was an awful thing to say."

"Sometimes the truth isn't pretty," Paige commented.

"Truer words have never been spoken," Etta said. "I hate feeling helpless and out of control. We've got to do something!" She stood and paced, having to edge around the pile of building materials in her living room. "I'm thinking how I can protect Jon from all of this turmoil and uncertainty. He's been feeling it since he was born, you can see it in his sweet eyes. How do I put the healing balm on that?"

"You know exactly what to do, Etta," Paige smiled brightly, "It's time to gather the Goddesses."

CHAPTER 31

The sky was dark and clear, winking with the magic of a million stars. The moon, a waxing crescent, appeared low on the horizon with Mars and Venus close by; the witch's moon. Lit with only candles, Etta's patio pulsed in a rhythmic dance of light. Crickets chirped, water tinkled in the fountain, and a breeze rustled the leaves overhead. One by one, clothed in colorful, ethereal dresses, they gathered. Instinctively knowing what to do; they shed their shoes, each setting their sacred offering onto the base of the fountain which looked like an altar.

A solemn Addy carried a mason jar filled with murky liquid. Della brought a small wooden box. Paige set a bowl filled with earth on the stone ledge. Mim walked silently to the altar and laid one fully blooming red rose onto the ledge. Patti, dressed in a grey kimono, brought a small piece of tattered lavender satin ribbon and laid it among the other offerings. Nothing was said as they waited in silence for *the one*.

Mim stood near the fountain, as the circle was formed. Looking to the side door she smiled at the site and rang a gong which resonated deeply into the night air.

Etta appeared in a simple white gauze dress, wearing a long pink scarf draped over one shoulder. Her hair swept away from her face. In her arms she held Jon wriggling in his favorite cookie monster t-shirt and a diaper. He smiled at the attention turned to him. Etta stepped into the circle and lifted Jon high into the air. He giggled wildly as the Goddesses began their gathering.

Etta spoke first, addressing only Jon, "My darling son, this is the night that we initiate you into our world. You were not born through us, but delivered to us. We honor your presence as a sacred vessel of love, hope and eternal joy. We draw to you; health, calm understanding and mending of your wounds, be they physical, spiritual now or in your past. We each bring to you a gift to protect you, surround you and to be with you always on your journey through life." Jon was placed in front of the alter within the circle. Puzzled as to what to do, he smiled when Della joined him on the ground.

Della took her box from the altar and sat on the ground next to Jon, "This is the gift of music. Spirits in song, to soothe, uplift and celebrate." She closed her eyes as she wound the bottom of the box and opened it. Twinkle, twinkle little star chimed out beautifully. She kissed Jon's head and handed him the box. He looked back into her face and grinned, exposing three tiny white teeth.

Addy retrieved her mason jar and sat next to Della joining them in the circle. Twisting the lid off of the jar, she handed it to Jon and helped him to dump it into the fountain, "Water from the creek. This water will retain the memory that you rose above it. This memory will keep you safe and your life journeys buoyant." She kissed Jon's head softly and he smiled patting in the water.

Patti sat next to Jon and reached for the lavender ribbon, "I bring to you the gift of friendship and love. This ribbon is from your grandmother's hair. I saved it and treasure it as a reminder of my love for her. The power of love surround you, Jon." Patti held the ribbon to his own cheek and then placed it into the music box. Patti kissed his chubby hand, Jon giggled, no doubt tickled by the meticulously trimmed goatee.

Joining the group, Mim sat with Jon and handed him the rose. "You are the heart I feel beating outside of my own body. You are the joy I didn't know existed in the world. I give you my love, protection and support, always. I bless you with a curious mind, that you will always find wonder in the world." Jon stood up and threw his arms around Mim's neck, puckering up for a kiss, "Muah". A caterpillar crawled out of the rose and Jon's eyes danced as he squealed into a full belly laugh. The magical events of the gathering surprised no one present, especially Jon.

Paige sat into the circle with her bowl of earth, "Jon." He looked into her eyes and gave her his full attention, "I bless you with the gift of belonging, strength and support. You were not born of the red dirt, but you will thrive on it. It is truly the most wonderful gift I have been given." Jon put his hand into the dirt and smiled at Paige. She kissed his head with her blessing.

Etta sat completing the circle and addressing Jon, by saying, "Jon, I bless you with the gift of mothering. It is the most sacred thing I have to give you." Mim reached for her hand and they exchanged a look of deep understanding. Jon ran to her, "Ma!" His earth covered hands left red streaks down her face. How appropriate. Etta lifted Jon up and the group circled around them, "Holy Mother, bless this baby boy that he may grow into a wonderful man. May he know he is supported and loved by this red earth. Let him be soothed and cleansed by the waters. May he be surrounded with love. May he be lifted up by the music and may he always find peace here with us. Let the highest good be done in Jon's behalf in

San Francisco and let hearts and hands be guided by you, Mother... And so it is. Blessed Be!"

Jon ran between the women basking in the attention and adoration. When they returned to the patio table there was one more gift waiting for him. A beautiful peach pie cooled on the stone table of Etta's back yard.

"GiGi," Jon said quietly clapping his hands.

The party went on until *the one* was overcome by the bedtime blues. Jon was laid down surrounded by the Goddesses who had blessed him for his lifetime. As his tiny hand relaxed in sleep, out fell a hardened red ball of dirt, which was left nestled next to him.

Quietly the party wound down. Mim sat quietly in the charm of Etta's back yard. Patti slipped silently next to her respecting the enchanted moment. More than forty years had passed since he'd broken her heart under the stars. Mim rested her head on his shoulder and sighed, "You know, the last time I missed a man this much... it was you."

~

"Will!" Etta yelled excitedly into the phone, "It's been days! How are things going?"

"It's the damndest thing," Will said his voice crackling with a bad connection, "We're on our way home. Oh no, we're going into a dead zone. I'll see you around three..."

Will's phone cut out and she was left standing there with nothing but a dead connection in her hands. Numbly, she tuned in to

Will. He felt excited and happy. An electric thrill of anticipation shot through her and she knew there was going to be a celebration. A few phone calls and the whole gang had gathered at Etta's house, huddled on the patio, waiting for news.

Will and Tony pulled into the drive. Will, busting out of the car and sprinted toward Etta with the baby on her hip. Gathering them into his arms he said, "It's all over, we won!" He was trembling as he kissed Etta and Jon repeatedly. When his tremble turned to an outright shaking fit, Etta sat him into a chair.

Tony spoke up, "We were in the court room, ready to fight to the end of this thing and Miles walked in looking like a million dollars with Linda on his arm looking, well, really pissed off. We thought we were in for a knock down drag out ugly battle. The judge read Mile's complaint and I read our answer. Seems Miles didn't have a private detective watching Jon. He was taking video the day Jon wandered. When the Judge realized that Linda and Miles had taken the video of Jon from the other side of the creek and never tried to save him, the judge granted our motion and everything is final. Jon is home to stay."

The group broke out into wild cheers of joy. Will held Jon in one arm and Etta in the other, grinning like a hero.

CHAPTER 32

Etta looked at the curtains with barn yard animals on them and pulled up the blinds revealing the nursery she'd completed. "I can't believe this furniture!" Etta reached for Will's hand.

"Amazing job, Bro." Will nodded to Jake.

"Look how perfect it fits into this room!"

Jon had crawled into the toy box. The only visible part of him was his bottom, legs and tennis shoes as he dug in a discovery of new toys.

Paige stood staring at the snapshot picture she was taking in her mind, so different from the life she'd left behind in Oregon. Jake wiped the guard rail of the baby bed, fussing with a rag he had in his back pocket, "Paige stumbled onto it in the attic the day we found out about baby Jon. It was meant to be."

~

"Two weddings in two months," Mim called out from the back of her closet, "We should all have our heads examined."

Tony looked perplexed into the chaotic jumble of colors and fabrics strewn inside the cramped cave of Mim's closet, "What are you looking for, Love?"

"Oh I shoved it back here years ago…" Her voice was muffled, barely audible.

"So you want steak for dinner?" Tony, trying to be helpful

called into the dark feminine abyss.

"Oh, oh, Ahhhh.... I think I have it!" Mim pushed her way back out into the light of her bedroom, hair frazzled and full of static, "YES! Yes, that's it." Admiring the swirls of colorful paint on the canvases Mim sat them on the floor against the bed. Two paintings, three feet tall and two feet wide hadn't seen the light of day in almost twenty years. "I think I'll just let them breathe." Mim smoothed her hair down and looked at Tony, "Now, what were you saying?"

Tony couldn't look away from the art. His eyes absorbed the details on the canvases. Tilting his head to one side his lips rose into a smirk of pride. He nodded to himself and then looked at Mim, "The nekkid years?"

She nodded.

"Brilliant. Masterful. Why aren't these hanging in a gallery or on your walls?"

"I knew when I painted them they weren't for me. I painted this one for Etta. And I knew I needed to paint a second one, but had no inkling I would have two daughters."

"So many emotions in these images." Tony commented.

"Yes." Mim said satisfactorily, "It's how I see love."

"That's how love should be." Tony reached for her hand, "I'm going to miss you."

"Oh, I'll miss you too, Darlin'." Mim cooed back to him absentmindedly.

"Why do I get the feeling that you're just waiting for me to leave?"

"Don't be ridiculous!" she ran her fingers through her bobbed hair avoiding his eyes, "Okay, you distract me." She finally looked at his face, " I have a lot to do in a short time and when you're here all I want to do is be next to you." She put her arms around him and squeezed, pulling him toward the door to his loaded car.

"We'll have to work it out." Tony announced, "Because, when I come back, I won't be leaving."

The kiss he planted on her lips buzzed sweetly, momentarily distracting Mim from the urge to run and lock her front door.

Hi You;

Thanks for reading my debut novel, Broad Street Goddesses. Paige, Etta and Mim all became my friends as I conjured them up to tell you this story. I procrastinated finishing the manuscript because I didn't want to say goodbye to them. I still feel that Georgia, Patti and Mim have more stories to tell and as I work to publish this book I am continuing the saga, plotting book two and three of the Broad Street Goddesses saga.

In 2009 I answered my own call of the red dirt as four generations of family roots drew me home to Nevada County, California. Something magical happens when I'm here. My creativity blossoms and I feel surrounded by inspiration. The houses and businesses I've created for this book are fictional in a very real town. This is my love story to Nevada City.

I live in my family home in the historic area of Grass Valley Ca. with my retired husband who fishes and our two rescue dogs, Barnaby and Bodie who adore him. Surrounded by my crazy, lovable family, most days you can find me bare footed, covered in paint or happily clicking away creating a new story.

If you'd like to stay in touch you can find me on facebook: https://www.facebook.com/pages/DeAnna-Carol-Williams
Or you can email me at DeAnna-Willaims@comcast.net

Safe travels on your journey,
De

Made in the USA
Middletown, DE
04 April 2020